MOVING UP ON MANOLOS

NINA WHYLE

CHAPTER ONE

'Malibu!' squeals my flatmate. 'Alex Canty has invited you to MALIBU?' It never fails to amaze me how my usually sensible and dependable flatmate becomes a quivering wreck at the mere mention of my friend, Alex Canty.

'Sex on legs' she ingeniously named him. At a lean six foot two with bleached-blond hair and a washboard for a stomach, she has a point. He looks every inch your Hollywood Heartthrob, which he is.

'I can't believe it. Alex Canty. ALEX CANTY!'

I slump across the kitchen table and close my eyes. Sian is going to be like this for some time so I might as well make myself comfortable.

The effect Alex has on women these days is staggering. Mind you, he seems to be coping with the attention well enough, judging by our lengthy telephone conversation this evening. Just how many parties does a person need to go to in one night? Five. Evidently.

Alex wasn't always so popular with the ladies. But he is no longer the lanky and incredibly scruffy friend I remember back in drama school. Who spent most of his days dreaming about being the next Bruce Willis. I would tease him he looked more like Woody Allen. It wasn't quite true back then but he certainly wasn't the hunk he is today.

1

As for me, I dreamt of taking the West End stage by storm … but uh … things didn't quite work out that way.

Oh, big deal!

I give myself a mental shake. So what if I haven't fulfilled my childhood dream? It's not as if I'm the only one out there wishing life had turned out differently. I'm a secretary for an insurance firm.

There really isn't much more to add – except there have been days when I've woken up in the early hours of the morning unable to breathe and wishing that I could start my life over. But who hasn't felt like that? At least Alex is living the dream. I'm happy for him, really, I am. I would love nothing better than to see him after all this time but it wouldn't be a good idea, (slightly embarrassing, if nothing else). It's about time my flatmate realised this. I peel myself off the table just as Sian pirouettes across my eye line.

'Uh, Sian!' I call out. She doesn't answer. I try again this time louder. 'Sian!' Still nothing. Oh, what the hell. 'SIAN!'

I yell at the top of my lungs, and before I bottle it, 'I'M NOT GOING TO MALIBU.'

Sian stops in mid-twirl, her arms splaying out to the side and one leg bent in an odd fashion. I have an urge to giggle.

'What do you mean, you're not going to Malibu?'

How does she do that? One minute she's on one side of the room, the next, looming down on me with her Monty Python killer-rabbit slippers, toe-tapping against the vinyl floor.

'Well?' she demands, eyebrows pointing upwards.

'I'm not going to Malibu.' I give my shoulders a nonchalant shrug, but my voice has lost its decisive tone.

'I gathered that much, but why the hell not?' Exasperated, she flops down in the chair opposite. 'What possible reason could you have for not wanting to spend three glorious weeks in Malibu holidaying with the delectable Alex Canty?'

Well, since you put it like that!

Avoiding my friend's incredulous gaze, I lean back in my chair until the two legs balance precariously on the floor. I stretch my arm out behind me and grab my glasses from the counter. With painstaking slowness, I slide them over the bridge of my nose. I try to think of a plausible excuse but my brain draws a blank.

'Well?' Sian says, clearly not going to let me off the hook.

'Tea. How about a nice cup of tea?' I utter in hopeful bribery. I drop the chair back on its four legs and leap to my feet. 'Earl Grey or Ceylon?' I wave the two questionable packets in the air.

Sian just stares at me like I'm out of my mind.

'Did you know that in Britain we consume around 145,000 tonnes of tea a year ...?'

'I know what you're doing,' she cuts in.

I blink through my glasses.

'You do it all the time.' She gives me an all-knowing, all-annoying smile.

'What's that then?' I ask crossly.

'Whenever you're trying to avoid a subject, you rattle off some silly trivia.'

'I do not—'

'Or you change the subject.'

'I can't help it that I have an ability to remember a lot of trivia facts,' I say, sniffily. 'You know some people would be fascinated with what I know. Consider it a sign of intelligence even.' Sian squints at me doubtfully. 'OK, proof of a good memory then. Did you know the elephant is the only animal with four knees?'

'You're doing it again.' she says smugly.

'I'm not,' I protest.

'Are.'

'Not.'

'Are.'

Oh, I give up! I turn away, busying myself with the tea.

3

'Earl Grey,' Sian chuckles behind me.

I roll my eyes. Maybe if I were more like Sian things would have turned out differently. Sian might be considered tiny at five feet three, but she is tall in every other sense of the word. And fearless; there's no way she would let a man treat her like a doormat and stampede over her dreams. Sian has the most potent self-belief this side of Simon Cowell but I'm not Sian and even though I stand at five-feet-eight – hardly the picture of a delicate violet – that doesn't mean I'm not as, uh … fragile as the next, uh … budding flower.

'Here.' I shove the mug of tea grudgingly into her hands.

She beams at me brightly. 'Thanks, hon.'

'Brrrrr,' I say, cradling my mug of tea to my chest. 'Is it me or is it cold in here?'

'And there you go again, changing the subject.'

If only I could.

It's the middle of winter and the central heating is on full blast. I also happen to be wearing a T-shirt, an old woolly jumper, and equally old grey flannel pyjama bottoms tucked into a pair of thick woolly socks to add to my panache! You would think I'd be feeling warm and toasty, but instead an eerie chill has crept into my bones. It always does when I think about my ex. I don't want to think about him, but he has this unpleasant habit of turning up uninvited. I blow into my mug, wishing I could blow away the unwanted memories just as easily. Instead, I end up with foggy specs. I take off my glasses and wipe them on my sleeve.

'So, when is Alex Canty expecting you?'

If only it were that simple. If only I could turn back the clock. If only I had gone to Malibu with Alex when he first asked me. If only I had never met Philip. If only, if only … Life is full of IF ONLY.

Straight out of drama school, I took a job as a waitress at a restaurant frequented by West End theatre thespians.

Philip was the restaurant manager. A dream boss to work for, he gave me time off whenever I needed. He also made it obvious from the start that he fancied me and well, to be honest, I was flattered. He was fairly good-looking in a clean-cut sort of way, and he just seemed – nice. And I needed nice. It was his persistence that won me over in the end. He was so sure that I was the one for him that I thought he must be right.

I can look back at it now and see that he caught me at a particularly vulnerable and lonely point in my life; my best friend had upped and left for Hollywood, I was struggling to find an agent, the bills were mounting up and I had a massive student loan to contend with. It seemed the most logical step to move in with him. Everything had been perfect for a time. I'm sure of it. He was supportive, charming, and when we did eventually sleep together, it had been pleasant rather than explosive. Nothing remotely comparable with the romances lining my bookshelves, but that's fiction. Real life is different.

Even now I have trouble pinpointing exactly when it started to go wrong between Philip and me. When his accusations stopped being small bouts of jealousy and turned into something more possessive and nasty. I can't remember when I stopped going out with my friends, only that I did. Philip would make such a fuss whenever I spent time with them, that to save aggravation I stopped seeing them and eventually they stopped asking. Then there were the spiteful comments after yet another failed audition. At first I made excuses for him: he was under a lot of pressure from work; he didn't mean the things he said. But as much as I tried to ignore his comments whilst I trudged from one audition to the next, it was hard to stay positive when being turned down because I wasn't what they were looking for. It pained me to accept that Philip was right; that I didn't have what it takes and the sooner I accepted it and got a proper job, the better.

Two years I put up with it. TWO *WHOLE* YEARS! I let him bully and manipulate me before I finally came to my senses and packed my bags. I learnt a valuable lesson. This I can say with absolute conviction. Never again will I let a man bully me and tear away at my personality.

Sian jabs me in the arm, waking me from my reverie.

'You haven't heard a word I've said, have you?'

I look up hastily. 'Sorry, miles away.'

Sian delivers me a thousand-watt smile.

'That's precisely where you should be. Miles away in sunny California.'

'I can't afford to go gallivanting halfway across the world,'

'Nonsense,' Sian counters. 'Didn't you say that Alex offered to pay for your flights? And didn't you say you'd be staying at his cousin's house? What's to pay for? And don't think I don't know about the money you have stashed away for a rainy day.'

I let out a gasp. She knows about that?

That's the bonus of having a monthly income and no social life to speak of. But I have plans for that money.

'Look, Sian,' I say, aiming for a veto on the subject, 'I'd rather wait until Alex's home is renovated before I visit. I don't want to stay with some stranger I've never met before.'

'You've got to be kidding me. It's Michael Canty.' Then, seeing my confusion, she adds incredulously, 'you do know who Michael Canty is, don't you?'

I stare back trying to remember what Alex said exactly. 'Some sort of writer?'

Sian gives me a pained look. 'Michael Canty happens to be a top-selling novelist.'

'Well I've never heard of him.'

'That's because he writes horrors.'

'I don't like horrors.'

'I know,' she laughs. 'But I'm sure he's not.'

'Not what?'

'A horror.'

I give Sian a weak smile. 'It's just not the right time. I have piano lessons on a Tuesday, then there's my work at the Bubble Theatre Group and, uh … I was thinking about starting a Cordon Bleu course, and uh … taking up Aikido …' I trail off because I'm obviously just making up excuses now. 'Besides, I've nothing decent to wear.'

'That's it!' Sian slaps her forehead as if it suddenly all makes sense.

I'm confused. 'It is?'

'I can't remember the last time you bought anything.' Sian seems thoroughly disturbed at the mere thought of such lax wardrobe attention. 'You can't possibly meet Alex looking like that!'

I should be affronted. I'm not.

'What's wrong with the way I look?'

Sian's face twists into a comical grimace.

'What's right with it, you mean.' She throws me a cheerful grin to take away the sting. 'Nothing a few quid and a trip to Liberty can't fix.'

'I think it's going to take a more than a few quid.'

'I'm glad we're on the same page,' she replies. A determined glint has entered her eyes. I need to act fast.

'There's no way I'm wasting my life savings on clothes.'

'What else have you got to spend it on?'

'A deposit on a flat.' Oops. I didn't mean to say that out loud.

Sian's mouth drops open and she is rendered speechless. Ten, twenty, thirty seconds … she just stares at me then her bottom lip begins to quiver and I think she's going to cry.

'I didn't know you wanted to leave me.'

'Not right away,' I add hastily. 'I mean I haven't even begun to look for a flat or anything.' I wave my hand in the air in a flippant manner. 'Just one day … you know … in the future.'

Sian's face does an about turn and she is all sprightly again.

'Well hold that thought,' she says cheerily. 'What we need to do is to concentrate on your imminent trip to Malibu. You are going to go to Malibu, aren't you?'

Honestly! Sian is like a dog with a bone when she gets an idea into her head.

'Oh, for heaven's sake! I'll think about it, OK?'

'Fantastic!' Sian leaps to her feet. 'I knew you'd see I was right.'

'But I haven't …' I let it go. I'll just have to let her think she's got her way then do exactly as I please.

'I'll go and get my magazines and put some ideas together.' And with a flick of her red mane, she flounces out of the kitchen.

I gather my own hair — thick and on the dull shade of brown — lifting it high off my shoulders then letting it drop back down with a heavy sigh. It would be nice to see Alex again and he did seem particularly persistent that I should visit him. In fact he seldom sounded more urgent. Maybe something is wrong? I shake my head. That's absurd. What could possibly be wrong with his glamorous life? Which is why I told Alex what I told Sian: that I would think about it. But my mind is set. I am NOT going to Malibu. Besides, Alex doesn't want me cramping his style. He's got a new set of friends. He should just forget about me. We have nothing in common any more. And to think I was even contemplating giving acting another shot. Who am I trying to kid!

My face suddenly pales and I stare at the kitchen door half expecting Philip to walk in. I try to laugh it off when he doesn't. Of course he won't, you silly moo. My laughter peters out to a small whimper. Even after all these years my ex still has the ability to make me feel like crap. I haul myself into the living room where I find Sian curled up in her favourite corner of the sofa ripping pages out of a fashion magazine.

'I've got loads of ideas ...' She holds up the torn pages. When she sees my face, she springs to her feet, the magazine pages dropping to the floor. 'You OK? You look like you've seen a ghost.'

To my astonishment I burst into tears.

'Oh, hon!' Sian rushes to my side. 'What is it? What's up?'

She drags me to the sofa where I collapse into a blubbering heap, tears steamrolling down my face. I tell Sian everything. All about Philip, his spiteful comments and controlling manner, and my failure to make it as an actress. 'And to top it all, I look a mess!' I wail, looking down at my very tatty, shapeless jumper and seeing myself as others might, frumpy and old before my time.

'My God!' Sian leaps to her feet, pacing the floor with tremendous rage. 'I knew it had been bad but I had no idea it had been that bad.'

I rub my red swollen eyes. 'Don't you see? If I was beautiful and talented he wouldn't have said those things.' I hiccup.

'Crap,' Sian spits out venomously. 'Oh he did a good job on you. I hate men who bully and manipulate women. It's enough to make me want to hunt him down and string him up by the goolies.'

She surprises me into a laugh.

'And you're not a failure.' Sian kneels in front of me cupping my hands. 'For one thing you left him. That,' she says, 'takes courage.'

I can't meet her eyes. 'Yeah, after two years.'

'But you left,' Sian reminds me. 'Remember that — you left him because you weren't prepared to put up with his bullying ways any more. That's what courage is all about. As for your job, if you hate it, quit.'

'And do what?'

'Act. Sing,' she says, as if it is the simplest thing in the world.

'I tried that, remember.'

'Maybe not hard enough,' she adds gently.

'That's not fair.' I put my hand to my head. I can feel the beginnings of an almighty headache coming on. 'I did try but I kept being turned down.'

'Well then, you move on to the next audition and you keep going. Jane, you have an amazing voice, it would be a shame not to use it.'

'You're just saying that because you're my friend.'

Sian is having none of it. 'Poppycock. I'm saying that because it's true.'

I look at Sian. Could she be right? Am I braver, stronger, than I give myself credit for? Sian believes it. The question is, do I?

And wasn't it difficult for Alex in the early days? How could I forget the anguished phone calls, the shared frustrations as he ranted at everything and everyone, the lack of opportunity, the positively useless agents?

'A holiday might be nice,' I say, feeling a sense of giddy hope burgeoning in the pit of my belly. 'A chance for me to rethink the future.'

'And where better to do it than sunny California?'

'Hmm, you could be right.'

'You know I am,' Sian counters smugly.

'And it would be nice to see Alex again,' I say, warming to the idea.

'Oh yeah, baby! Hey!' Sian leaps to her feet. 'Stand up.'

'What?'

'Stand up,' she instructs bossily. 'And take those damn glasses off.'

'I won't be able to see.' But I do as I'm told. Red-faced and squirming, she looks me up and down, her forehead pleating into a concentrated frown.

'What?' I cross my arms defensively.

10

'Jane, you are beautiful, you do know that?'

I pull a face to the contrary.

'I'm serious. You might hide yourself in hideous clothes but you can't hide the fact that you are beautiful. You have the perfect hourglass figure, great complexion, beautiful green eyes, long legs and big boobs. You're FHM's wet dream.'

'Sian!' I exclaim with embarrassment. And it is totally untrue.

'You've just let yourself down in the wardrobe department. You shouldn't swamp yourself in baggy clothes. You need to show off your curves, not hide them.'

'They're comfortable!'

'They're offensive.' she counters, ignoring my open-mouthed protest. 'What we need to do is revamp your image. The better you look, the better you'll feel, and the more desirable you will become.'

I snort hysterically. 'Oh, and exactly how do you intend to perform this miracle?'

CHAPTER TWO

WOAHHHH!!! Hands stretched out in front of me I hurtle towards the wall, landing against it with a grateful thud. Not my most graceful of entrances.

I feel woozy and unsteady on my feet. Thanks to the three (or was that four?) glasses of champagne I guzzled on the flight. Not that I'm counting. It isn't every day I get to sit in first class. Besides, I promised Sian I'd be more daring for a change – live a little. Because I am, after all, smart, gorgeous and talented … I dissolve into a fit of giggles. Perhaps I'm taking Sian's positive-thinking exercise a bit too far. An elderly couple passing by cast over a disapproving look; I pinch my lips together to stop myself from hooting with laughter.

Just for the record, Sian can perform miracles. You wouldn't recognise me. I don't recognise me. I'm wearing superfine skinny black jeans, a blush silk camisole, a vanilla-coloured silk-crepe jacket and am standing in, (albeit haphazardly) a pair of – drum roll if you please – canary yellow and blue four-inch Manolo Blahnik peep-toe heels! How's that for a fashion overhaul?

I nearly had a heart attack when I handed over my credit card. Sian said that you cannot put a price on style. And these really are the most exquisite shoes I've ever seen. Pity

I can't walk in them, although I seemed to manage easily enough when I boarded at Heathrow. Champagne and high-heels are clearly not a great combo!

The changes didn't stop at my wardrobe either. Sian coaxed me into swapping my glasses for contact lenses. This was greeted with rapturous applause from approving work colleagues. My boss even accused me of wearing coloured lenses. I thought that was the most hilarious thing ever. Emerald indeed! They now feel a bit on the dry side and a little uncomfortable. I root inside my bag, (Mulberry in case you're interested) for some saline solution.

It was my hair that became the final stage in my transformation. For as long as I can remember I have always had long hair and generally scraped it back in an unexciting ponytail. Never in a million, trillion years could I imagine cutting it, and yet cutting it seemed a final way of saying goodbye to the old me and hello to the new, confident me. So, I let the hairdresser chop away. It now lies jaw-length and shiny against my face.

Even now, catching my reflection in the glass, I am stunned by the stylish woman staring back. It doesn't look like me and yet it is. Amazing what a good hairstyle and some decent clothes can do. The make-up was a little trickier to master but I love a challenge and I found a stunning shade of cherry-red lipstick, the type of shade that exudes confidence. It works too. I definitely feel more confident (ish) when I'm wearing it.

Putting one shaky Manolo-clad foot in front of the other I wobble my way towards some stern-looking men in passport control. By the time I clear the slow-moving queue (fashionably late, naturally) and teeter over to the baggage carousel, luggage is already spilling from the chute. I immediately spot mine tipping out from the top as if to say, TAH-DA! Well you can hardly miss the leopard-print suitcase. I can't even blame this purchase on Sian, as it was entirely mine and mine alone. I think I took Sian's 'find your inner tigress' literally. I brace myself as the suitcase chugs towards me. Just when it's within my reach I lean forward to grab it but I'm unprepared for the sheer weight of my indiscreet prowling bag, and untrained in the art of balancing in high heels. Suddenly, I find myself being pulled forward and I'm going to hit the carousel face-first when an arm grabs me from behind and gets me, and my prowling bag, back onto solid ground.

Ohmigod! Ohmigod! OHMIGOD!

My face is burning with mortification but I'm OK. I'm not face down on the carousel. I'm OK.

'Thank you so much.' I look up and my gaze is instantly drawn to two very bushy eyebrows.

'You're very welcome,' the voice booms.

I know it is rude to stare but I can't help it. His eyebrows are thick and black and really bushy; like a pair of black furry caterpillars having a stand-off, completely at odds with his thick white head of hair.

'Heels,' I say, hoping this is enough explanation. He seems to understand.

'Lovely,' he replies.

I let out a grateful laugh. 'When I think what could have happened had you not ...' I shudder. 'Actually, it doesn't bear thinking about.' An image of myself sprawled out across the carousel pops vividly into my head.

'It isn't every day I get to help a damsel in distress.'

'Thank you, I think.'

'And one so beautiful.'

Beautiful indeed. He exaggerates. 'Well, thanks, again.' I thrust out my hand.

'My name is Jane. Pleased to meet you.'

'Bob,' he says. 'Bob Edwards.'

His voice resonates loudly around the lounge; several heads turn in our direction. Wow, he is loud. He takes my hand in a bear-like grip and pounds it up and down. And wow, that's some handshake. He lets go and I wiggle my fingers to encourage circulation.

'What brings you to LA? Or can I guess … actress?'

'Me!' I titter. 'Well, funny you should say that …'

By the time we've reached the arrivals I've somehow given Bob the impression that I have a successful stage career in London. It just sort of popped out. I guess the champagne is still loose in my system. Of course, I fail to mention that those stage appearances were like a zillion years ago. Moving swiftly on, I tell him I'm here visiting a friend, Alex Canty. He's impressed. He says he knows Alex Canty. But really that doesn't come as a surprise; you'd have to be living in the refuges of a Mongolian missionary to not know who Alex Canty is.

Pity he isn't in the arrivals hall, waiting for me like he promised.

'Timekeeping isn't one of his strong points,' I say, scanning the crowds and finding myself distracted by a man that can only be described as heart-stoppingly gorgeous.

I'm mesmerised.

Sian would be impressed with my choice of words and the fact that I'm checking a guy out. I haven't checked a guy out in … Well, a very long time. I'm unable to resist a come-hither look. I think Sian would say I'm making progress.

The gorgeous stranger is dressed casually in khaki green cargo pants and a black T-shirt. However, there is nothing casual in his stance. He reminds me of a brooding Mr Darcy in spite of the modern attire. An image of him wearing a pair of breeches and nothing much else pops into my head, surprising me into a giggle.

'Sex on legs.'

'Sorry?'

Flustered, I drag my gaze away. 'I'm … uh,' I clear my throat. 'Alex is late.'

Fortunately, Bob appears oblivious to my breathless state. 'A gentleman should never keep a lady waiting, especially one as delightful as you.'

I give him a winning smile. It isn't often one is paid so many compliments. So what if he's old enough to be my dad? It's nice to be appreciated.

'Would you like me to wait until he turns up?'

I shake my head. 'I wouldn't want to inconvenience you. I'm sure he'll turn up.' Eventually.

'It wouldn't be an inconvenience,' he gallantly informs me, laying on the charm that I'm finding endearing. 'On the contrary, it would be my pleasure.'

'I'll be fine,' I insist. 'Honest. But thank you.'

'If you're sure?'

'Positive.'

'Well in that case ...' He takes out a business card and hands it to me. 'Call me if you get stuck. Call me anyway and let me take you to lunch.'

I take his card and pop it into my bag.

'I would love that. Thank you.'

And I mean it too. I'm pretty sure there will be days when Alex needs to go off and do whatever important stuff famous actors do these days. It'll be nice to have the company.

Bob picks up his luggage and bids me a farewell salute as I watch him disappear into the crowd. I'm just thinking what a lovely man he is when there is a tap on my shoulder.

'Jane Allen?'

The unfamiliar voice makes me jump and squeal at the same time. For the second time today, I topple into the arms of a complete stranger. This time, my reaction couldn't be more different. Instinctively, my hands go out in front of me to cushion my fall, but instead of hitting the ground my palms land against a chest. A chest I can't help noticing is rock hard beneath my fingertips. Two large hands grip the top of my arms sending a jolt of electricity searing through the fibres of my jacket, and my nose is beguiled by a subtle scent of oranges and sandalwood. I step closer and press my nose against the chest and inhale, before coming to my senses. I gasp, and pull away.

Well, I was right about one thing: he is even more attractive up close. My eyes are momentarily drawn to the small scar on his chin. Not so much Mr Darcy as Indiana Jones. I wonder what world-saving adventure he had to fight himself out of to get such a distinctive marking.

I offer up an apologetic smile. I notice he doesn't smile back. In fact, now I have him in my vision he is looking at me in a less than favourable light. He has mastered this to perfection with the slight beak of his nose and acerbic twist of his lips.

'Jane Allen?'

Nice voice, shame about the aggressive tone.

Remember you are smart, gorgeous and talented ... A nervous giggle erupts from my lips.

'Are you drunk?'

My mouth flops open. I quickly snap it shut. 'I beg your pardon?'

'Drunk?' he reiterates.

So I did hear him correctly. 'Of course, I'm not drunk,' I say, bristling with indignation. Even if I were, God forbid, tipsy, it is hardly a crime. He doesn't have to look at me with such disapproval. He isn't my father!

'You startled me, that's all,' I say. 'You shouldn't creep up on people.'

'I don't creep.'

Whatever!

'If you don't mind I happen to be waiting for someone.'

I swing away from him, bristling. I can't believe I thought he was gorgeous. What a jerk. I can still feel his presence behind me so I turn back round.

'Can I help you?'

He smiles. Actually it's more of a smirk.

'You didn't answer my question.'

I grit my teeth. 'Yes, I'm Jane Allen.'

'I'm Michael Canty,' he says.

'How nice for you,' I retort but as soon as the words leave me, a horrible realisation dawns on me. No! No! NO! It can't be. Michael Canty, one of America's bestselling horror novelists, and a bit of a dish, recalling Sian word for word. Not that I care much for horrors, all that blood and gore; a person must have a warped mind to write such depraved stuff, and my brief encounter with this man is a pretty accurate observation.

'Alex's cousin?' I say with dismay.

'Got it in one.' He seems as pleased to see me as I am to see him, positively grim-faced.

I force myself to smile and extend my hand. 'Why didn't you say? Pleased to meet you, Mr Canty.' For an unpleasant second, I think he isn't going to take my hand.

'You can call me Michael,' he says, coolly slipping his hand into mine.

'Jane,' I respond, equally coolly but feeling anything but. You could fry an egg on my back and steam beansprouts on my brow!

His handshake is warm and firm. Peculiarly, my skin tingles long after I've tugged my hand free. 'Alex couldn't make it then?' I hug my arms in front of me.

'How very observant.' His tone is derisive. I have no idea why he is being so mean. 'Alex asked if I wouldn't mind picking you up.'

'And do you?'

'Do I what?'

'Mind picking me up?'

His response isn't quick enough and I know I've hit the proverbial nail on the head.

'I'm a bit busy,' he replies.

'Thank you so much for taking time out of your busy schedule, I'm so very much obliged.' My sarcasm doesn't go unnoticed.

'That's quite all right.'

I even think I see the beginnings of a smile, or I could have imagined it. He frowns way too much.

'So how do you know Bob?' The change of questioning surprises me. It takes me a moment to realise he's talking about my new friend. 'You mean Bob Edwards? Do you know him?'

'By reputation.'

And that means what exactly? I wait for him to elaborate but he doesn't and I'm not about to ask, even though I'm dying to. 'We met at the baggage carousel.' He continues to frown.

'You should watch that, if the wind changes …' I joke. He produces a slight smile but blink and you'd have missed it.

'He helped me with my suitcase. A perfect *gentleman*.' I over-emphasise. 'We're going to have lunch …' I falter when a bored look glazes over his face.

'As much as I'd like to stand here and discuss Bob's attributes …' his voice is condescending, '… we need to go.'

He picks up my suitcase, holding it as if it weighs nothing more than feathers, and stalks off. So much for the happy welcome I was expecting!

Even the sight of his well-built frame carrying my leopard-print suitcase barely rouses an inner snigger. Biting back the sob of frustration rising in my throat I hurry after him, my heels clink-clanking against the concrete floor.

His hurried steps are too quick for me and the distance between us quickly widens. It doesn't help that my handbag keeps sliding down my arm and knocking against my leg. I'm going to wake up with a massive bruise there tomorrow. (Note to self: must learn to pack handbag lightly for optimal 'chic-ness' whilst walking.) And if I'm not careful I'm going to fall arse over tit and break an ankle or something. As the distance between us increases I begin to panic.

I stop for the millionth time, hitch my bag back onto my shoulder, and shout out his name. When he doesn't turn around, even though he must have heard me, I decide enough is enough. Didn't I promise myself I wouldn't be pushed around? Didn't I promise myself I wouldn't be treated like a doormat? Isn't this supposed to be the new, improved Jane Allen? Confident, hard as nails Jane Allen. Can't you hear me *ROAArrr!*

I almost give in and break into a run when he disappears completely out of sight. I tell myself to stand firm, that he'll be back when he notices I'm not behind him, and when he does I'll give him a piece of my mind. I cross my arms and give myself a determined nod of the head.

You hope he'll come back; he's got your suitcase. Unless he's not who he says he is and he does this act all the time, being offensive and stealing women's luggage ... OH NOOOO ... my beautiful clothes!

Then I see him. Judging by the thunderous expression on his face he's not happy. My resolve wavers but I resist the urge to flee. I cross my arms defiantly. Tigress. Remember. Didn't I read somewhere that a tiger's roar can paralyse a human being?

'What's wrong?' he barks. His voice is so harsh that it makes me wince.

Tigress. Remember.

'You're walking too fast. I can't keep up.' I force myself to look into his black stormy eyes.

'If you had chosen to wear appropriate footwear you wouldn't need me to slow down.'

'Well I realise that now.'

'Good. Perhaps next time you won't be so stupid.'

It still comes as a shock to me that people feel they can talk to me any way they please. Do I have the word 'mug' stamped on my forehead? How dare he call me stupid! And how dare he mock my beautiful Manolos! My anger, starting from my four-inch heels, rises until it envelops my whole being.

'That's it!' I hiss through clenched teeth. 'I have had just about enough of you. You have been nothing but disagreeable to me since we met.'

And to think I had romantic illusions about him. Well they're squashed to oblivion. He might be good looking, but his manner stinks.

I thrust my finger at his chest, deliberately taking my time to pause after each word.

'If you hadn't wanted to pick me up you should have said as much to Alex. I am quite capable of getting a taxi. Now if you'd just give me back my suitcase, I'll bid you good day and goodbye. I wouldn't want to take up any more of your precious time.'

Tears of frustration fill my eyes but I blink them back and reach over for my suitcase. I will not give him the satisfaction of seeing me cry.

'Though I'd be interested to know what Alex will make of your behaviour,' I say. With one final tug ... 'PLEASE. CAN. I. HAVE. MY. SUITCASE. BACK?'

He lets go and I stumble backwards, but I don't fall. I look at him, my eyes full of hate. I'm stunned when I see two red blotches staining his cheeks.

'I'm sorry,' he mumbles.

I don't trust myself to speak. I'm barely managing not to cry.

'I'm sorry,' he says again. 'There's no need to get a taxi, my car is just outside.'

'Worried what Alex will say?'

'No,' he replies. 'I've just had a lousy day. But that's no excuse to take it out on you,' he adds quickly. 'I really am sorry.'

He takes my suitcase and, too shocked by his apology, I let him. Words are easy, actions count for far more in my book. I will just have to wait and see if the sincerity I think I caught a glimpse of can be trusted. Right now, I just want to get out of here. My skin prickles with self-consciousness as I become aware of the small crowd we have attracted.

'OK, apology accepted.' I take off my Manolos (resolving to wear something more appropriate next time) and stuff them into my already overloaded bag.

The cool concrete floor instantly soothes my swollen feet. The downside is it makes me four inches shorter. I could really do with the extra height right now, especially with Mr Hothead looking at me with those self-satisfied eyes: as if I've just confirmed how stupid I am for choosing to wear high-heels on a transatlantic flight. I narrow my gaze, daring him to pass comment. He doesn't.

With the little composure I have left, I stride purposefully away. I don't even bother to check if he is following me. I'm far too busy trying to stop myself from shaking. It must be the aftershock. I can't remember the last time I stood my ground like that. If ever. I really must invest in another pair of Mr Blahnik's; they're doing wonders for my psyche.

I've never liked confrontation at the best of times, but it does feel good to stand up for myself. He must be sulking because it takes him an age to reach my side. When he does I refuse to look at him but I can feel him watching me.

'We need to turn here.'

I don't respond.

'Jane?'

I don't want to make it easy for him, but I do want to get out of this airport. Wordlessly, I follow him out of the air-conditioned terminal.

A blanket of hot air immediately hits me and I start to sweat. Not to mention the piping hot ground burning my feet. I hop from one foot to the other.

'OW! OW! OW!'

My poor feet!

'Would you like me to carry you to the car?'

I stop hopping and gape at him. I'm not sure what shocks me more, the fact that he's actually smiling, or, the thought of being held in his arms. It's only when my soles start sizzling like raw meat on a griddle that I remember to hop.

'How about it?'

'And have you break your back?' I say with forced gaiety.

'You'd be a featherweight in my arms.' He is still smiling and it's the sort of smile that softens his strong features. Two deep grooves have dented the side of his face, tiny lines fan the corner of his dark eyes, and they are actually twinkling at me. Beware a wolf in sheep's clothing, I warn myself, because I certainly don't want to think what it would feel like to be in his arms. Not if I want to live to tell the tale.

'No need to come over all chivalrous.'

His smile dissipates.

'Where's your car?'

He points to the covered car park in the distance. 'Over there.'

I groan.

'Sure, you don't want me to carry you?'

'Quite sure,' I reply somewhat sniffily. 'A little dirt on the feet doesn't do any harm.' Dirt maybe not, but scorching ground certainly does.

Ow! Ow! Ow!

I know I look ridiculous skipping from one foot to the other and a surreptitious glance in Michael's direction confirms this – his smile is a mile wide.

So much for the glamorous entrance I was aiming for. It was bound to happen. From the moment I dumped the frumpy image for this glamorous new look, I've been convinced people will see through the façade and spot me for a total fraud.

I'm relieved when we finally reach the covered car park and I can stop hopping.

'You OK?' he asks, another smile playing on his lips.

'Fine,' I wheeze, clutching my waist. 'Absolutely fine.'

He directs me to an expensive-looking car and I act unaffected, like it's an everyday occurrence, me, travelling in first class and sitting in luxurious cars when in reality I'm usually pressed against someone's armpit on the Victoria line.

He unlocks the door and holds it open for me.

'Thank you,' I mumble, sliding into the seat, careful not to put my feet on the cream interior. I root inside my bag for some facial wipes.

By the time Michael has stored my suitcase in the back of the car and settled into the driver's seat, my feet are clean and the used wipes stuffed into the bottom of my bag. I stretch my feet and wiggle my tortured but brightly painted pink pedicured toes in front of me.

'Nice!' Michael remarks.

I know he's mocking me and I should probably ignore him but I'm curious.

'How did you know it was me at the airport?'

He turns from the wheel and gives me a smile. I tentatively smile back. Perhaps there is hope for us yet. Michael reaches inside his pocket and hands me a photograph. It takes a moment for my dry eyes to focus. A younger Alex is doing a fine impersonation of an ape. And me? I'm not sure what I am trying to be, but the effect is memorable: eyes crossed, cheeks puffed out, and thick, heavy, black liner circling my eyes. I look like a deranged panda. I can't believe that of all the photos Alex could have chosen ...

'You haven't changed at all,' he says, starting the engine and putting the car into drive.

My mother always said, 'If you can't say anything nice, say nothing at all' but oh, how I wish I had a witty comeback, something clever to wipe the smirk off his conceited face. Predictably my mind has gone blank. The only thing left to do is strategically ignore him for the rest of the journey. I lean back against the leather headrest, close my eyes and think of the many ways I'm going to kill Alex

CHAPTER THREE

The next time I open my eyes the car has stopped in front of a large wrought-iron gate. Heavy-lidded I watch the gates swing open and the car roll forward. Not yet ready to rise from my slumber, I nuzzle into the soft, warm fabric, breathing in the smell of oranges and sandalwood, mingled with ...

Oh hell!

I bolt upright in my seat, rubbing my eyes in dismay. Michael is staring straight ahead so I can't read his expression. I don't need to tell you how mortified I am. I open my mouth to speak to try and make light of the fact that I fell asleep on his shoulder but nothing comes out.

He brings the car to a stop and jumps out. When he's gone I slump down and let out a low pitiful moan. I wish Sian were here to make me see the funny side.

'You snore.'

I look up and Michael's head is poking through the open window. I gape at him gormlessly, still unable to find the words. I'm not positive but I'm sure I hear him chuckle as he disappears round the back. Red-faced, I try to convince myself it isn't the end of the world. I mean, I only fell asleep on his shoulder. *Possibly snored*, my mind torments. Still, it could have been worse I could have dribbled.

Groaning, I slot my feet back into my Manolos. Better than Cinderella in a glass slipper competition! My Manolos serving as my Prince Charming. Who needs him anyway!

I go to open the door but Michael is already there. Such a display of chivalry, anyone would think he was a nice guy.

'Thanks,' I mumble.

'You're welcome,' he replies.

With him standing there waiting I swing my legs to the side, just like Joanna Lumley showed me on the Graham Norton show, and climb out of the car in a lady-like manner. It would have been more impressive if I were wearing a skirt.

'I don't snore, by the way,' I say as I follow him round the car, squirming as soon as the words are out. He doesn't respond other than to raise a sardonic brow.

'I don't.' I rub my nose, feeling put out.

He still doesn't say anything so I opt for a change of subject.

'You have a nice house.'

Well I say house – mansion would be more accurate. It is a large, impressive white building with huge windows. He must be very successful at what he does. I'm so enthralled by the architecture that I'm not looking where I'm going and I don't notice Michael stop. As if things couldn't get any worse I slam into the back of him. Michael stumbles forward, regains his balance. Me, I end up on my hands and knees on the ground.

'Those heels will be the death of you.' He grabs me by the arms and unceremoniously lifts me off the floor.

Don't cry. Don't cry.

'You stopped,' I say, wiping the gravel from my hands. 'I wasn't looking.'

'That much is obvious,' he says. 'I thought I'd been charged by a rhino.'

Charming!

'Anyone would think you've never worn a pair of heels in your life.'

Yeah, well, it's been a while.

'Can I make a suggestion? When we get into the house can you change into something you can actually walk in?'

I suppose he has a point. He just doesn't have to be so smug about it. For no other reason than I think it's that or cry, I start to laugh. It's a strange bleat of a noise. Michael's bemused expression only makes me laugh harder and soon I'm laughing so hard that I give myself a stitch.

'Let's see if we can get you inside in one piece.' He grabs me firmly by the elbow and leads me across the gravel forecourt, my laughter petering out. The warm pressure of his fingertips sends out tiny sparks of electricity through my jacket and up and down my arm. It takes all my concentration just to put one foot in front of the other. I'm relieved when we reach the front door and he lets go.

'Do you like dogs?'

'Dogs?' My ears tune in to the frantic barking coming from inside the house. I'm not sure I like the sound of that!

'Depends on how big they are,' I say, truthfully.

'It's OK, he doesn't bite.' He pauses. 'Except strangers.'

'Is that so?' I give him an indifferent look. If I hadn't spotted the twitch of his lips I would have insisted on going back and sitting in the car.

Michael unlocks the door and I take a tentative step behind him, bracing myself for the possibility I might have to make a run for it. Michael lets out a chuckle. To my absolute delight, and relief, a lively brown and white springer spaniel bounds out in front of us. Its tail wags with uncontrollable excitement.

'Hey there, boy!' Michael bends down and ruffles its hair, and in particular a spot behind his ears. I stand for a moment, mesmerised by master and dog.

'We have a visitor.' Michael glances up at me. 'Digger, this is Jane. All the way from England.'

I smile at the dog, hoping he can sense that I am avid dog lover.

'Digger. Kill. KILL!' I shoot Michael a panicked look. The dog doesn't move and Michael starts laughing.

'Aren't we the comedian all of a sudden,' I retort.

I ignore his laughter and crouch down. 'Hello there,' I coo, holding out my hand.

The dog tilts its head to the side then casually saunters up to my hand and nudges it with his wet nose. Expelling a silent sedimentary breath, I scratch him behind his ears.

'Aren't you a handsome boy!'

He swiftly rolls onto his back and puts his paws in the air; they limply splay out to the side.

'Some guard dog you are,' Michael grunts with affection.

I laugh, dropping to my knees, and give Digger my undivided attention.

'You're adorable, aren't you!'

'When you've quite finished charming my dog, perhaps I can show you to your room?'

I pick myself off the floor.

'How could I forget, you're a very busy man,' I say, slightly sarcastically.

'You do realise you have dog hair all over you?'

I follow his gaze and groan, brushing the hair off my jeans.

'As a kid I had a knack of getting my best clothes ruined. It used to drive my mother crazy. I can picture her now, eyes rolling despairingly skywards.' I stop. Why am I telling him this? I pretend to cough and brush at the dog hair on my jeans.

Michael turns and heads inside.

Digger and I follow obediently behind him.

If I were a cartoon character my head would be spinning on its neck right now. I am gawping every which way, trying to take it all in. It's an amazing house. I love it. A grand, antique-looking chandelier hangs from the ceiling, there's lots of modern artwork on the walls (I'm sure I spy a Picasso or something, definitely original), tanned leather sofas, a massive flat-screen TV, a large pool table and at the far end I can see a huge window, which I'm guessing overlooks Colony Beach.

I lean over the banister, one leg half off the ground to get a better look. This place is a far cry from the tiny Victorian flat I share with Sian, with its peeling wallpaper, hideous seventies patterned carpet and cheap furniture. In fact, it's exactly the type of house I would have if I had the kind of money he obviously has. Michael clears his throat loudly. I peer up to find him standing at the top of the stairs looking at me in that way usually reserved for wayward children.

I run up the remaining few steps. Not so bad for a high-heel novice!

'Do you always take such a long time to walk up the stairs?'

'I didn't know it was a race.'

He opens a door. 'Your room.'

'Thank you.' I step inside and come to an abrupt stop. Three thoughts immediately spring to mind. This room is enormous; Christ, and it's bigger than my entire flat, and it's exquisitely decorated.

'Nice,' I say inadequately.

Michael circles around me and deposits my suitcase on the bed.

I take off my shoes and squeeze my toes into the cream carpet, revelling in the lush velvetiness between my toes.

'Closet is over here. Bathroom to your right, it has a shower and Jacuzzi ...' Michael starts talking but I'm only half listening. I bypass the king-size bed, but pause long enough to run my fingertips across the satin sheets. Ooh ... I'm going to enjoy waking up in those. I make a beeline towards the enormous window covering the length and breadth of one wall. My eyes bulge. Alex said this place was amazing. He hadn't been exaggerating.

'Is this the Pacific Ocean?'

'Yes.' Michael comes to stand next to me. 'I don't think I'll ever tire of looking at the water.'

We stand like this for a moment, side by side, looking out at the magnificent sight, only now that he is standing close I have a little trouble focusing on the spectacular view; my vision starts to blur. Damn contacts again! I wish he didn't stand so close, it makes me feel all nervous and jittery inside.

'My sister and I used to spend our summer holiday in Hayling Island. We would spend all day on the beach, only coming in when the sun went down. But these beaches don't look like that, they're pebbled, we always had to be careful not to stomp our feet on the rocks but it had the most beautiful shells ...' I'm babbling but I can't seem to stop myself. 'My parents would despair when we came back with yet another bag full of smelly, occupied shells. The shells hatched underneath my pillow one year and scared my sister into peeing the bed ... it was the top bunk ... that was unpleasant ...' Stop wittering like an idiot I tell myself.

I look at Michael and he is looking at me with a tiny half-smile on his face. I find myself blushing.

'Colony Bay is private, so feel free to use it.' He walks away. 'And that goes for the swimming pool too.'

I look down at the large, kidney-shaped swimming pool. I could do with a swim right now; either that or a cold shower.

'Hungry?' Michael asks.

I tear myself away from the view and walk over to Michael and Digger.

'Not really,' I shrug.

'You're not one of those women who starve themselves, are you?'

I stop and place a hand on my hip. 'Do I look like the type of woman who does?' Now why did I go and say a thing like that?

He gives me a long, leisurely look and I can feel myself squirming.

'No,' he says, after what seems like an eternity.

Meaning what, exactly? Is he saying I'm fat? I stop myself. Don't even go there.

'I'm going to make myself a sandwich. If you want one I'll be in the kitchen.' His departure is quick and abrupt.

I fling myself backwards onto the bed and groan. My brain immediately hits the rewind button and starts spooling back, stopping at each embarrassing event: falling asleep on his shoulder; falling over – twice; hopping barefooted at the airport; rowing in arrivals. I roll over and bury my face into the pillow.

What happened to the cool, sophisticated woman who boarded the plane at Heathrow Airport? She didn't bloody well exist!

It's all an act and it gets worse. I realise I might fancy Michael. Of course, you knew that already, but then he was so horrible and now … well now he doesn't seem so bad … Oh God, I don't know what to think.

Best not to think at all.

I drag myself off the bed and fetch my suitcase. Unpacking takes me all of ten minutes.

Now what?

Face.

In the bathroom I survey my reflection and groan. The immaculately turned-out woman who boarded the plane in London is now dishevelled, but not in that good, sexy way. It takes me a good twenty minutes to restore order, and plenty of confident-boosting red lipstick.

I give my reflection an exaggerated thumbs-up. It's really goofy. I think I'm becoming the absolute epitome of a sad, travesty-stricken caricature of myself.

For a moment I consider hiding out in my room and waiting for Alex to return, but that wouldn't be very courageous of me. Remembering that I am a smart, talented, gorgeous woman I slip into my Manolo heels ... Did I mention they were four inches? Whatever was I thinking? I should have gone for a two- or three-inch heel, eased myself in gently. But that would have been too easy, and with my calf muscles flexing, my feet won't dare to complain. I will conquer four inches, no sweat, and boy, don't I look hot!

CHAPTER FOUR

It's only when I reach the bottom step that I realise I have no idea where I'm going. 'Uh … hello?' I call out. My hesitant voice bounces back to me. I try again, only louder and with more gusto. 'HELLO?'

There is a sudden sound of scampering feet. I look up to see Digger bounding towards me, skidding to a stop in front of me, his tail wagging uncontrollably.

'Well, hello there, handsome.' I bend over to ruffle his ears. 'Have you come to show me where the kitchen is?'

He cocks his head as if giving my question considerable thought. I almost think he understands me, on some bizarre level, when he rolls onto his back, expectantly. Laughing, I drop to my knees.

'OK. Here's the deal,' I say, scratching his belly. 'I'll tickle your lovely hairy belly then you show me where the kitchen is, OK?' The dog looks back at me, contentment dribbling down his chin.

'You know some people would regard talking to yourself as a sign of madness?'

Michael's quiet voice makes me jump.

'I wasn't talking to myself, I was talking to your dog,' I say, keeping my eyes fixed on the dog and not at him. 'I bet you talk to Digger all the time.'

'Yes. But everyone knows I'm mad.'

Hmmm, can't argue with that.

'Come on. Up you get!'

I scramble to my feet.

'I was talking to Digger.'

I cough to cover my embarrassment. 'Yeah, I knew that!'

'I see you didn't take my advice.' His gaze drops to my feet.

'Well I figured I haven't done nearly enough falling over for one day,' I say, meeting his amused eyes.

I notice he is still wearing the same khaki-coloured trousers, but he has changed his top and is now wearing a faded grey T-shirt with some obscure band I've never heard of emblazoned across his chest. He hasn't shaved, his hair is damp from a shower and it has begun to curl up at the ends. My sensitive nose tingles with the aroma of freshly bathed skin and the familiar scent of oranges and sandalwood – it's intoxicating to the point of drunkenness. I lick my dry lips. Gosh, he really is knicker-dropping gorgeous!

It's weird that someone I barely know is having this kind of effect on me. I can't stop staring at him.

'Is the offer of a sandwich still open?' I ask.

'Sure. This way.'

Like everything else in the house, the kitchen is large and stylishly decorated; cool metallic and dark wood. It is ultra-modern, ultra-masculine-looking. I wonder how often it gets used.

'So what sandwich would you like?'

'Oh, I'm not fussy. Whatever you're having.'

'Grilled vegetables and hummus?'

I was expecting a regular cheese or ham sandwich. Guess he's a bit of gourmet – he needs something to offset those dubious manners.

'Grilled vegetables and hummus sounds lovely,' I say, delightedly.

'Lemonade?'

'Great, thanks.'

'Slice of lemon?'

I nod. 'Yes please.'

While Michael busies himself with the sandwich I stand in the middle of the kitchen feeling a bit like the lemon on his chopping board just waiting to be beheaded. It would help if I could think of something to say. I clear my throat nervously.

'Do you want a hand?'

He doesn't turn around. 'I think I can manage a sandwich. Why don't you sit down?'

I do as he suggests, tucking my legs under a large metallic table. Digger settles companionably by my feet.

Michael hands me the glass of lemonade and a bowl of mixed olives then returns to his chopping board. I stay sitting at the table, one hand stroking Digger, the other holding the lemonade and absent-mindedly selecting olives. The only sound coming from Michael is the chop-chop-chopping sound as he slices through the vegetables at chef-like speed. He doesn't appear to have a problem with the silence like I do.

'So how old is Digger?' I ask, aiming for any degree of small talk.

He doesn't immediately answer and then it's as if he takes pity on me. 'He's five.'

'That's thirty-five in dogs years,' I say chattily.

He doesn't respond.

'I've always wanted a dog but I suppose it wouldn't be fair to keep it cooped up in a flat all day.'

Again, silence. This is literally like pulling teeth. 'Have you been to London?'

Finally, he turns around. 'Yes. A few times.'

'Have you been on the London Eye?'

He gives me a tight smile. 'Yes.'

I groan. I have no idea why I asked him that. I should probably just shut up. I am an idiot.

'It's a bit pricey, isn't it, but it's a great way to see London. So, were you there for business?'

'Yes.' But he doesn't volunteer any more information.

'It must be wonderful to do what you love and get paid for it.'

He leans his body against the swanky Boffi kitchen counter (I've become an expert on interiors since becoming a bored secretary), and pops a chunk of artichoke in his mouth.

'And do you enjoy your work, Jane?'

'It pays the bills.'

'You don't like acting?'

'Oh, I love acting,' I enthuse, then realise my mistake. I take a moment to compose myself. 'I work as a secretary for an insurance firm.'

'I thought … Alex said …' He looks confused.

'I haven't acted professionally for a while … and before I knew it three years flew by!' I risk a little laugh. 'I am a member of an amateur dramatics society but recently I've been thinking about giving acting another shot, or at least I think I am, it's sort of why I am here.'

I can't believe I've confided in him. This is more than I've told anyone. Probably because he's a complete stranger. I also think my anxious twittering is annoying him because he is frowning again. But then again frowning seems to be his natural disposition, grumpy faced writer-man that he is.

I have been telling myself not to expect anything from this holiday. That my life is not going to dramatically change overnight, but I can't help feeling that something exciting is going to happen to me.

'Alex did say he would introduce me to some agents …' I tail off. I get the distinct impression he has judged me on something and decided I'm guilty.

He whittles off a sliver of grilled pepper and slides it slowly into his mouth then grabs two plates and places one down on the table.

'So how long has it been since you actually acted?'

The sandwich looks scrumptious. I take a bite; mmm, it is.

For a moment I consider lying but what would be the point. 'Um, well, it didn't really take off after graduating, just the odd day here and there.'

'How long were you trying before you quit?'

'I didn't quit!' I protest. I'm certainly not going to enlighten him on the whole Philip saga. 'You know nothing about it.'

Is that the best I can come up with? This isn't the school playground. I might as well start sulking now.

'Things just went a bit pear-shaped for me,' I confess. I reach over for another bite of my sandwich. He continues to eye me with the suspicion of a hotshot prosecutor, and I feel the heat gathering in my cheeks as I chomp down on the sandwich. To make matters worse my mouth ignores my brain's intention of shutting the hell up.

'Not everyone gets to fulfil their childhood dream. I mean it's not like I'm the only one out there wishing life had turned out differently.' The age-old argument that has always comforted me in the past sounds piteous and weak now, and I'm conscious that I am revealing far more about myself than I mean to.

'As I said things happened ...'

'A man, you mean?' His look is unflinching and self-satisfied.

'Yes, a man,' I admit peevishly.

What would be the point in denying it? I still can't shake the feeling he is judging me and I want him to understand. But understand what, exactly? That I'm not completely spineless? It didn't happen for me before, what makes me think it'll happen for me now? I might as well give up.

Philip's words chill me and I'm angry for letting him creep into my thoughts.

'And you've been working for this insurance firm ever since?'

'Yes,' I snap. 'Is there something wrong with that?'

'You tell me.'

I'm not sure how to answer him so I take another bite of my sandwich. It's really tasty.

'Does it make you leap out of bed in the morning?' he probes.

'Huh? Uh, no …' But honestly, how many people can say that?

'What makes you think you can make it as an actress now?' His question jolts me. 'It's a tough industry to break into and if you didn't succeed before …'

That sounds like something Philip would say. But he doesn't know me. He doesn't know what I am capable of. I owe it to myself to give it another shot, a proper shot this time. He's not the first, and I doubt he'll be the last person to question my ability. If I'm to succeed in this industry I'm going to have to toughen up. I draw in a shaky breath.

'I'm wiser now, more ready for it.'

'So, are you prepared to do anything?'

'Absolutely. Anything.'

'Anything?' He cocks his brow.

'Well, not anything,' when I grasp what he's implying. 'I'm not going to sleep my way to the top, if that's what you think.'

'You wouldn't be the first.'

'That doesn't really happen?'

He looks at me as if I'm being naive.

'Well, good luck.'

'Don't you mean break a leg?'

'Now why would I want that?'

And I know this sounds ridiculous, but I'm positive his eyes travel the length of my legs and my heart does a thumpety-thump. I know, ridiculous, right, because my legs are safely tucked under the table.

'Help yourself to anything. I'm off to my study.' He abruptly swings away.

'You're leaving me?'

'And I don't want to be disturbed unless it's life or death. OK?'

'But ... err ... what will I do?'

He stops and gives me a faint smile.

'Anything you like. You don't need babysitting, do you? You're so much wiser now!'

'Hospitality certainly isn't your calling,' I grumble.

He treats me to an indifferent smile and exits with an obedient Digger following behind.

Alex mentioned some people find Michael a bit moody but his blowing hot and cold is slightly unnerving. I should learn not to care but it's hard not to. I like to think I get on with most people but when you can see you're not particularly liked and your presence is unwanted, what do you do then? Maybe it's me; maybe I bring out the worst in people.

I stop myself. Those kinds of negative thoughts are not going to do anyone any good and the sooner I disregard them for the twaddle they are the better. I devour the rest of my sandwich, which really is delicious, then head over to the sliding doors.

I just have to accept that not everyone is going to like me, no matter how hard I try. Shaking the cloud of insecurity from my head, I slide the door open and step out into the glaring mid-afternoon sun. Now here's something to smile about.

I make my way across the decked terrace, my heels making a clickety-click sound against the concrete slabs – I smile. I've never worn heels around a poolside before. I like it. I feel like I should be wearing a kaftan and sipping a mojito! Standing tall, shoulders pulled back, back erect, I am a glamorous, confident woman. But secretly I suspect I am more of a precarious pelican about to slip on a concrete slab.

I glance over at the pool and while I'm tempted to have a quick dip, I decide tomorrow will be soon enough to expose my lily-white body. Besides, I want Alex to see me looking presentable for at least five minutes before I slip back into bad habits. Instead I settle myself under one of the large, bright yellow umbrellas that is fringing the poolside and stretch out. The warm sun feels glorious on my skin.

CHAPTER FIVE

I hear my name being called and its persistence filters into my sub-consciousness. I roll away from the sound but it follows with a chuckle.

I might have known!

My eyes fly open and Michael's face is just inches from mine. If I wanted to I could reach up and kiss him! Alarmed by this random thought I pretend to cough and haul my body up. Michael is forced to stand up. I push my hair out of my face, feeling flustered. Trust him to be the one to catch me snoozing again.

'I thought you had tons of work to do?' I sound crotchety. Well I am.

'I do, but an intermittent snorting sound was distracting me.' His voice is grave, but there is no mistaking the poorly disguised humour seeping through.

'I do not snore. Must be your imagination.'

'I'm afraid my imagination is purely visual, not aural.'

'You should do stand-up. I'm thinking nineteen fifties summer season Blackpool.'

He laughs. My mood is appeased slightly.

'So, what do I owe the pleasure?'

'I thought you might like to know that Alex is here.'

'Alex! Here! Oh crikey.' I leap to my feet, toppling forward and straight into Michael's arms. If I'm not careful he's going to think I'm doing this on purpose. I pull away and straighten up.

'How do I look?' His expression is poker-faced. 'Oh, never mind.'

'Do you always find it easy to fall sleep?' he asks.

'Must be a side-effect of your riveting company,' I reply with a chuckle, quickly dodging past. Now I resemble John Cleese in the ministry of silly walks; one of my legs is still asleep, unaware it's four inches higher than normal.

Digger is already at the front door barking with excitement and I rush to join him, flinging the door open just in time to see Alex climbing out of a bright red flashy sports car. He looks the epitome of a handsome movie star: tanned, gorgeous and trendy in faded blue jeans and a white T-shirt. No wonder he tops the *100 Sexiest Males Alive* polls frequenting the glossy magazines. I stop myself from running up to him and jumping into his arms, a) because I haven't learnt to run in heels and b) I want to soak in my best friend's reaction.

'Hello, Alex deary,' I call out in a cheeky Python-esque manner.

Alex peers up and ever so slowly slides his dark glasses down the bridge of his nose. Seeing me, he grins. 'Jane, is that really you?'

'The one and only.'

We stand like this for what seems like ages, both wearing identical goofy grins. The last time Alex saw me I was thirty pounds heavier, wearing DM's, ripped jeans, and let's not forget the heavy black eyeliner.

Alex is the first to speak. 'Are you going to stand there or are you going to give me a hug?' His voice catches with choked up emotion.

Taking tiny baby steps, I attempt a run across the forecourt, trip and catapult myself into Alex's open arms.

Laughing and squealing, he swings me around. I can hear Digger barking enthusiastically in the background.

Alex hugs me tight. 'God I've missed you.'

'Me too.' I squeeze back, tears pricking the back of my eyes.

'It's been too long.'

'Far too long,' I agree.

Alex puts me down, his blue eyes glistening with unshed tears and then, as if he can't bear the thought of letting me go, lifts me back up and starts spinning me round and round until we're both dizzy.

'Alex, I'm going to throw up!'

He puts me down but doesn't let me go.

'I suppose I have to let myself out.' An imperious nasal voice breaks through our embrace and we pull apart. So enthralled in seeing Alex I hadn't noticed the woman sitting in the passenger seat, but I can't fail to notice her now. I watch in awe as the blonde star uncoils from the seat and slides out of the car, her silky hair cascading gloriously down her back and glinting gold in the sunshine. She is wearing the tiniest pair of white shorts, showing off her tanned slender legs to perfection. An equally tiny white T-shirt displays a very flat tanned midriff. A candyfloss-coloured cardigan is wrapped casually around her shoulders and on her feet, white flip-flops. She looks effortlessly stylish, as if she hasn't had to try too hard. I look like a dishevelled pig farmer in comparison.

Except on closer inspection her lips look a little augmented to me, and those are definitely not her own boobs, they're more rigid than the metalwork of the car she just slid out of.

'So you're Jane Allen,' she says in sugary tones. 'I've heard so much about you.'

'Don't believe a word he says,' I say chattily.

44

'Quite!' she says, raising a single elegant eyebrow. I feel a bit deflated that we're not going to be friends. I have the distinct impression she doesn't like me.

'Jane, this is Kimberly Roberts, Kimberly this is Jane Allen,' Alex announces as we shake hands. I don't need any introduction, I know exactly who she is: Alex's co-star in *The Dr's Shifts*. Sian hates her.

'Hello,' I smile pleasantly. 'Pleased to meet you.'

She gives me a flicker of a smile. Nope, she most definitely doesn't like me.

I guess being popular in Malibu is going to be hard work.

'Alex,' Kimberly coos, slipping a possessive arm into his. 'How about that ice-cold drink you promised me.'

Seeing Kimberly and Alex together it's easy to see why they are so often linked romantically in the press, and I wonder if there is something more to their relationship than the on-screen chemistry. I must remember to ask him about that later.

'How did it go?'

I jump out of my skin. Michael! Slowly I turn around, pretending my heart isn't palpitating to a drum and bass mix gone mental. He walks leisurely down the steps towards us.

Michael and Alex are both tall and broad and have that smouldering thing going on with their eyes, but whereas Alex's eyes are warm and inviting, Michael's are suspicious and alarming; and never more so than when they are looking at me. What have I done to warrant the black scowl? Probably still smarting from the joke I made earlier.

'I'll tell you about it later,' Alex says, disengaging himself from Kimberly's grasp.

'How did what go?' Kimberly looks at Alex then at Michael.

'Oh nothing,' Alex dismisses hastily.

Kimberly seems to want to press him further but Michael grabs her attention. 'Kimberly, you're looking stunning as always.' He plants a light kiss on both cheeks.

She gives him a dazzling smile.

'Hello, Michael, how's the book coming along?'

'Slow,' he groans good humouredly, leading her towards the house.

I look across at Alex and he gesticulates sticking his finger down his throat. I let out a giggle.

'Not as stunning as you, Jane,' he says, looping an arm through mine and giving it a squeeze. 'I'm really glad you're here.'

'Me too.' I squeeze back, feeling myself welling up again. I hadn't realised how much I missed having Alex around. He's still the same old Alex with the same naughty grin and twinkle in his eye.

'When you two have quite finished smooching perhaps you will join us.' Kimberly's sugary tone reveals annoyance.

Alex smiles pleasantly. 'I just can't get over how marvellous my Jane looks. Not that you weren't marvellous before,' he says with another shameless wink.

'No need to go overboard.' I poke him in the ribs, aware that Michael and Kimberly are less than appreciative of the affectionate display of our reunion. Talk about frosty atmosphere, an Arctic expedition has better weather prospects. But I refuse to be intimidated by the Botox-Viper starlet or the moody writer.

'Thanks for meeting Jane, you're a true gent, Mr C.' Alex turns to me. 'Have you two had fun?'

I remain tight-lipped, sneaking a peek at Michael but he seems indifferent to what I may or may not say.

'Sorry about not meeting you.' Alex grabs my hand. 'I wanted to but ...' He stops himself. 'I'll explain later.'

I follow his gaze and Kimberly is watching us with the eyes of a narked hawk. Whatever it is, he doesn't want to tell me in front of her.

'Get down, Digger.' Kimberly brushes Digger's paws off her white shorts, only Digger thinks it's a game and jumps right back up again.

'Oh get off you stupid dog!' she screeches, pushing him away with exasperation.

Alex slaps his hands on his knees. 'Hey, Digger!' Digger runs to Alex and jumps on him. Alex ruffles his ears.

'He shouldn't jump up like that.' Kimberly glowers at me as if it is somehow my fault.

'Fucking hell, Jane!' Shocked by Alex's dramatic outburst I turn at once. He has a look of complete astonishment on his face.

'What! What is it?'

'I've just realised something.' He can barely get the words out. 'Your hair!'

I laugh and touch it. 'You like it?' I toss my head from side to side as if I am in a shampoo ad.

'Love it,' he enthuses. 'Though I'd never have guessed in a million years you would get it cut.'

'My drink!' Kimberly says, all but stamping her feet.

'Yeah, yeah, coming.' Alex pulls me by the hand and we follow them into the house.

Half an hour later we are all sitting outside on the decked terrace sipping champagne, Alex's idea, in celebration of my arrival.

The evening air is now considerably cooler. Not that dissimilar to the general mood of the party. I would have preferred to have Alex all to myself so we could catch up properly but Kimberly and Michael have joined us. It's not quite the riveting company I was expecting. Well, maybe Kimberly's bionic bust and face are actually riveted. I can't quite make out any movement or natural facial expression yet. I'm allowed to be bitchy as she hasn't made the slightest effort to be nice to me.

It isn't hard to see why men might find Kimberly attractive – she's got that whole California-babe thing going on: long blond hair, skinny figure, big boobs and a smile that is just too lovely for, for, for … reality.

She leans over and whispers something in Michael's ear and it must be funny because he throws back his head and laughs. He has an attractive laugh, deep, rich, sexy.

'You're not what I expected.' Kimberly interrupts my thoughts. 'You look much bigger in your photos.'

Just which photos has Alex been brandishing around? Miaow!!

'I was bigger,' I say. 'I only need to look at food and I put on pounds.'

'I've never had to worry about my weight,' Kimberly churns out with a sickly, saccharine nonchalance.

'I don't suppose Alex showed you the photos of him dressed up in high-heels and make-up?'

Alex bursts into laughter. 'You don't still have those do you?'

Michael and Kimberly are staring at him but while Michael looks amused Kimberly looks somewhat mystified.

'I think the tabloids would be eager to get their hands on a few choice photos of the younger cross-dressing Alex Canty. I seem to remember you were partial to a particular red dress.'

Alex gapes at me with a slight look of worry.

'You wouldn't?'

I wiggle my brows. 'What's it worth?'

'My complete and utter adoration from this day forth!'

'I'll settle for total and eternal servitude.'

'Have I told you how much I admire you as a person, as an actress?'

'OK. Your secret cross-dressing is safe with me.' I wink and tap the side of my nose.

I steal a glance at Michael and his eyes seem to probe mine, searching for goodness knows what. I return his gaze but nerves get the better of me and I look away.

It's been ages since I've been attracted to anyone and I really have forgotten what to do. My guess is he doesn't find me the slightest bit attractive. This is why I have to get this silly infatuation out of my head. Besides, I'm not here to meet anyone. I'm here to … find myself. Does that sound lame?

'You really are the most marvellous person I know, and beautiful.'

'Huh?'

'And I'm not just saying that because you could ruin my macho image.'

If Alex is trying to make Kimberly jealous, it's working. I can almost feel the hatred burrowing into my skin.

'OK, Alex, no need to go overboard, I've already told you your secret is safe with me.'

'You do look different from your photos,' Kimberly cuts in mordantly.

I send a silent thank you to Sian. Alex turns to Michael and Kimberly.

'Did you know Jane was the star at drama school?'

'Yes, you have mentioned it a few times.' Kimberly's lips tighten as if all her collagen dissipated instantly. 'And what is it that you are doing at the moment?'

It's a casual enough question but I know better than to believe she is genuinely interested in anything about my life. 'Nothing at the moment.'

'Tell us about that play you were in,' Alex urges.

My local amateur dramatics where I played a menopausal goose seeking the meaning of life. It sounds sillier than it was. I suppose it was trying to be a symbolic statement about forgotten femininity and just ended up on the pantomime side of Mother Goose. The audience was full of kids by the second Saturday. It was not the aspiring woman's topical piece the playwright hoped. The less they know about that the better. I wish my memory of it were burnt out too; every time I see Big Bird I shudder in a hot flush. Besides, I don't need Kimberly to have another reason to look down her snotty plastic nose at me.

'I'm between jobs at the moment,' I say, avoiding Michael's gaze. Alex looks at me curiously. I will tell him. I will. Just not in front of Kimberly.

'It's a very tough industry to succeed in,' says Kimberly smugly.

Both Alex and Michael shift uncomfortably in their seats.

'What do you do when you're not acting, wait tables?'

Kimberly's act of sincerity is exactly that – an act (her acting skills are atrocious), and I'm getting sick and tired of her high and mighty attitude; she only plays a one-dimensional character in a TV show. I quell the impulse to throw the contents of my glass in her face and smile politely. 'I work for an insurance firm.'

'Oh,' she expels from her nose, clearly delighting in this piece of news.

'I didn't know that.' Alex looks at me with surprise.

'Got to pay the rent somehow.' I avoid his questioning eyes and take another sip of champagne.

'Acting is a dog-eat-dog world and only the toughest survive,' Kimberly says. Her artificial sweetness is really irritating me now.

'Or those who have Daddy to help them get the part,' I retort in the same honeyed tone.

She sucks in a furious breath – as much as her taught features can muster – and Alex chokes on his drink. It gives Kimberly an excuse to take her pent-up fury out on his back with a couple of sharp slaps. It's no secret that her dad, a well-known TV producer, got her the part. I take a peek at Michael and to my surprise he is hiding a smile.

'My dad didn't get me this job,' she retaliates hotly. 'I had to audition with hundreds of other girls.'

'Speaking of acting,' Alex intervenes coolly. 'My news.' He pauses dramatically as all eyes swivel to him. 'This is my last season on the show.'

Alex's news does manage to defuse the tension between Kimberly and myself, but Kimberly is now looking at him as if he had just told her something positively indecent. 'What do you mean, last season?'

'I've been thinking about it for a long time and it's now official ...'

'But ... but.' Kimberly is genuinely distraught. Her brows actually crinkle. And then, as if the wrinkle police have just caught her, she deliberately smooths them out. 'But you can't leave. What about us?'

'More champagne, anyone?' Michael hoists the bottle from the ice bucket.

Kimberly shakes her head furiously.

'Jane?'

I'm too dumbstruck to speak. Sian is going to be absolutely distraught.

'Jane?' He holds the bottle in front of me.

'Uh? Oh yes, champagne, thank you.' I hold up my glass for him to pour.

'I don't see why you have to leave the show,' Kimberly bleats. 'They've offered you more money, haven't they?'

'How do you know that?'

'I, um ... just something I heard.'

'It's got nothing to do with wanting more money, Kimberly,' Alex says stiffly. 'I've been doing the show for five seasons. I need a change ... a new challenge.'

'But what about your fans?' Kimberly beseeches. 'People love Mel Keaton. Just think about all those who will be devastated if you left.' She turns to Michael. 'Wouldn't they?'

'I'm staying well out of it.'

51

Michael has said nothing to release the tension but I'm well aware that he has spent the majority of the time frowning at me. He probably blames me for the way the evening is turning out; the reasoning's of a prolific horror writer are so far totally unfathomable to me. Between him and Kimberly it's a wonder I haven't disintegrated under their hostile gazes. But Kimberly does have a point; millions of people will be devastated if Alex goes. Perhaps that's why Alex had been so persistent that I visit him, a chance to talk over his career plans, a bit of moral support?

'I suppose you knew about this?' Kimberly spits the words out in a vengeful flurry.

'No.' I shake my head. 'This is the first I've heard of it.'

She glowers at me in disbelief.

'It's true, Kimberly, Jane knew nothing about it. It was my decision. It's something I've been thinking about for a long time.'

'But what about us?' Poor woman looks like she's on the verge of tears.

'We'll still be friends,' he replies.

'Friends!'

The atmosphere is getting far too intense for my liking. I stand up, stretching out an exaggerated yawn. 'If it's OK with everyone I think I'll turn in for the night.'

'Yes. Of course you must be exhausted.' Kimberly gives me a fake smile.

'Nonsense, you haven't finished your champagne,' Alex says.

'Don't think I can stomach any more ... alcohol.' Or Kimberly for that matter.

'You never were very good at holding your liquor.'

'I could drink you under the table,' I boast.

'Or on top of it,' he grins.

I know exactly where he is heading with this little statement. 'I don't know what you're talking about,' I croak a tad too wildly, nearly falling over myself in an effort to clamber over the small table and put a hand over his blabbering mouth.

'Let's just say Jane likes to get up on tables when she's had a few drinks,' Alex says, prising my hand away.

'It was a very long time ago,' I inform my unimpressed audience.

'Personally, I hate to see a woman drunk,' Kimberly contorts from her surgically designed mouth, souring the moment.

I force myself to smile and lift myself off Alex. 'You're quite right, which is why I'm off to bed. Goodnight, everyone.'

'I'll come with you … tuck you in.' Alex jumps up, grabbing me in a way that suggests all sorts of nudge-nudge, wink-wink antics. I don't know what his game is but Michael and Kimberly are less than impressed and neither am I. As soon as we are out of sight I wrench my arm free.

'OK, what's going on?'

'What do you mean?'

'Don't come over all innocent with me. You know exactly what I'm talking about. "I'll come up and tuck you in …"' I mimic, stomping up the staircase.

Alex laughs. 'I'm just messing about.'

'Tell that to Kimberly and Michael.' I stop at the door to my room. 'Where do you think you're going?'

'Ah, Janey … don't make me go downstairs.' He kneels down and swipes a reed from the dried plant arrangement by the door, placing it firmly between his teeth; demanding an audience as he morphs into a half-witted Huckleberry Finn character and performs the most ridiculous monologue ever written.

'If only I knew about cogs and stuff, Martha might be givin' me her corn bread, now she's givin' it to Wily Stan. He don't love her like I do, just coz he can read don't mean he's smart or nothing. I read, I read the stars, I read the moon, I read her face when she let me near the chickens that day. I like chickens, they have a lot to say to me and I have a genuine liking for their seed. Why oh why won't Martha …'

Giggling, I stop him before he drones on any longer.

'Enough, chicken boy!'

Alex wrote this monologue after a mad drunken night when he was still very much under the influence of vodka and *Forrest Gump*. It was our first year at drama school and our end-of-year practical exam. He passed it off as a retro comic monologue … The moderators weren't impressed as it was the realism exam.

'All right … five minutes,' I concede, opening the door and flinging off my shoes and then, remembering that they are Manolos, racing to rescue them and placing them upright in the middle of the floor; pride of place, winking at me in the moonlight.

'But I know you, Alex, and I know you're up to something.'

'Me!' He flutters his eyelashes at me as he walks into the room on his knees. 'Up to something! I take offence, Janey. You know I'm just a lost boy in this big ol' world, don't know how the cogs and springs work.'

'Enough,' I say, not wanting a repeat performance. 'Well whatever it is, it's probably best I don't know. I don't want to give Kimberly and Michael any more ammunition to hate me.'

'Who hates you?'

I throw him an 'are you blind?' look. 'Did you not see the hostile gazes being fired my way?'

'From Kimberly?'

'Yes. Kimberly,' I say. 'And Michael.'

'Oh I wouldn't worry about Michael, he just comes across that way with people he doesn't know but he's going to love you when he gets to know you.'

I pull a face. 'He constantly scowls and has a habit of twisting his lips into a condescending smirk.'

Alex laughs. 'He's got a lot on his mind.'

'His book, I know.'

'Believe me, his bark is worse than his bite, just pull him up on it.'

'Oh I will. I notice you haven't given me the same reassurance about Kimberly.'

'I'll handle Kimberly.'

We sit chatting and messing around for another hour and then I really do have to kick Alex out before he falls asleep on my bed.

CHAPTER SIX

I open my eyes and I know I'm on holiday because there is
no whooshing of wind or rain against the windowpane.
Instead, a gorgeous beaming ray of sunlight is streaming
through the blinds creating a pretty strobe effect across the
sheets, warming my face. I stretch out my arms and legs,
languidly enjoying the way the satin feels against my skin.

Back home I love nothing better than to snuggle under
my duvet on a grey and cold day (Hungarian goose down,
twelve tog, my homage to the Menopausal Play stint!), but
this is an entirely different feeling altogether. I glance over
at the travel clock. Wowser. Ten a.m.

With a spurt of energy I scramble out of bed and bunny
hop to the bathroom. I'm surprised at how refreshed I feel,
considering it took ages to fall asleep. I spent far too long
mulling over the events of yesterday, and in particular
thinking about Michael. Try as I might, I can't get him out
of my head. The warm tingling sensation in the pit of my
stomach when he stands close, the jolts of electricity when
he touches me, the strength of his arms as they close
around me, his strong, broad chest against the palm of my
hand, his sweet musky scent ...

OK. You get the picture.

I shower quickly, pull on a tangerine-coloured bikini, a pair of khaki shorts, crisp white vest-top, slip my feet into a pair of white Havaiana flip-flops and go in search of the source of the tantalising aroma of roasted coffee beans and cooked bacon.

Alex is alone on the terrace, placing a plate on the table.

The feast before me is impressive: warm rolls, croissants, bacon, eggs, sausages, fruit and coffee.

'Wow. Who's coming for breakfast?'

Alex's head snaps up. 'Jane! You're up! I was going to bring you breakfast in bed.'

'What with, a forklift? This isn't all for me?' I look at Alex and he beams at me proudly.

'I couldn't remember what you liked so I thought I'd do a bit of everything.'

I gaze at him, speechless. 'I can't eat all this!'

Alex looks disappointed.

'Oh, Alex!' I put my arms around him giving him a hug. 'Thank you, it's a lovely gesture.'

'Hope I'm not interrupting anything?' A deep voice encroaches from behind. Alex and I swivel round.

'Morning,' Alex chirps cheerfully.

'Morning,' Michael grunts.

My throat is too tight to speak. I was hoping that when I saw Michael again I wouldn't feel quite so attracted to him but my heart starts hammering and my skin begins to tingle.

'Another all-nighter?' Alex says.

'Uh-huh.'

'You mean you haven't slept at all?' I blurt out.

'I crashed out for a couple of hours at my desk.' Michael gives me a peculiar look. Then slowly he looks me up and down and I'm aware that my lily-white legs are on display. A pink glow of self-consciousness sweeps across my cheeks.

I drop to my knees, hiding my legs under the pretence of stroking Digger. 'Morning, Digger.'

'So what do you think?' Alex chuffs, marvelling at his handiwork.

'I think this is the first time I've seen you in the kitchen,' Michael replies.

I laugh. That sounds more like the Alex I remember.

I sit myself down at the table. 'You could feed a cast of thousands with this lot.'

Again I can't help noticing the difference between the two men. While loyalty makes me favour Alex's easy-going charm and handsome face, I'm forced to admit that Michael has the edge on magnetic moodiness.

'So who else is coming?' Michael sits down, helping himself to coffee.

'That's what I said,' I say, grabbing a croissant.

Alex swoops down and picks up a croissant. 'I did get a little carried away.'

'All this food!' I exclaim. 'What a waste.'

'Oh, come on, guys, where's your sense of adventure?'

'Where's Kimberly?' Michael's eyes quickly search the rest of the poolside terrace.

'Gone home, I hope.'

I giggle, and Michael throws me a look. My giggle trickles off to a gurgle and finally stops.

'So she stayed, did she?' I ask Alex.

'Why don't you wake her up?' says Michael.

'Do I have to?'

There's a long silence between the pair as they exchange a look. Alex gets up from his chair.

'All right, all right, I'll see if she's up. But I don't know why I'm bothering, she doesn't eat …' His voice trails off as he heads out of the room.

I hope Alex won't be long. I am a prickle of nervousness and haven't a clue what to say to Michael. I needn't worry because he disappears behind his newspaper and ignores me. Perfect.

I pour myself some coffee and take a sip, the hot liquid burning the roof of my mouth. Michael looks up.

'Hot,' I muffle off my burnt tongue, setting the mug on the table to cool down.

'Coffee usually is.'

'Droll,' I burble, my tongue still reeling.

His lips surprise me with a smile then he ducks behind his newspaper again.

I load a roll with bacon and take a hefty bite. Digger, I notice, is watching me intently. I slip him a strip of bacon, then another, then another. When I look up Michael is watching him.

I blush. 'I only gave him the one piece, that's OK, isn't it?'

'Yes. Just don't make a habit of it.'

'No, no I won't,' I say, quickly taking a bite of my roll. My stomach flickers with nerves as he watches me. A piece of roll slips out of my mouth. Whoops.

'Have you been writing long?' I mumble through a mouthful.

Michael heaves a sigh and gives up on reading his newspaper. 'A while,' he replies.

'You must be very successful.'

'I do well enough. Have you read any of my books?'

'God no!' I exclaim.

He laughs, not the least offended. 'I take it you dislike horrors?'

'Um, well, no,' I fluster. 'I mean, you're obviously very good at what you do. I'm just not into guts and gore.'

'It's not all about guts and gore. There is the suspense element and the dark depths of one's own mind,' he says with amusement. 'I leave it ambiguous and let the reader choose the horror.' He's mocking me.

'But you have to admit you do have to think up some pretty ugly things to write those kind of books.'

He now seems more amused than ever.

'It's just not my cup of tea.' I shrug my shoulders.

His dark eyes start to dance. 'No doubt you prefer a fine romance instead?'

'What's wrong with that?'

He sighs. 'I hate to be a bearer of bad news but there is no such thing as true love.'

'I take it you're not the romantic type?'

'Got it in one.'

Why am I not surprised!

I bring my coffee to my lips and take a tentative sip. It's just the right temperature. I do love my morning coffee, but at home I usually need at least two or three cups to get me going.

'You don't like women very much, do you?'

'What has that got to do with romance?' He sounds positively entertained with my notions, and if I'm not mistaken, a little patronising. 'As it happens I like women a great deal.'

My cheeks are boiling hot – I'd never be able to play poker, my tell is uncontrollable. Note to self: must learn not to blush at everything he says. I take another sip of coffee to wash the sticky lump in my throat.

'But you don't believe in love?'

'No I do not.'

For a moment a poignant sadness hangs in the air.

'I suppose you believe in Mister Right charging into your life on his white horse and sweeping you off your feet?'

'I'd settle with a white Porsche.' I am being flippant but Michael doesn't smile.

'I find it hard to believe that there's "the one",' he continues a little brusquely. 'The world is far too big and haphazard a place for silly girlhood ideas about fate and, what is it, oh yeah, destiny; that always makes me laugh.'

I sigh deeply. 'I suppose you're right.'

'I'm a realist. I believe in lust, obsession, and unrequited infatuation. But love ...' He looks at me with surprise. 'You're agreeing with me?'

I nod. 'Sad, but yes.'

He seems genuinely gobsmacked by my confession. 'I hadn't expected you to agree with me. Women rarely ever share my views on the subject. You don't believe in love?'

'Neither do you,' I exclaim.

'But I'm a renowned cynic.' He angles his head to the side and furrows his brow thoughtfully. 'Someone must have hurt you badly.'

I frown into space for a second.

'When a moment is enjoyed coincidentally by two people it doesn't need to be discussed, developed ... it's not a lecture topic to be dissected for ever more. If there's a next moment then fine ... if not ... then fine too.' I'm impressed with myself, I manage to sound both wise and mature. 'I'm not interested in falling in love just enjoying myself!' I meet his incredulous gaze with defiance. Well I can hardly tell him the truth. I can't tell him that although getting together with Philip was a colossal mistake there's still a small part of me that hopes one day I will find someone to love and cherish and he would love and cherish me wholly in return, but I also have to be prepared for the reality that it might never happen.

'So that's how it is.' He looks at me, his expression unreadable. 'I'll have to remember that.'

And what's that supposed to mean? I frown at him.

'I thought you two told me you weren't hungry,' says Alex, sitting down.

He's beaming from ear to ear. I didn't realise that while I was talking to Michael I was also feeding Digger.

'It's delicious,' I say, sneaking a look at a contented and now snoring spaniel. Alex reaches over, filling up his own plate, and Michael disappears behind his newspaper.

'So have you seen anyone from drama school?' Alex asks, tucking into his food. I shake my head. I lost contact with everyone. I suppose I could have got back in touch when I split with Philip but I was too ashamed.

'Why, have you?'

'Pete's married.'

'No way!'

'Fell madly and deeply, and more to the point drunkenly, in Vegas,' Alex grins. We spend an all too brief moment reminiscing about the old days when Kimberly swoops down.

'Morning, all!' she crows.

She is wearing the same white shorts from yesterday and a man's shirt tied in a bow at the front. She is immaculately made-up (she must keep her entire bathroom cabinet in that large bag of hers) and her hair is scraped back in a pristine ponytail. Her face is even more taut than yesterday.

'Kimberly!' Alex is scowling. 'Is that mine?'

'Looks good, doesn't it?' she giggles, giving us a self-congratulatory twirl.

She sits down next to Michael and gives me a superficial smile. 'Did you know you have a coffee stain on your top?'

I look down and right enough there's a decorative coffee splodge across the front.

I bet she ate her sibling in the nest. Oops, rephrase that, pushed them out.

For a moment we all eat in silence. Well, Michael, Alex and I eat, Kimberly just watches us. I notice Alex growing considerably agitated and fidgety; it's as though his left leg is being periodically electrocuted.

I press my hand on his knee. 'What's wrong?' I mouth.

He doesn't answer me.

I catch Kimberly watching us and snap my hand from Alex's knee, even though I've nothing to feel guilty about.

Alex pushes his chair away from the table and jumps up.

'Come on, Jane, let's go for a swim.'

I look up in shock. 'I can't go swimming after I've eaten this lot. I'll sink.'

Alex sighs and sits down again.

Kimberly looks at my empty plate and I can't work out if she's envious at the sight of solid food being gorged by female-kind or utterly disgusted by it. She really seems nauseated by the whole 'edible' idea.

'What about a walk then?' Alex's look is pleading and desperate. A previously sleepy, contented Digger is now fully awake, his tail wagging uncontrollably. I heave myself off the chair. 'All right, that I can do.'

'I'll come too,' Kimberly says, getting to her feet. 'I could do with burning some calories this morning; a glass of champagne sticks to a woman's frame.'

'I thought you had somewhere to be.' Alex doesn't bother to hide the irritation in his voice.

'Not until later.'

'No offence, Kimberly, but I haven't seen Jane in ages and I want to catch up. Alone!'

I gape at him, even squirm a little. I almost feel sorry for the woman. The look on her stony face tells me she doesn't want my sympathy – if looks could kill.

'Uh, we don't have to go this minute …' I sit back down.

'Yes, we do, Jane!' He grabs my elbow and pulls me to my feet. 'Let's walk this lot off.'

'But how am I going to get home?' whines Kimberly.

Alex doesn't disguise his exasperation. This is a side of his character that I have rarely witnessed. 'A taxi is an ingenious creation,' he snaps.

'I'll take you,' Michael offers, looking at me as if this is somehow my fault.

'But don't you think you should get some sleep?' I say with dismay.

He gives me an odd look and I bite my lip. Get a grip, Jane, he might think you care. Well I do. I'd say the same if it was anyone about to embark on such a foolish venture. 'I mean, is it wise to drive when you haven't slept all night?'

'She has a point,' Alex adds.

'I can get a taxi,' Kimberly pouts, as if she's making some great sacrifice.

I wait until we're on the beach before breaking away from Alex.

'OK. What was all that about and don't try to fob me off again.'

Alex grumbles unintelligibly, unclipping Digger's lead.

'Come on, Alex, out with it.'

'It's nothing really. I'm just trying to put some distance between myself and Kimberly.'

'Well, why the hell did you bring her back with you yesterday?'

'She invited herself. I couldn't get out of it. Anyway, she said she wanted to speak to Michael.'

'Michael!' What could she possibly want to talk to Michael about? 'Are they very good friends then?' I try to sound casually interested while ignoring the nervous dread filling my tummy.

'No!'

My relief is pathetic.

'So what's the story with you and Kimberly then?'

'She's got it in her head that we are destined to be together.'

I can't think of anything more hideous.

'And do you return these ... erm, sentiments?' I ask carefully.

Alex pulls a face. 'Fuck no!'

I giggle. I can't help it, Alex looks appalled by the very thought.

'The tabloids speculate about it all the time ...' I say.

'And I always vehemently deny it,' he replies.

I giggle again, but Alex isn't laughing. 'It's not funny, Jane. Look, do you mind if we talk about something else? Why don't you tell me about what you've been up to?'

I look at him and he looks so glum that there's only one thing for it. I narrow my eyes and liberate the odd but naughty Miss Marple-cum-Sméagol character Alex and I created for our improvisation class. When his lips twitch I know I have him.

'Pray-tell Aunty Janey where the hidden locket is. Come, come, you pretty young thing, do the girls like you, do they? Do they?' I rub my legs in a disgusting perverted manner. Alex is really laughing now.

'Your life sounds much more intriguing, bronze boy. Tell me more and I shall look into a local hedge. It is there we will find the locket and the answer, oh young shaven, plucked one of Malibu.'

'Oh, Jane, I'm so glad you're here. I'd forgotten how damn funny you are.' He throws his arms around my shoulder, hugging me close. 'Now tell me about your flatmate, why won't she talk to me on the phone?'

I sigh happily. 'She's your number one fan and you make her nervous. Personally, I can't see what all the fuss is about.'

Alex trips me up and I stumble forward, giggling.

'It's for my hunky bronze body and good looks.' His grin is shameless.

'No one likes a big head.' Then, I decide to tackle the question millions would pay good money to know.

'So, no girlfriend then?'

Alex shakes his head. 'Footloose and fancy-free.'

'And Michael?'

I thought I threw in the question casually enough but Alex's curiosity is displayed by the virtue of one inquisitive eyebrow.

'No, he's not my type, darling! Why do you ask?'

'Just making conversation.' Alex narrows his eyes but I can't seem to leave the horror subject alone.

'Does he have a girlfriend?'

Shit, too obvious?

'No, he doesn't.' He starts grinning inanely. 'You know you and him would be a perfect match. Don't know why I didn't think about it before.'

'Me and Michael!' I splutter. 'What on earth ... how could you ... he doesn't even like me.' My voice rises to a squeak.

'Whatever gave you that impression?'

'You must have noticed him scowling.'

'He always scowls.'

'And he was horrible to me at the airport.'

'Michael was?'

I decide to tell him exactly what happened and when I'm finished Alex is staring at me with open-mouthed disbelief and, if I'm not mistaken, anger. 'I'll have a word.'

I feel a jolt of horror. 'No. Don't!'

'But, Jane, he shouldn't have spoken to you like that.'

'He did apologise,' I add feebly. 'Oh, Alex, promise me you won't say anything.'

Alex doesn't look happy about it but he agrees. He takes hold of my hand and we follow the shoreline like a couple of giddy teenagers, kicking the sand with our feet as the sun beats down on us, reminiscing over the good old days.

When we eventually return to the house it is completely deserted. Hot and sweaty from the walk, I strip down to my bikini and step towards the edge of the pool. Alex joins me, stripping down to his swimming shorts and showing off his fit physique. Sian would want me to take a photo. I do owe her one. Hmm, maybe I can convince Alex to get his kit off for the camera.

'Ready. Steady. Go!' And without waiting to check if Alex is ready, I dive into the pool and start swimming. I can feel him closing behind me but I am determined to get to the other side before him. 'I win!' I slap the side of the pool, grinning giddily.

He is only seconds behind. 'Cheat,' he laughs, coming up for air.

We spend the rest of the day alternating between sunning ourselves by the poolside and jumping into the water when the heat gets too much. In all that time there is not a peep from Michael. Not that I am looking. Well, OK, I might have eyed up the writer's room a couple of times.

CHAPTER SEVEN

After a leisurely shower, I grab too many fluffy towels and consequently trail them out in a weird tail appendage. Despite going to great lengths not to burn – SPF50 – I still managed to miss a couple of crucial spots, in particular the lower bum cheeks. But my bum isn't going on display tonight unless somebody gets the tequila out. OK, that happened once and I was intoxicated enough to think I'd positioned myself in the bushes; one trench looks the same as another when you desperately need a pee with tequila glasses on. Oh, and then the jeep moved. Fifty spectators is a successful show in fringe theatre. You could say it was quite a controversial piece.

My first film premiere. I'm so excited.

As I pull on my Manolos (figure I should get some practice in, the last thing I need is to trip on the red carpet – oh God, that would be so embarrassing), Beyoncé's 'Single Ladies (Put a Ring on It)' comes onto the radio and I start to dance along. I am hot and sultry ... hmm ... maybe I shouldn't bother with a dress at all. I start laughing uncontrollably. Of course I would never, ever do something so ... attention-seeking. Besides, I spent a small fortune on the canary-yellow ruffled dress (Notte by Marchesa); an obligatory purchase when Alex first mentioned the thrilling words 'Film Premiere'.

Descending the staircase I stop to marvel at an oversized vase full of the most fragrant lilies. Michael Canty has taste ... hmm, maybe he's gay. I congratulate myself on this logical conclusion about the surly writer when he suddenly appears in front of me. He is standing on the step below and our eyes are almost level. My stomach does an immediate loop-the-loop.

'You've caught the sun.' His words sound intimate for a comment that is altogether harmless and my poker-tell cheeks turn a deep crimson as he leans forward to peer into my face.

OK, not gay.

I'm dazed by my body's pathetic reaction to him.

'Aren't you going to the premiere?' I swallow. 'Of course you're not.' I answer for him, taking in his sweatpants and T-shirt.

His smile is disarming. 'Not my cup of tea.'

Funny!

'You look ... lovely,' he says.

I blush.

'The premiere will be good exposure for you. You're bound to make some good contacts wherever Alex goes.' The way he says it makes it sound like he disapproves. What does he know, anyway, and why does he have to be so relentlessly judgemental?

'Right ... well ... bye then ...' I move to step away at the same time he moves and we crash into each other, my hands falling against his chest. 'Sorry ...' I chew down nervously on my lip. I have so many facial tics he probably thinks I'm a Tourette's sufferer. I pull my hands away, feeling flustered under his scrutiny. When I look at him I have a fleeting feeling he wants to kiss me; it feels almost trance-like.

'Oi! Jane, get your arse down here. Car's arrived,' Alex calls in a mock-cockney accent.

Michael and I jerk apart.

I half-stumble and half-run down the staircase, not daring to look back at him.

'Don't wait up,' Alex shouts to him, wrapping an arm around me. I still can't bring myself to look up. What the hell is wrong with me?

I'm glad Alex pulls out a bottle of champagne for the drive because my nerves are jumping all over the place. My mind keeps rerunning the scene: was he or wasn't he going to kiss me?

'Just remember to keep your face relaxed,' Alex instructs, 'and stand a little to the side when you pose for the camera.' He squeezes my hand reassuringly. 'There's no need to be nervous, you'll be fine.'

'They'll be looking at you, not me.'

'I don't think so, gorgeous, not in that little number. It's all about the dresses.'

The limo comes to a halt at the front of some barriers and Alex gets out first. I hear the crowd go wild. Alex holds out his hand and I gulp back the nerves. 'Come on,' he says, 'it's only friendly camera fire, let's dazzle them.'

Easy for him to say!

We are instantly struck by blinding flashbulbs. Alex gives my hand another reassuring squeeze as flashes fire off all around us and keeps a firm grip as he pulls me up the red carpet, only letting go to sign autographs.

The deafening noise of cheering crowds is overwhelming; hundreds of cameras clicking ferociously, ravenous reporters wrestling for soundbites.

Crikey … yikes … gulp!

The photographers and TV crews are crammed in so tightly behind the barrier it looks like a factory farm and they do look a lot like crazed animals.

Several microphones get shoved in Alex's face, and each time he calmly smiles and answers their questions.

'What was it like working with Bernice Stoker?'

'Amazing, cool, great.'

'How was it working with Woody?'

'Yeah, he has a reputation; Woody should have been in West Point,' Alex jokes.

'Are you dating anyone?'

He winks. 'That would be telling.'

'Who's your friend?'

'This here is the wonderful Jane Allen.'

The flash goes off in my eyes. All the while I have a fixed smile on my face, at the same time trying not to blink like a confused camel.

'They don't want pictures of me,' I hiss into Alex's ear.

''Course they do.'

The flashbulbs continue to follow us like fireflies, and as Alex is refusing to let me go I have no choice but to pose with him, pretty sure I'll be cropped out of the frame when it goes to print.

Posing for the cameras is a peculiar out-of-body experience and not altogether unpleasant. I remember to smile, and turn slightly to the side and put my hands on my hips so my waist is exaggerated, but it's a relief when we finally get inside.

Alex grabs two champagne flutes from a passing waiter dressed as a French mime artist and I slug mine back greedily.

'Alex Canty! The man to ensure continual revenues even on the DVDs.'

A man with a paisley cravat swoops down on us, followed by a small wiry man dressed head to toe in black. I instantly recognise the director Woody Pettigrew.

'Joel, who do you think I am: Howard Hughes or your local Chase Manhattan branch?' Alex grabs the man's hand and gives it a vigorous shake.

Joel laughs.

'And Woody, why are you still sober?' Alex spurs.

'Who says I am, dear boy-child,' the director swiftly retorts, patting Alex heartily on the back.

Alex pulls me into the crook of his arm. 'This is Jane. She's my very best friend in the world,' he tells them. 'We were at drama school together. She's a very talented actress and singer, and dances like a dream. The world is missing out on something tremendous, something better than space exploration, better than sex! Better than sex on Viagra ...'

Joel and Woody laugh raucously.

'Thought that might get your attention, you old foxes.'

It's all highly embarrassing.

'OK, Alex, don't overdo it.' I grasp the producer's hand first, 'Very pleased to meet you, Joel,' and then shake the director's hand, 'and very pleased to meet you too, Woody. I adore your films.' I try to sound professional and level-headed.

'Jane is a bit of film buff,' Alex informs Woody.

Woody gives me a sceptical but warm smile.

While Alex and Joel start bantering their masculinity I turn to the director, unsure what to say. But, as ever, it doesn't take my mouth long to catch up and review the situation; it's like it's spring-loaded.

'I loved your film *Driving Menace*,' I say. 'And *The Day We Say Goodbye*.'

Woody is pleased that I've seen them and when I tell him my all-time favourite is *Blue Night*, an obscure indie film, he's really impressed and we have a discussion about the merits of *Dogma's* artificial forced simplicity against the poetic French realism. The reason I know so many films is because my social life for the past few years has consisted of a tub of Ben & Jerry's and a DVD. Ten minutes later Woody and I have become the best of friends. Alex says that we're both offbeat and nerdy.

After three glasses of champagne I need a pee, and with only a few minutes to spare before the film starts, I hastily make my way through the crowded room. While I'm sitting there, I hear Alex's name mentioned and my ears twist towards the sound, honing in on its signal.

'Do you think that's his new girlfriend?'

'I guess so. She's probably one of those real actresses from London; they don't allow enhancements there, that's why we stay here – and you have to learn more than two lines at a time in London.'

'She has that funny accent too. I hear he likes intellectuals, she looks like she thinks about stuff, Leanne … right?'

'I like to think about Alex, does that count?' The giggling fades as the two girls leave..

CHAPTER EIGHT

The film is great. Alex is great. Not that I expected anything less.

He wasn't the main lead, but his charisma made it into a memorable quirky role and his character was so different from his TV part.

'You were brilliant!' I beam like a proud mummy.

'You really think so?'

'Don't be bashful! You know you were.'

Alex gives me what is possibly the coyest look I've ever witnessed. I can tell he's pleased and I do understand his desire for new challenges. The leap from TV stardom to the big screen can be pretty daunting but George Clooney managed it. Talk of the devil, the man himself walks straight past me; I try not to ogle after him, which is like asking Homer Simpson to put down the doughnut. Yummy!

Arriving at the after-show party is a surreal experience. It's being held in a mock castle up in the Hollywood Hills, themed knights in shining armour holding trays of glittering beverages immediately greet us. Alex opts for a green concoction while I go for a red number because it matches my lipstick. How divine!

Alex taps a passing waiter on the shoulder. A man covered by a hinged metal visor stops and holds out a tray full of canapés. We both grab a napkin and start loading up with smoked salmon blinis, tartlets of all descriptions, crostinis blushing with their rich toppings ... it is an absolute wonderland of miniatures; food and drink are in freefall. In fact I've never seen such lavish presentations of finger-food. Hollywood is the place where even the finger-foods have dreams. For what is essentially a buffet is now a delicious gallery of edible art. There's even a caviar bar where you can help yourself via the optics. Can you imagine it? Not nasty gin being dispensed but CAVIAR! A feast for the eyes! Fortnum and Mason's food hall has relocated to Hogwarts, everything so accessible, ample and, most importantly, flowing.

Three yummy little red numbers later, and I am tipsy. So is Alex. Did I say tipsy? I meant loaded.

We stumble onto the dance floor and trip about, feet following after loosely limbed bodies, whilst performing our own version of the tango and clearly demonstrating why one should be sober attempting it. Alex throws me off in a dramatic gesture and I land on Woody's table. Well, on his lap to be exact.

'English actresses are so much more natural, free and spirited,' Woody Pettigrew announces to his table companions.

'Spirited being the appropriate word choice!' I wink at them all while leaning backwards.

It seems that they think this is a funny skit so Alex and I carry on with gusto.

After twenty minutes of dancing we quench our thirst with another cocktail and I propel myself unsteadily towards the toilet, making my way past the multiplying crowd, elbowing and pushing equally drunk stars and non-stars.

As I get through to the last tier of tables a guy points at me. Beautiful people encircle him, some sitting, others standing. He lets out a sardonic laugh then addresses me directly.

'Very funny, saw you dancing; are you a comedienne on cable?'

'I think I saw her on NBC,' purrs his sidekick.

Awkwardly I bow and hastily continue on my route, slightly baffled. I wonder if the drinks have a more potent component mixed in; 'Hollywood Style', if you know what I mean.

I reach my destination, conclude my business, and attempt to reapply my make-up. One look at the mirror and I freeze. A massive red dribble is stained down one side of my mouth. It must have been the blasted raspberry stack stuck on the side of my glass. I stand dumbfounded in front of my drastic reflection and a revelation hits me: that guy was the star from the *Twilight* film; oh crikey, I've let myself be a complete clown. He must have thought I had vampire make-up on to take the piss, maybe I should apologise. No … then he'll think I'm a dribbling idiot, best just leave it alone.

A woman taps me on the shoulder. 'Are you OK, sugar?'

Shakily I whisper, 'Yes, just mortified, err … you know, had an idiotic moment amongst strangers.'

'Well you're in the right place for that. Have a ball, no one cares here.'

I take comfort in her words until I realise she's now chatting to the hand-dryer, all googly-eyed. I rummage around in my clutch bag for make-up but to my horror it has all fallen out. Somehow I have a swimming hat and a star-shaped wand though.

My newly found insane friend has a Dior bag gaping open and everything in it a girl might need. Now what's the best way to approach this?

Well, here goes, I haven't a shred of dignity left so I introduce myself to the hand-dryer and enter into their surreal conversation. The hand-dryer agrees I should borrow her cosmetics but leave the Botox syringes intact.

Feeling slightly more composed I strut back to Alex. Before I can say anything he shoves another red number in my hand, which I quickly offload onto a passing tray along with its wicked raspberry totem pole. Think I ought to sober up, and fast. Hiccup!.

CHAPTER NINE

I glance across at the travel clock. Fuck. Four a.m. and I'm still awake. I can't sleep. I've tried. But I am hot, sticky and my legs keep twitching restlessly to the techno music still pounding loudly in my head. I turn wearily onto my front, thumping the pillow and pushing my face into it, begging for sleep. No good. I try turning onto my back, kicking off the sheets. But it's no good; my body is still buzzing from the after party and, most probably, the potent alcohol fuelling my insomnia. I'm just going to have to get up.

It was, however, a brilliant night, totally surreal, but a total blast. I swing my legs out of bed and wander over to the window. The pool looks as inviting as ever, its lights beckoning me like a magnetic water siren.

A swim might help me sleep.

But it's the middle of the night, the sensible voice inside me contests.

I remind myself I'm supposed to be experiencing new things, and haven't I always wanted to try skinny-dipping?

The tiny voice inside squeals in alarm but I squash it down and head for the great outdoors. Be brave, warrior.

The terrace slabs are refreshingly cool against my bare feet and an even cooler air blows against my bare legs. I move over to the pool, looking around nervously, as if somebody could be lurking behind a sun lounger or spying from a bush with a long lens. Not that I could see if they were, I'm not wearing my contacts. I giggle with nerves.

Maybe I should keep my knickers on?

Coward! The voice inside my head taunts.

I've come this far, I can't chicken out now.

Gingerly I tiptoe over to the pool edge and step out of my knickers, before quickly whipping off my T-shirt and taking up the classic diving position. I sway back and forth a few times; having cocktails doesn't really enhance your balance. Maybe this isn't such a good idea. I don't want to drown. I hold out my arms and they flutter about; if anyone was watching I'd resemble a drunken butterfly. A naked drunken butterfly, I correct, before diving ungracefully into the pool.

The water is invigorating, especially good between my legs. Several leisurely lengths in I turn on my back and float, the warm water lapping against my naked skin; I feel deliciously naughty and exhilarated. Why have I never done this before? It's an amazing feeling.

'Can anyone join in?'

Shock pulls me under, resurfacing seconds later with a mouthful of water. What the hell is he doing here? I search for him and can just about make out a big blurry silhouette. Fuckety-fuck, I wish I had my contact lenses in. I'm also beginning to have difficulty coordinating my arms and legs and slip under the water again.

'Jane, are you OK?'

I resurface, coughing up more water. It probably doesn't help that my head and body are still foggy from too many cocktails.

'Are you sure you're OK?'

'Yes,' I say, spluttering up another mouthful.

'Good. For a minute there I thought I might have to come in after you.'

My stomach contracts and I lose coordination again, slipping under. I hear his deep laughter reverberating through the water.

'You're supposed to be in bed,' I say crossly, when I finally resurface.

'I was writing,' he says. 'Deadline to meet.'

Treading water, I finally seem to regain the proper use of my arms and legs. I eye Michael from a safe distance, not wanting to get any closer.

'Well, don't let me stop you.'

'Writer's block,' he says. 'A midnight dip might just be the answer. Mind if I join you?'

'NO!' I blurt. 'I – um ...' I stumble in desperation. What do I say? You can't come in because I'm stark bollock naked? I swim tentatively towards him and wait at the bottom of the steps, crouching down to shield my modesty.

'Actually, I was just getting out.'

'Oh that's a shame.' He picks up my towel and holds it out for me. Now that I am closer I can see his mouth is pulled back into a wicked grin.

'You coming out or staying in?'

I open my mouth and close it again. Panic flutters around my body.

'You can just drop the towel there, thanks.'

His mouth twitches but he doesn't move. In fact he doesn't look to be in any hurry.

'Spoilsport.'

My mouth flops open and I sink beneath the water's surface, choking. Oh God ... he knows. The treacherous audacity of the man!

My cheeks are so hot that steam is coming off them. Oh God. Oh God. Does that mean he saw me jump in? How much could he really have seen?

'There I was, innocently looking out my study window, and then ...'

Oh God ... Everything then.

'Although it all happened much too quickly for my liking!'

'I didn't have you down as a peeping Tom,' I say, testily.

He crouches down and runs his fingers lightly across my moist arm, his dark eyes meeting mine.

'As an actress you must be used to getting undressed in front of people.'

My heart is racing ten to the dozen, and I'm quivering with nerves, or is it excitement?

'Well?' he says, cocking his eyebrow and pulling himself to his feet. 'You staying in or getting out?'

This is excruciating. He is so cocksure of himself that I wish I had some clever retort. But he's right, I am an actress and if this was a film set and I was ... what? A temptress? No, a sexy alien lady emerging perfectly from the pool and devouring her mate. Yes, that's it. I'll show him. I ignore the distant warning bell in my head and step out of the pool, standing in front of him, my naked skin gleaming white.

Well I managed to wipe the smirk off his face.

Breathe, I tell myself. Chin up. Stomach in. He still has hold of the towel and shows no sign of giving it to me. I fight the urge to yank it from his hands and look straight into his face in what I hope is a cool, confident, sexy manner. But inside I am trembling, my heart is beating frantically and there is a heat rapidly inflaming my body and making my legs melt from the ground up. I notice the twitch of muscle in his jaw and I realise he's not as cool and controlled as he makes out. This gives me more confidence and a brief moment of pure, feline satisfaction.

Then doubt wiggles in. Suddenly my legs don't feel as shapely, the curve of my belly not flat enough ... Do I measure up to his standard of beauty? The look in his eyes tells me I do. He wants me ... of that much I am sure. But he doesn't even like me.

He steps towards me, wrapping the towel around my shoulders. A shudder racks my body as soon as he touches me. Once again, I can hear the faint muffled sound of alarm bells going off in my head, telling me to leave now, but I am too paralysed to move, trapped by lust. And then he kisses me. He is kissing me and I am kissing him back, exploring his mouth and feeling more alive than I have ever been. I haven't kissed like this since I was a hormone-driven teenager.

I wrap my arms around his neck, our kissing growing more urgent, more intense. I'm aware at some point of the towel dropping to my feet; I press my naked body into his and feel his hardness press against my stomach ... oh boy!

He pulls away and I moan my disapproval, and then moan in delight as his mouth encircles my breast. 'Is this what you want?' His voice is gravelly and full of lust.

I close my eyes and arch against him. 'Yes.' My voice doesn't belong to me – it sounds raspy and wanton.

His mouth torments me with each flick of his tongue until I can bear the exquisite torture no more. He returns his mouth to mine and I kiss him back with the same ignited passion, running my hands under his T-shirt, lifting it up and pressing myself against him, rubbing my breasts against his chest, feeling the thin matting of his hair. I hear the sharp intake of his breath as he pulls me closer, our hips welding together. A deep animalistic moan spills from my lips. I have never felt this driven by desire, this possessed by a need to touch and be touched.

'No!' Michael suddenly howls like a distressed animal, pushing me away. I stumble backwards, completely stunned.

'Alex!' he says.

I stare back at him, desperately confused.

'What about Alex?' My voice is still husky with desire. 'He doesn't need to know,' I add helpfully.

'Is that so?' he snarls.

What am I missing here?

With hands that feel like lumps of ice I reach down and grab the towel from the ground, wrapping it tightly around me.

'You're tempting, I grant you that.' His mouth twists cruelly. 'But this is wrong. Wrong.'

There it is. His words loud and clear. Wrong.

'You kissed me!' Not the best retort, but true.

'I did, didn't I?' He seems surprised by this. 'I hadn't expected you to ... to ...' he shambles for a moment then recovers, '... be such an easy conquest.'

'Why are you being like this?'

'Perhaps when it is handed to me on a plate it is less appealing.'

His words are like a slap across my face. Anger now boils my blood. I don't need to listen to any more of his schizo-crap; who does he think he is? I bring the towel closer to my chest, as if it could somehow shield me from his cruel words.

'Thank you so much for that insight, excuse me,' I say with scorn. And with nothing further to add I turn on my heel and push pass him. My legs buckle, but somehow I manage to get to my room.

I grab a T-shirt from a drawer and tug it over my head; clambering into bed I pull the sheets over me.

Oh, the humiliation!

I bury my face into the pillow. I should have resisted him. I should have not been such an easy conquest, recalling his cruel words.

Enough! I tell myself. I am made of stronger stuff. I am smart, gorgeous and talented. Tears slide down my face.

If he isn't man enough to act on what, as he had so eloquently put it, 'was being handed to him on a plate', then he doesn't know what he's missing.

I nearly convince myself that I'm OK but my bravado is just an act and the tears start falling thick and fast. I wrap my arms around the pillow, hugging it close, willing sleep to take me. Everything will be better in the morning..

CHAPTER TEN

The next morning, I wake up with the sense that somebody is in my room. Michael?

I bolt upright with such a force that I knock the coffee cup out of Alex's hand and even his speedy reflexes can't stop the hot contents spilling over my T-shirt and sheet.

I leap out of bed, lifting the wet cloth away from my skin.

Ow! Ow! Ow!

'Nothing like scalding hot coffee to wake you up in the morning,' I manage to quip, running to the bathroom.

'Fuck, Jane, are you OK?' Alex barges over just as I am lifting the T-shirt over my head.

'Alex!' I screech, holding the wet material in front of me, the little good that it's doing.

He barks out a nervous laugh. 'Oops, sorry.'

'Get out!' I yell when he just stands there. 'And stop gawping.'

Alex brings a hand over his eyes and starts backing out the door. 'Sorry,' he says, laughing loudly.

'Out!' I croak.

He grabs blindly for the doorknob. 'I'll see you downstairs.' I can still hear him chuckling long after I've showered and dressed.

'Coffee.' Alex places it on the kitchen table in front of me, trying not to laugh.

'Thanks,' I grumble, picking it up and ignoring his immaturity.

Besides, I have more pressing thoughts. Ever since I sat down I can't stop staring at the door, expecting Michael to walk in any minute. It's making me all jittery, jumping at every noise and inconsequential sound. I am absolutely dreading seeing him but I can hardly avoid him in his own house. What do I say? Should I just pretend nothing happened? It was just a kiss, after all, a kiss that shouldn't have happened, nothing to be embarrassed about. I can blame the booze. I'm sure I was still drunk from the party. Anyway, I've decided not to speak to him. He doesn't deserve it. With any luck he'll be locked up in his study and I won't have to speak to him.

'Jane? Jane?'

I look up and Alex is clicking his fingers in front of my face.

I swat his hand out of the way. 'What are you doing?' I say a little harsher than intended.

'Look, I'm sorry what happened ...'

'What?' Oh God, Michael's told him.

'Sure, no big deal, we're both adults—'

'I've seen you naked plenty of times. I had a whole summer of putting you to bed, Ms Excess!'

'What are you talking about?'

'What are you talking about?' We both stare at each other and then the door swings open and my skin breaks out into a sweat. I'm too afraid to look but my eyes swivel to the door. To my relief it's just Digger.

The dog saunters into the room and heads over to his water bowl. I turn back to the door, waiting for his master to follow, although I still haven't worked out what I'm going to do. After what seems like an eternity staring, Michael still hasn't made an appearance.

'Look, Jane, I really am sorry. It's just you reacted so quickly I didn't have time to move the coffee. You practically launched yourself out of bed, what were you expecting, an ambush?'

I drag my gaze from the door. 'Once you've been trained by the KGB, sleeping can be a torrid affair!' 'You know the score, Alex, once a spy always a spy – I sleep with one eye open!'

Digger comes over and nudges his wet nose against my hand.

'So what do you want to eat? I can make us a fry up?'

I wrinkle my nose at the thought. 'Think I'll pass. I'll just have some cereal.'

'Suit yourself.' He passes me a cereal packet.

I pour myself a bowl and follow Alex onto the sun deck, noting that my legs are trembling. They only stop shaking when a quick glance around tells me Michael isn't here either. I take a gulp of coffee.

'Oh, I forgot to tell you, Michael flew to New York this morning.'

Coffee spurts out my mouth. Alex jumps out of range just in time.

'Bloody hell, Janey, what is it with you and coffee this morning?'

The news should make me feel better, but for some reason my stomach twists in pain.

'What's he doing in New York?' I try to make it sound blasé, hoping the forced fluidity of conversation covers my true curiosity.

'He has an apartment there and usually heads there when he needs to make a deadline … which means …' Alex gives me a wide grin, 'we have this whole place to ourselves.'

I match his wide grin with one of my own.

'I'm not filming until tomorrow,' he continues, 'so I can devote all my time to my favourite person. So, Jane, deary, what do you fancy doing?'

We spend the rest of the afternoon lounging by the pool then Alex takes me to Nobu for magnificent sushi. The paparazzi are there and take photos of us eating and walking out of the restaurant, which feels really surreal out of the context of the film premiere setting. When Alex heads to bed, early, as he's filming tomorrow, I change into a silky night ensemble (La Perla, very decadent), slide open the enormous balcony doors and decide to give the funky hammock a go.

On my first attempt I nearly catapult myself off into the night air. Second attempt I get the strings so badly twisted that my leg is starved of blood. I manage to detangle myself and try for a third time. Luckily I get my derriere positioned properly with the numbed leg ready to reattempt a mount. And success!

It swings gently to and fro and the motion almost makes me sleepy. I turn my head, ready to nestle down into the cushion, when I spy a contraption embedded in the wall. Genius, it's a phone so you don't even have to bother with the tricky dismount. And it's bound to be tricky with my coordination. I love these fancy homes and their fancy things.

I pick up and dial my home number.

'Hi, Sian, it's me.'

'Jane!' she squeals down the phone. 'OMG! Right, tell me everything, what's it like? How was the premiere? Did you get to meet anyone famous? What's the house like? What's Michael like? How gorgeous is Alex? How's the wea—'

'Wooah there … easy, savant girl.'

Sian giggles. 'OK, OK … begin and don't leave anything out.'

You would think I was completing a police report with the questions Sian asks, even down to what the celeb dogs were wearing and how Alex takes his coffee.

'And there definitely isn't a girlfriend in Alex's life?' she pushes, leaving no stone unturned.

'He's not dating Kimberly, if that's what you're asking. She's horrible. Up close you can't see any movement, it's even worse than her acting. I think they must use CGI on the series.'

Sian chuckles with satisfaction so I relinquish a little inside gossip for her ears only. 'She's desperate for Alex but he's repulsed by it.'

'I never liked her ever since I saw her being interviewed, fake and arrogant. She's a snake masquerading in designer clothes. Is Alex happy that you're there?'

'Oh yes, we're having a blast, just like old days but sunnier and in more exciting settings.'

'I am soooooooo jealous. And what about Michael Canty?'

I lose my flow and for a moment just umm down the phone.

'Jane, I think the connection is going ... Jane?'

'Oh, he's all right, a bit moody; he's gone off to New York to finish his book.'

'Well, writers are more temperamental than artists. Is he as handsome as he looks in his picture?'

'If you like that sort of look.' My enthusiasm has wavered and I try to buck myself up by changing the subject. 'Alex and I got really hammered at the premiere ...' I tell her all about the red dribble faux pas – Sian truly enjoys other people being happy and that's why she's the best girlfriend you can have.

'Sian, you know if you hadn't sorted me and my drastic wardrobe out I wouldn't be having nearly as much fun. I would be the laughing stock.'

'Oh shut up, Jane, don't think I didn't enjoy spending all your money so you'll have to stay with me for ever and ever. It was all a self-serving cunning plan. Oh, and you were on the second page of *OK!* magazine and in the *Daily Mail* in the DVF dress. You looked incredible, by the way. They were calling you his mystery woman.'

'Bloody cheek,' I fume. 'We were just playing up for the cameras ... well he was anyway.'

'It's caused quite a stir here. You know you can tell me, I won't sell your story.'

I hear her controlling a giggle. 'Sian, you're incorrigible. I'm just kicking back in a hammock, you'd love it here.'

'Next time you can get Alex to invite me then. Can you get a photo of him when he comes out of the shower?'

'SIAN!'

'I mean in the shower!'

'Good night, you horny devil.'

CHAPTER ELEVEN

'All I seem to be doing is eating.' I undo the top button of my denim shorts and sigh. We're sitting on the steps of Alex's trailer enjoying the sunshine. Alex is in his Mel Keaton costume, consisting of a pair of green scrubs and a doctor's white overcoat which has a hanging stopwatch and a real stethoscope attached, although he has discarded the white overcoat and rolled up his sleeves. He picks at a green salad with as much enthusiasm as a limp slug.

'Don't worry, it's all low fat,' he grumbles.

'You're joking!'

'No.'

'But it tastes so good,' I enthuse.

His head jerks with disdain. 'Jane! It's rabbit food.'

'But it's so fresh.'

'I could murder a burger and chips.'

I laugh. 'You're just grumpy, your abused body is craving grease.'

'Actually, I've got a lot on my mind,' he replies, cryptically.

'Surely the hungry caterpillar plot isn't still confusing you,' I quip, but he doesn't react.

'Anything I can help with?' I ask gently, but he just stares into the distance.

Well, I'm having a lovely day, even if Alex isn't. In fact I've had a lovely week. We've spent most of it lazing by the pool or swimming in the sea, taking Digger for long walks and playing practically every single game that Michael's beach home offered up. We've eaten out at swanky celebrity-filled restaurants; every day Alex has dragged me out for a fancy meal even though I've offered to cook on numerous occasions. He still can't get used to the idea that I know how to cook more than the beans on toast and pot noodles from our college diet.

We've been to Fig & Olive in Melrose Avenue, to the Ivy in Beverly Hills, and wherever we went there was always some celebrity lunching a few tables away.

A million miles away from my old life back in Stockwell.

I could really get used to this lifestyle but I know it's not going to last forever so best make the most of it. I'd also like to say that all this activity has meant I haven't thought about Michael but that would be a lie.

I look over to Alex, who continues to sit there glumly swirling his salad around with a fork, and I wonder if perhaps he's nervous about the next scene. He has every right to be. I'm not sure I like the idea of him being submerged underwater for so long.

'You know you don't have to do the next scene,' I say. 'I mean, that's why you have a stunt double.'

I can't fathom why Alex insists on doing his own stunts, but as an alpha male I shouldn't really be surprised; primitive instinct gets them every time.

'What are you wittering about?'

I feel a flash of irritation. 'I was just saying if you're worried about the next scene, get your stunt double to do it.'

'I'm not worried about that,' Alex replies wearily. He rakes a hand through his hair. 'We're friends, aren't we, Jane?'

'Of course we are,' I say, wondering what an earth has got him so twitchy. 'Look, Alex, you know you can tell me anything.'

'I know,' he says.

'Talking through a problem is the first step to solving it.' Now who sounds like a self-help book?

'It's Kimberly.'

'Kimberly?'

'I slept with her.'

'You did what! You idiot.'

'It was ages ago! And it was just the once.' His tone is defensive. 'I was drunk and she was, well ... she was ...'

What? Waiting like a stalker? She probably spiked his drink then pounced on his jugular like a frenzied vampire. 'I think I get the picture, so what's the problem?'

'She's got it in her head that we are meant to be together.'

'I don't think I follow.'

'For richer, for poorer, in sickness and in health.'

'Oh.'

'I'm not ready for any of that stuff. Besides, I can't stand the woman.'

'Is she really that bad?' From my point of view, which is evidently different to any young, hot-blooded male, she is about as inviting as nuclear fallout.

Alex's face twists in agony. 'She's a psychotic bitch.'

Seeing as Alex isn't holding back ... 'She does look a bit frozen. In fact very similar to an ironed Barbie doll,' I point out.

'And as hospitable as Himmler at a bar mitzvah.'

I manage to make him laugh.

'Oh, Janey, I knew you would understand. That's why I told her we were lovers.'

'YOU DID WHAT?' I screech so loud that some crewmembers wandering past curiously look over.

'She just wasn't taking no for an answer and, well, I told her we used to be lovers and that I'm still in love with you.'

I'm so shocked that I can only stare at Alex, my mouth opening and closing in disbelief.

'I thought this would be the best way of showing her that there is no her and me. You're an enigma, she didn't know anything about you, she couldn't mess ... I mean ... I thought it would make her see sense, but it hasn't really stopped her hounding me.'

'Why didn't you just tell her the truth?'

'I've tried but she just won't listen.'

'No one will believe it,' I tell him stiffly.

'That's where you're wrong. The magazines are already intrigued by the new mystery woman on my arm.'

I groan. 'Don't remind me.' I had Sian on the phone again last night telling me she saw another picture of me with Alex. Then it dawns on me. 'Does Michael think we're together too?'

'Yes. Well, I didn't want him to try and talk me out of it. I figure the more people think we're together the better, and I knew Kimberly would grill him.'

Well this might explain a few things. 'When exactly did you come up with this master plan?'

'Just before you arrived I told him that I wanted to rekindle our relationship.'

Something clicks into place. Maybe that's why Michael reacted the way he did. But he still kissed me. He initiated it even though his cousin told him he was in love with me. What does that say about him? But for the first time since that disastrous night, I feel a glimmer of ... not happiness exactly, but self-righteousness. Perhaps he was just as affected by the hypnotic chemistry as I was.

'You know you're not my type,' I rib Alex.

The worry lines on his forehead disappear and he starts to grin, relief no doubt, that I've let him off the hook so easily.

'I'll have you know that a lot of women think I'm rather a good catch.'

'Really,' I say with mock indifference.

Alex jabs me in the arm. 'You should see my fan mail. Well, not the X-rated ones.'

'Now you're simply showing off.'

He laughs.

'So how long do we have to continue with this pretence?'

'Until Kimberly gets the message and cools off, which I'm hoping won't be long since the papers have a few pictures of us saying we are madly in love ...'

'They're saying what?'

Alex shoots a finger in his ear. 'Hey, watch the volume there, you're going to burst an eardrum.'

'I'll burst more than an eardrum. Why on earth would they say we are madly in love?'

Alex avoids my gaze and I know there's something he's not telling me.

'What have you done?'

'I haven't done anything,' he insists, then, after a pause, 'That's why one has a PR agent.'

I put my face in my hands and groan.

'Just that we've been pictured together eating out at different restaurants, and they just put two and two together.'

'There is no two and two,' I tell him crossly.

'I don't know why you're getting so upset; some women would love to be in your shoes and it's not like you've got a boyfriend.'

No need to rub it in.

'That's not the point,' I say. 'And save the wounded puppy-dog face, it won't wash with me.' But Alex throws his arms around me and plants a noisy kiss on my cheek.

'You're impossible.'

'But you love me, right?'

'No! You are a conceited pain in the arse.'

'Jane Allen!' thunders a voice.

I look up in surprise. 'Bob!' I leap to my feet. 'Fancy seeing you here.'

His genial face reveals disappointment. 'You didn't call.'

My cheeks blush with pleasure. 'Oh, I thought you were just being polite.'

'I am never polite. Hello, Alex.' The two men shake hands.

Alex knows Bob, wow what a small world.

'I can't stop now,' he bellows, glancing at his watch, 'but give me a call and we can have lunch.'

I beam cheerfully. 'That would be lovely.'

'Actually I'm having a party this weekend, you should both come along.'

'Would love to,' Alex replies for both of us.

'Thank you, Bob,' I add.

We wave him goodbye and both sit back down. 'That's the man I was telling you about, the one who saved me from an ominous collision with the carousel.'

'That's the carousel guy?'

'What?' Alex is giving me the strangest look. 'Have I got mayonnaise on my face?'

'No, you haven't got mayonnaise on your face,' he says, looking disbelieving. 'Jane, do you have any idea who that man is?'

'Yes, of course, silly, I introduced you to him. That's Bob Edwards.'

'Yes, I know who the bloody hell he is, that's the bloody point, but do you?'

Now it's my turn to look at Alex as if he has sprung two heads.

'Do you know who Bob is or, more to the point, what he does?' He's talking to me as if I am a small child.

'Err ... no I don't.' I poke out my tongue in honour of his condescension. 'Why?'

'Jane! Bob Edwards IS Hollywood,' he cries out dramatically. 'He runs this place, for starters.'

My mouth starts opening and closing but no words come out as I realise how much of a big deal this is.

'He's not just involved in film and TV, but he also backs Broadway productions.'

I have lost the power of speech.

Alex laughs. 'Here's your opportunity to dazzle Bob Edwards. He seems to like you; you should ask him for a role.'

'Don't be silly!' I finally manage, my voice cracking with disbelief.

'What have you got to lose? If you impress him he could get you a role on Broadway or, better still, right here in Hollywood. You can come and live with me, get yourself a tourist visa, do some student films, and hey presto there's your O-1B visa.'

'I'm not sure ...'

'What do you mean, not sure? You said there isn't much waiting for you back in London. Besides, what's happened to the spunky Jane I know and love?'

'Fizzled, fried and frightened.'

Alex looks slightly taken aback and I submit. 'I suppose there's no harm in having lunch ...'

Even if I could dazzle Bob Edwards, could I live in a different country? It's a daring thought to relocate and move to a strange city. Could I leave my family and friends and try to break into the toughest business in the world? I didn't make it in England, what makes me think I can make it here?

'Jane, I can read you like a book.'

'Really! OK, Derren Brown, what was I thinking?'

'I didn't make it in England, what makes me think I could make it here. What about my friends and family, blah, blah, blah.'

I playfully punch him in the arm. 'Very impressive, Mr Brown!' Talking about it and doing it are two different things – I'm just not sure I have it in me.

'Oh, I didn't know you'd be here today.'

I don't need to turn around to recognise the owner of the high-pitched whine; it's the same voice that was screeching at the top of her lungs at some undeserving soul in the dressing room earlier. It amazes me that such a beautiful ... well, a meticulously modified creature-woman could make such an ugly sound.

'Hello, Kimberly.'

'What a day!' she exclaims dramatically, her mouth curving up into a wicked seductress smile, as though her appetite is about to be satisfied. 'What did Bob Edwards want?' she asks Alex.

'It wasn't me he wanted. It was Jane. Oh, didn't you know he's a good friend of Jane's?'

That's pushing it but it's fun to see the surprise trying to surface on Kimberly's face.

'Really?' The disbelief in her tone is too much for me to resist.

'Yes. Bob and I go way back,' I taunt.

'You do get around, don't you,' Kimberly coos cattily.

'Don't I just.' I dispense with sardonic comportment, unwilling to be intimidated by the blonde star.

'Sorry, Kimberly, Jane and I were just leaving.' Alex grabs my hands and pulls me up. 'I want to show her the underwater tank before I'm called back to wardrobe. Come on, my love.'

I try to smile lovingly into Alex's eyes as he leads me away.

'Don't let me stop you,' the plastic creation crackles with an over-compensating air of nonchalance that she doesn't quite pull off.

CHAPTER TWELVE

I take a look in the colossal wall mirror by the front door, satisfied I've made the right decision: multi-striped maxi dress, gold gladiator sandals, huge shades, and a large straw floppy hat – very Boho chic! Only took five different outfit changes to pick 'the look'.

It's important I try and make a good impression.

I drop a kiss on Digger's head, close the door to Michael's mansion and climb into an awaiting taxi.

I took Alex's advice and gave Bob Edwards a call; unsurprisingly, I got his PA who took down my number and said she would call me back. I put the phone down and resorted to reality … I mean, what was I thinking … everyone in Tinseltown says 'give me a call', 'we must do lunch', they don't actually mean it. Five minutes later she calls back with a place, date and time.

'Chateau Marmont,' I say to the driver.

Yep, that's right. I'm meeting Bob for brunch at CHATEAU MARMONT. I can't believe it. The pinnacle of all hotels in Hollywood, the beacon of auspiciousness – or inauspiciousness, depending on your viewpoint – such a juicy star-studded history: the kaleidoscope of film, music and TV stars that have stayed there, died there or gone mad there is spellbinding. I'm confounded by this turn of events.

Me! The scruffy failed actress from Stockwell with a big hotshot producer in an iconic venue of Hollywood ...wow! I give myself a pinch to check this is really happening.

I can't wait to be contained in the same walls as Vivien Leigh or drink from the same bar as Lindsay Lohan. I must remember to contain my awe. Note to self: must act cool. Do not fiddle with stuff. No blushing. No biting. It's beginning to sound like madness already. I can already feel my hamster cheeks filling up; and I haven't even got there yet. Darn, I'm excited.

It is evident from the way the maître d' treats me, as if I am an irreplaceable Ming vase, that Bob Edwards is an important man. Of course I know that now, because I Googled him and have a whole different perspective. How can one man be so powerful? I have no idea why he has singled me out, only that he has and I might as well do my best to impress him – who knows where it might lead.

I stroll into the restaurant trying not to look at the other diners, although I'm sure I spy Jake Gyllenhaal.

'There you are,' Bob booms, getting up to air-kiss me loudly on both cheeks.

'Why, am I late?'

'Not at all, what would you like to drink?'

'A kir royale would be lovely.'

'Kir royale it is.' Bob motions for the waiter who swaggers over to us. Something about the swagger looks kind of familiar, but then in my peripheral vision I see the actor Adrian Grenier from *Entourage* walking past and I'm distracted, which, let's face it, is understandable. But remembering why I am here, and who I am with, I turn and focus my attention on Bob.

'I like a woman who's on time. A mark of a true unspoilt professional,' he twinkles at me.

'I was looking forward to seeing you again,' I reply earnestly.

'Me too,' he says, taking a sip of his drink. His top pocket suddenly beeps and he pulls out his phone. He glances at it then looks at me. 'Sorry, Jane, I need to take this.'

'Sure … go ahead.'

He smiles apologetically then swiftly turns to his phone. 'Tom, what is it?'

I use the opportunity to look around me, soaking up the magical ambience and, OK you got me, to spot any other celebrities. I mean it's hard not to in a place like this and Sian would be disappointed if I didn't at least make an effort. I see a household face and I'm just trying to place the name when a waiter steps in the way; I peer at his profile just to see if any recognition jolts my memory, and then it's like a bolt of lightning strikes me.

NO BLOODY WAY!

That doesn't quite describe the sensation, which immobilises me to my chair and makes my stomach plummet into pure panic. Freaked out, sweating profusely, it can only be … Philip the Pessimistic Pilchard! What's he doing here? I finally get away from it all and here he is. It must be his doppelganger, that's the only feasible explanation. I should get some sort of regression therapy, now I'm hallucinating, it can't be healthy for one's sanity. Maybe I'll try floatation therapy, no … psychic herb healing, I think that might be best as I am a bit claustrophobic and that would only lead to another trauma that might need an alternative therapy on top of the floatation therapy, and who ever heard of having therapy for therapy …

I screw my eyes tightly together and open them again just in case I am seeing things. Philip's doppelganger heads towards me.

Oh God, he must have caught me staring.

'Can I get you anything?'

A cold chill runs down my spine. It's him. It's Philip. I am not hallucinating. He's standing there right in front of me. I search for the birthmark under the right side of his chin, fitting the last piece of the puzzle and confirming I am not going loco. Philip, the man who knocked my confidence and made my life a living misery, is standing right in front of me and he doesn't even recognise me. I feel myself shrinking away.

'Madam?' he says again. This time he looks at me more closely.

'A glass of still water, please,' I say quickly, adopting an American accent.

'Right away, madam,' he says.

He hasn't recognised me! My open-mouthed disbelief follows the back of him.

Did he really drive me into becoming a repressed bland mousy woman that disappears into the walls, gets digested into the mirror, no one notices her and no one knows she exists? I must have changed so much, mentally and physically.

'Nice accent,' Bob says, sliding his phone into his pocket.

'Just thought I'd try out a few vocal exercises,' I say hastily.

'Are you OK? You look white as a sheet.'

'Do I?' My hand is trembling as I run it over my forehead. 'I feel OK.'

But I don't feel OK, far from it. But now is not the time to have a meltdown.

'So, Bob, do you like living in the hills?' I say, continuing with my American accent.

Bob chuckles. 'It's mighty awesome, ma'am,' he jests.

He starts to talk about his production company but I can't really concentrate: any second Philip is going to return with my water and I need to think fast and smart. I wonder what Bob would say if I threw a drink in the waiter's face. A waste of the fine pink bubbles, granted, but a confusing rage races through me.

My body tenses all over when I sense the presence of a waiter arrive at our table. I take a deep breath and look up. But it isn't Philip. It's a different waiter. What happened to Philip? I surreptitiously swivel my head round, looking for him. Does that mean he recognised me? Or was he really a figment of my imagination and I am going crazy after all? For a few dizzy seconds I can't think straight. I am cracking up.

'Jane, are you sure you're OK?'

'What? Err ... yes, sorry, just thought I saw someone I recognised.' I pull myself together; the last thing I want to do is piss Bob off by being distracted every five seconds like a highly-strung mare.

Over the course of brunch I manage to compose myself without further psychotic tricks of my obviously paranoid mind. It must be paranoia because Philip never wanted to go to LA, he said LA was full of airheads and pretentious money launderers posing as artistes.

Conversation with Bob is an enlightening experience. He tells me about his ex-wife, who systematically sniffed her way through a few of his millions and when he booked her in to the most expensive clinic money can pay for she started to bribe the doctor and had an affair with him all at the same time. She then bankrupted the doctor by claiming half the clinic after they married in Vegas with no pre-nup (clearly there's no love lost). Thankfully Bob's two children have managed to remain sane despite the split and their unscrupulous yet resourceful Machiavellian mother. I'm mesmerised.

'There's a story waiting to be scripted.' I gawp at Bob.

'Far worse than one of those soaps I use to produce back in the eighties.' He belts out an enormous laugh. 'Think of that, an addict running the most exclusive rehab clinic on the planet! Thought you might like the irony of that one, English lady.' Bob is incredibly good humoured, stoic and he's great company, a far cry from Mr Moody writer pants.

When the conversation turns to my career plans, I tell him I want to do a musical; no point being shy in coming forward. He then tells me a friend of his is looking for a new Roxie Hart. Oh wow. Only one of my favourite musicals of all time.

'I love *Chicago*,' I enthuse.

'I can get you an audition if you want.'

Just like that!

I feel an explosion of delight. 'You can do that?'

'For you, my British butterfly … Yes.'

I don't quite know what to say.

'How do you know I'll be any good?'

'Aren't you?'

'Yes.'

'Well then?'

'Thank you, Bob, that would be wonderful,' I say quickly, in case he changes his mind. 'Truly, that's ever so kind of you.' I manage to remain relatively calm.

'Please stop, you'll get me all self-important! It's only an audition – you have to do the rest.'

'Of course.' I nod vehemently.

I want to ask him, why me, why has he chosen me to help?

Self-doubt is threatening to creep in and wrap itself around my larynx at any given moment. But I know better than to reveal my insecurities, and anyway, it's difficult to have that conversation when people start coming over to talk to Bob. I'm glad to see that most of them waited until our food was out of the way.

I pick up my coffee and take a sip.

'You're very popular,' I remark. It is about the fourth time Bob has been interrupted by someone wanting to pitch, audition or give him a script.

'I am, aren't I,' he bellows. 'I wonder why.'

'It must be your devilish good looks,' I reply in the Miss Marple-Sméagol voice. He regards me in silence and I wonder if I've gone too far. To my relief he throws his head back and laughs.

'And the multi-million-dollar company I own, oh merciful one,' he deadpans. I can't believe it, he gets my humour; he really is as sharp as a Japanese knife on blowfish day. 'So you do character work too, eh? A triple threat you are, m'lady.'

'Well ...' I give a bashful shrug as my cheeks fire up. I know, I know what you're thinking but I can't help myself, it's like having let a noisy fart slip out unexpectedly and being forgiven by God all at the same time!

'So what are your plans for the rest of the day?'

'I'm going to be a tourist,' I tell him.

'Wonderful idea,' he says. 'What's on your list?'

'Mann's Chinese Theatre, and the, uh, The Hollywood Museum.'

'Marvellous, marvellous, you should get acquainted with this town, especially if you're going to live here.'

Live here? What gave him that impression? Although now he comes to mention it, it might not be such a bad idea, and Alex has already said I could stay with him. How would I tell Sian? Maybe I'll get that naked picture of Alex in the shower for her – that should do the trick.

'You should stop off at Musso and Frank. It's the oldest restaurant in Hollywood.'

'I'll have to look it up in my tourist guide.'

Bob writes down the address for me then settles the bill.

'It has long been a hangout for screenwriters and celebrities: Charlie Chaplin, Paulette Goddard; the Warner brothers were regulars, and the Rolling Stones were also known to drop by when they were in town.'

As we walk through to the spacious lobby together to my delight I see Jennifer Aniston talking with friends – not

105

the 'Friends' but her ... oh, you know what I mean. I'm getting quite accustomed to these celebrity liaisons. If I could just go over to her and get her autograph, I could ask her about Brad Pitt, Angelina Jolie and whether even after all this time she would like to put them both in a publicity blender, but Bob is already heading for the door and I have to hurry my steps to catch him up.

'Well, my British butterfly, apparently time flies when you're having fun.'

I walk with Bob towards a shiny limo. Standing in front of it are three assistants, all with palm pilots on the go.

'Especially with these three techno ball-breakers as heavy reminders!' he whispers to me. 'Can I drop you somewhere?'

'No, that's OK, I feel like walking.'

Bob is amused. 'Are you sure?'

'Yes, quite sure and thanks for a divine lunch.' Now don't I just sound all lovey and showbiz. Impulsively I give him a hug and two pecks on the cheek.

'The pleasure is all mine,' he says.

'And I'll get my secretary to call you about the audition.'

'That's really great, thank you.' Swiftly an assistant appears in front of us and hastily hands Bob their phone.

'Well, thanks again for everything. I had a great time. Bye!' I say, as another assistant ushers him into the waiting limo. I blow him a double-handed exaggerated kiss and high kick a palm tree, showing off those dancing pins of mine. CRUNCH my hip snaps back. Arghh! I am going to have to limber up before the audition.

I watch the limo disappear around the hillside's tropically green corner, pull my floppy sun hat on and start walking. Downhill may be the direction I'm heading but I feel as if I'm flying above everything. And whether it really was Philip or just a figment of my imagination I'm not going to let it spoil the rest of my day. Bob said he would recommend me and that's got to be reason enough to get excited.

This could be just the new beginning I need.

To say I crammed a lot into one day is an understatement; I jammed in a week's worth of sightseeing into a matter of a few hours. Mann's Chinese Theatre was buzzing with tourists clicking ardently away with their cameras at the various stars' footprints in cement. I followed suit and pulled out my own camera and started clicking away: it sounded like a plague of angry crickets. Next stop was The Hollywood Museum where I took an elevator down to the basement to see Hollywood's scariest characters. It was a lot smaller than I expected and all the movie memorabilia was crammed into a tiny space. Then I walked east along the boulevard and followed the Hollywood Walk of Fame. Apparently – I haven't quoted one statistical fact since I got here so it's about time – the Walk of Fame started out in 1960 with over 2,500 blank stars, and only about 2,130 of them have been filled so far! These numeric pearls go into my mental basket for future use against Sian's teatime interrogations. I finish off my sightseeing and drop into Musso and Frank Grill.

As soon as I step inside it feels like I've been transported back to the 1930s. It's an old-fashioned-looking restaurant, dimly lit with wooden panelled walls and high-sided mahogany booths cushioned in red leather, which I notice match the red jackets worn by the waiters. It looks like the kind of place Humphrey Bogart would have hung out in; he probably did, going by Bob's accounts.

A good-looking waiter with a dazzling 'only in Hollywood' smile shows me to a velvety booth. In fact, all the waiters are good-looking and the charismatic barmen look part and parcel of the furniture, exuding the joint's provenance from their weathered faces. I realise I must be waking up to mankind, enjoying the view – plastic 'n' all.

Sian would be proud of some of the lewd thoughts I've been having whilst sucking on my straw.

CHAPTER THIRTEEN

I really think that I have made progress. I'm finally over the self-doubt, self-loathing, self-pitying. You just have to look at me. Tanned. Energetic. Refreshed. I am having the best time too. Philip is just a blip in an otherwise brilliant week, if it even was him. I'm beginning to think it really was a horrid, panicked, hallucination. Alex has taken me to all the swanky celebrity pebble-dashed places. We've been photographed everywhere, there was even a photographer in the cloakroom at one nightclub hiding behind a shocking Lady Gaga contraption of a shawl. This business of pretending to be Alex's lover is not without its complications though. I had Mum on the phone demanding to know what was going on. So I told her the truth, that nothing is going on romantically, except she doesn't believe me. Since when do mothers rely more on tabloids for the truth than the words out of their own daughter's mouth?

Talk about a power shift. I'm not a politician habitually lying over some dark sordid affair.

As for Michael, he's still there at the back of my mind like a nagging wasp that won't go away when all you want to do is eat your ice cream in peace. Idiotically, I'm reading one of his novels, which is probably not the most effective way to banish him from my mind, but Alex dragged me into

Michael's study and told me to choose one; he said it might make me see him in a different light as he made such a bad first impression.

His writing den is peculiar, to say the least, except it somehow manages to emanate calmness. He has nonsensical stuffed animal heads mounted on all the walls; I don't care what anyone says, but that's odd right there. I snooped about a bit, studying the strange ancient curiosities scattered on the overloaded bookcases. Then I wandered over to the French doors and saw that his view overlooked the swimming pool area and I couldn't get out of there fast enough. I grabbed the first book I could find: *The Beast*, a book about 'isolation'. Jeez, that should make a happy read!

I skim the literary reviews on the back cover. *The human soul destroyed through its own malevolence. The most intriguing work yet from young writer M. Canty. He encapsulates evil with the dexterity only a magician's fingers can conjure.*

NO WAY! I'm fascinated; I thought it was just run-of-the-mill generic horror junk he wrote. It seems our moody maverick has a flair for the dark stuff. Pity he enrolled in the Darth Vader School of Charm.

The characters are entirely absorbing, especially the hero of the book – an everyday man, nothing particularly brave about him – who quite suddenly finds himself in an abysmal situation that causes him to fight for life, but not as we know it. I'm surprised to say I'm enjoying it. Enjoy is the wrong word. Terrified out of my mind is more accurate, it's giving me nightmares.

I thought it might on some strange level bring me closer to Michael as if reading his book will make me understand the man, give me some secret insight. I clearly don't know what's good for me. Truth be told, I am no closer to knowing him. If anything, it has made me a little concerned for his psyche.

110

I check my watch. Three o'clock. I've been reading for four hours straight. The book is certainly immersive, but the sun lounger is giving me a numb bum and I need to get up and walk, stretch out those creaking hips. I grab the Frisbee and pull on my baggy T-shirt and denim shorts. Digger immediately jumps up from his sleeping position before I even utter the one word guaranteed to spin him into a total frenzy. 'WALKIES!!'

I'm in no hurry as we walk along the beach but Digger races ahead. I hold my face up to the sky, feeling the warm breeze from the Pacific Ocean on my skin. I feel so happy. This holiday has done something to me; it has brought me back to life. I know this sounds cheesy but it's nonetheless true, it has made me realise that I haven't been living at all. I've been in limbo. In any case, I'm determined not to let myself live in limbo any longer. Tonight is Bob Edward's party, and although I haven't heard from him since our brunch, I'm going ask him about the audition.

'Hey, Digger,' I call out, Frisbee poised in hand. An alert Digger waits patiently for me to throw. I direct it straight for the water and Digger is immediately on its trail, leaping into the sea and catching the Frisbee between his teeth with the ease of a four-legged athlete. He runs back to me and I grasp the Frisbee from his jaw, but Digger is not letting go of his sacred plastic disc. We continue like this for ages, playing in and out of the water until my lungs are bursting and I can run no more. I collapse in a heap on the sand, panting heavily.

My shorts and T-shirt are soaked and covered with sand but I don't care. Sometimes it is just too much hard work trying to look pristine, and to be quite honest rather boring.

Digger jumps on top of me, nuzzling his wet whiffy fur all over me. Eau de stinky dog … nice!

He suddenly leaps off and runs away. This dog has far too much energy. I lean on my elbows.

'Digger!' I yell. 'Where are you …?' The words die away. Digger is running towards something … someone. I squint, trying to make out whom it could …

No way!

This isn't how I imagined our next meeting. I'm supposed to be dressed up looking utterly gorgeous. I need red lipstick, a sexy dress and impossibly high heels.

Perhaps I am hallucinating again?

But as he gets closer I know I'm not that lucky. I would get up if my legs would move, but I can't move so I remain exactly where I am, sitting on my bum. I don't trust myself to stand. My legs are trembling too much.

Michael stands over me, his large body casting a shadow against the sun. For a moment neither of us speaks and his eyes lock onto mine. My stomach twists into a knot.

'Hello, Jane.' He greets me with trepidation.

'Hello,' I manage in a business-like tone. My chest feels tight.

'You look …'

'A mess,' I offer up unapologetically. 'You're back then?' I say, stating the friggin' obvious.

'Yes. The book is finished.'

'That's good.' I look away. The silence lies heavy between us. I'm so lame. I had a million clever things worked out in my head; things that I was going to say when I saw him, but now he's here standing right in front of me I can't think what they were.

'Nice tan.'

'Thanks,' I mutter indifferently.

Another heavy silence.

'Have you been enjoying your holiday?' he asks.

'What do you want?'

It just burst out of me, but really, what did he expect? Does he really think I could forget all the horrible things he said to me?

Perhaps when it's handed to me on a plate it's less appealing.

112

'I need to apologise,' he says evenly. 'I said some terrible things.'

'You seem to make a habit of it,' I retort. 'And yes, you did.'

'You're not going to make this easy for me?'

'And why should I?' I didn't mean to be this feisty but it just keeps erupting automatically. 'Actually you know what ... don't bother.' I scramble to my feet and start walking. 'You've got nothing I want to hear.'

Michael grabs my arm.

'Get off me.' I yank my arm free. 'Don't you dare touch me!'

He backs off, Digger cowers and the pent-up fury deflates like a pin to a balloon. I put my hand out to Digger.

'It's OK, Digger. I'm not angry at you.' Digger looks at Michael then at me before he cautiously saunters over to my hand, nudging his wet nose against it. I look at Michael; tears start to prick the back of my eyes. I sniff them back.

'Look, we both know it was a mistake.'

'A huge mistake,' I add.

'You're Alex's girlfriend.'

'Ah – yes.' I momentarily forgot about Alex. 'Would you rather I move to a hotel?'

'No. You can stay. It was a moment of madness for both of us,' he says.

Yes, that's exactly what it was. But why does it feel like my heart has been ripped out and hung out to dry?

We walk back to the house in silence and it's horrible. I want ... I want ... I want him. There's no point denying it. But how can I tell him without giving the game away?

And I thought I had more sense.

Here is a man who treats me like a desperado and has the audacity to think he sets the tone of the next scene. A patronising excuse of a man who can just go on as normal, as if nothing happened.

It's a relief when I can escape to my room and have a good cry. I'm not even sure what I am crying about. 'A moment of madness.' How his words irritate me. He shouldn't have made a play for me if he thought I was Alex's true love, who would do such a thing? Only egotistical megalomaniacs with a fixation on being punished for temptation; why doesn't he just join the priesthood and be done with it.

I steam around my room, pacing faster and faster. I'm outraged all over again. I should learn my lesson; I clearly have poor taste in men. I'm not to be trusted. I have to keep my distance from men in general and especially Michael. There's no way I'm ever going to be a pushover, Michael is … he is …

'Ffff-uck!' I howl.

I walk straight into the edge of the bed and stub my toe. OW! OW! OW!

I grab my toe, hopping on one foot and suddenly lose my balance and fall onto the floor, grazing my knees on the carpet.

OW! OW! OW!

I roll onto my side hugging my burning knees and clutching my throbbing toe.

'Janey, what an earth are you doing?'

'Alex!' I turn my head to the door where Alex is standing, a bemused expression on his face.

'Haven't you ever heard of knocking?'

'I heard yelling. What the hell are you doing on the floor?'

'I banged my toe on the bed.' I lift my throbbing foot up for inspection.

'Ewww, pongville.' Alex holds his hand to his nose, backing away.

'My feet do not pong.'

He laughs, bending down to help me up. 'You really should be more careful. Did you know your knees are bright red?' I ignore his hand and sulk.

'Yes, Mr Observant, I'm quite aware. Anyway, what is it you want?'

Alex shrugs his shoulders casually. 'Oh nothing much … just thought you'd like to know I got the part.'

'You what! Oh Alex, that's fantastic news!' I scramble to my feet and throw myself into his arms, my throbbing toe, red knees and bad mood forgotten.

He laughs and swings me around. 'I know, I can't believe it.'

'You're finally going to be the action hero you always wanted to be.'

'Sci-fi, Captain Jane, there is a world of difference; well, worlds and galaxies to be precise.'

I look at his face. It's lit up like all his Christmases have come at once, and I have a vivid image of him saving a world from extinction in a tight spandex jumpsuit with a shiny communicator badge (or combadge, if any Trekkies are peeking) just like Jean-Luc Picard in *Star Trek*, his phaser at the ready. Sian is going to be frothing at the mouth.

'I'm so happy for you, this is what you've always dreamt about.'

Alex's grin is so big it's taking up his whole face.

'I know. All those years at drama school playing the comic sidekick, never the lead … Always cast as the archetypal ass.' Well, he didn't actually help that course of events after Vodka-Gump.

'Now we just need to get you your big break and all will be right with the world.' He says it like it's going to be easy. 'You do realise there's going to be all the movers and shakers at Bob Edward's party tonight. Do you have a dress?'

'I've got lots of dresses,' I boast.

'I mean a sexy dress, a hot little number to show off your two ample assets.'

I frown at him. 'How exactly is that going to help?' Even though I have an image of dirty favours and sleazy contracts.

'It wouldn't do you any harm to look smoking hot.' Alex wiggles his nose.

If he didn't have all the charm and charisma (that eludes his cousin) I'd hit him and knee him in the goolies, that's if my knees didn't throb so badly. I am so clumsy. I really should have gone to a Swiss finishing school, though I'd probably have been expelled. The only time I have grace is when I dance on stage.

'That's not exactly how I want to go about getting noticed. I have morals, you know.'

Alex ignores me. 'Has Bob called about the *Chicago* audition yet?'

'No! Not yet.'

'Well you can ask him tonight.'

'You think I should—'

'Yes, you should.' Alex gives me a stern look. 'You have to be assertive, put yourself out there.'

'Oh, I know that. I do … I will.'

'Good. Then you can start tonight.'

Tonight!

My belly suddenly scrambles with nerves. I'm really not that good with big crowds, and how do I network, exactly? I'd feel awkward just introducing myself to a complete stranger, far more when targeting them for conversation solely due to their connections; sordid ambushing is not my style. I don't even have a style of bamboozling. Oh God! Now I have to work on my bamboozle style – it took me long enough to get a style of dress, let alone an inconspicuous self-serving sales pitch. How do you drop into the conversation, 'get me an audition and a part, please; where did you say you were from?' Subtlety is not my forte, and I'm certainly not a smooth operator. My nerves are currently short-circuiting. Alex thankfully interrupts, preventing my fear machine from starting up fully.

'Bob wouldn't have suggested it in the first place if he didn't think … you had something special,' Alex stipulates persuasively.

'How could he know? He's never even heard me sing.'

'He's probably just got a good feeling about you.'

I wring my hands anxiously. 'You don't think he wants to get me into his bed?'

'Don't be so cynical. You need to pounce on the opportunity. I didn't get on a first-name basis with one of Hollywood's most powerful men when I first got here.'

Alex is right. It's all about who you know in this business and networking is a second career. Being in the right place at the right time. And fate works in mysterious ways, contrary to Mr M. Canty's beliefs. Meeting Bob was fate, stumbling onto the carousel belt was fate telling me to stand up and grab it … or hang onto someone with sensible shoes on. I heard Cameron Diaz got her break at a Hollywood party, and Charlize Theron was standing in line on Hollywood Boulevard when an agent gave her his card. It's just the run-in with Michael I can't seem to shake off.

Damn M. Canty … he is another negative that just needs to be swiped out with a double positive.

'You're right, Alex, I'm just not used to selling myself.'

'Bob would never waste time, and even if he just likes you socially you can meet his associates – what can be the harm of that?'

'Nothing,' I mumble.

'He invited you. You didn't fish for the invitation, that's his intention, now stop double-guessing people, it's not in your character.'

Alex never said a truer word and he knew me when I was still me (if that makes any sense).

'You're absolutely right. Now go.' I start steering him towards the door. 'I've got the most important party of my life to get ready for.'

CHAPTER FOURTEEN

'This isn't a good idea!'

I'm staring at my reflection in the bedroom mirror wondering what on earth possessed me to buy this dress. Ah, that's right, Sian insisted that the Hervé Léger bandage dress was essential in any starlet's wardrobe. It's a bright ocean blue and so short some might consider it not a dress at all, a small top at best. It certainly isn't a dress for the timid or the wallflower, that's for sure. Confidence and boldness, that's what this dress requires. I strike a sexy pose in the mirror then ruin the effect with a geeky thumbs up.

Oh God, I can't do this …

Yes you can, I tell myself rather forcefully. I stick my bottom lip out and give my reflection a 'can do' pout.

Only a few months ago I was slobbing around in tracksuit bottoms and an old jumper with a tub of ice cream for company, feeling sorry for myself; now look at me, getting ready for a swanky Hollywood party.

I adopt another sexy pose, batting my eyelashes and pouting like a diva in an outrageously sexist rap video. That's better. Confidence, that's all I need. And if I don't feel it – fake it. That's Sian's motto and it's done wonders for her.

And why not show a little leg — I didn't do all those squats and lunges for the fun of it. I just hope the redness on my knees fades. I totter over to the bed in my Manolos and grab my black sparkly clutch. As I let myself out of the room I see Alex coming towards me in a smart DJ and I stop, striking a pose.

'Smokin' enough for you?' I say, in a sultry voice.

Alex gives a long, drawn out wolf-whistle.

Giggling, I give a little twirl. 'Just something I threw on.'

He laughs. 'You're going to be the belle of the ball.'

'This place is like a palace!' My mouth drops like a loose pendulum.

'It's all right if you're Russian and own a gold mine,' Alex deadpans.

I don't care what Alex says, the house is amazing. It's the size of Paddington Station. There is door after door leading off this giant hall, where there's a chandelier so major that I shouldn't think even Versailles Palace could match it. I've never been in more elegant surroundings.

An Armani-clad butler shows us to the party, which is well under way. There's a big influential crowd, according to Alex: a hundred of the top movers and shakers of show-business talent in Los Angeles are gathered here tonight. Everywhere I look famous people are dressed in their finest, air-kissing and laughing merrily.

The large party spills out onto the swimming pool area, which is sparkling in cleverly designed node lights. Bartenders are shaking cocktails, a classical pianist is jamming with a drum and bass DJ, sending out a furious rhythm that thumps loudly in my head and I think I'm a clubby Jennifer Grey in *Dirty Dancing*, though possibly more Bridget Jones being thrown into a vampire's lounge.

'Stay put, I just need to talk to that lovely lady producer.'

'Where are you going?' I hate to admit it but I feel all twingy with nerves. 'Don't you dare leave me by myself.'

120

'You'll be fine. I'll be back in warp speed.'

'Alex, don't you dare ...' But it's too late, he's gone.

Oh God, I think I'm going to be sick. I lift a flute of champagne from a passing waiter and gulp half of it down then consciously start sipping. I am standing alone, all too aware of myself. I hate you, Alex Canty, I seethe murderously under my breath.

'Is that you, my English butterfly?' thunders a familiar voice.

'Hello, Bob.' I turn around, genuinely happy to see a friendly face. Bob air-kisses me loudly on both cheeks.

'Glad you could make it,' he booms. 'And may I say how positively exquisite you are looking tonight.'

'You may,' I say joyfully. 'And may I say how dapper you are looking. Mr Bond, I presume,' I purr in a Russian accent. Bob chuckles appreciatively.

Like most of the men here he is wearing a DJ, and it makes him looks very distinguished. Even his bushy eyebrows look like they've been trimmed, and his thick white hair is brushed back neatly.

'Your home is stunning.'

'Thank you. You must know it's the set from *King Solomon's Mines*; any minute now it'll collapse. So watch the walls, Jane! Where's that man of yours?'

'Who, Alex?'

'Yes.'

'He's been kidnapped by a producer.'

'We can't have that.' He puts a hand on my elbow. 'Let me introduce you to a few friends of mine.'

'I should probably wait for Alex ...'

'Nonsense! Leaving a beautiful woman alone by herself is simply asking for trouble, and why are you holding an empty glass? That won't do at all.' A waiter magically appears in front of us.

'Here.' Bob hands me a full glass of champagne, my second, not that I'm counting. He leads me through the crowd, nodding and smiling at numerous people along the way.

'How did the sightseeing go the other day?'

'I had such a swell time!' I joke in my newly adopted Americano style. Bob takes my arm as I skid slightly on the shiny floor.

'I must introduce you to Pat Goldstein. She's around somewhere ... Ah yes, there she is. She's the lady who is casting Roxie Hart.'

Oh God! This is really happening. He meant every word.

We reach a small group of people and they all stop talking.

'Everyone. Let me introduce you to Jane Allen. Jane this is Barry Bukowski, head of Maroon Matinees productions.'

'Hello, Jane.' He turns to me with a warm smile. 'What line of work are you in?'

Oh wow, the head of M & M's, as it's known in the biz.

'Hi, Barry.' I shake his hand in my most professional manner. 'I'm an actress.'

'Of course you are. Could hardly doubt otherwise.'

'I'd say so, goddess, simply heavenly,' slurs a man next to him.

'And this man posing as a gentleman is Howard Mears from Stardust Agency.'

'Which agency are you with?' inquires Howard.

'Oh, no one at the moment.'

'Really, that is very interesting,' he says, checking out my boobs.

I thrust out my hand. 'My face is up here.'

Everyone laughs. Bob coughs a chortle.

'I was just admiring the view.' Seedy boob man explains with playful arrogance.

Dirty old man. He's early fifties – I hazard a guess. Quite good-looking but a little too oily for my liking, and his small beady eyes hold mine for a little too long. I shake his hand, which I notice are chubby and hairy, totally at odds with the rest of his thin and wiry body. He looms forward and I catch the whiff of whiskey on his breath.

Bob elegantly intervenes by pushing him gently but firmly aside.

'Now, now, Howard, I think there's a thirty-five-year-old bottle of single malt with your name on it hidden in the back of the pool bar where your wife happens to be at this very moment. Looks like she's found the next gladiator there too.'

No sooner than the words 'bottle' and 'wife' are uttered, he is gone.

'He's not a bad sort, Jane, he just gets carried away at parties,' says a woman who looks a bit like Helen Mirren. She's about six feet tall, immaculately made up with sparkling blue eyes.

'And I think it's a while since he's seen a real pair of boobs,' she adds.

'Oh, right.'

'This is Pat,' Bob informs me.

'Pleased to meet you.' We shake hands and I am engulfed in a cloud of Chanel perfume.

'You sound just like you stepped out of a Jane Austen novel.'

'Surely not, I'm from South Carolina, ma'am,' I articulate in an exaggerated American accent.

She smiles as if she's humouring me and I squirm.

'Why don't we go sit over there? Bob has been most insistent that I meet with you.'

I feel like the arbitrary lamb being lead to slaughterhouse via poolside. My only companions now are nerves.

Bob gives me a wink and I smile back gratefully, trying to control my jumpy companions. My heart is racing.

'Bob, darling!' trills a young woman bearing down on us; blonde with boobs that look like they could float the *Titanic*, and fish pout lips, which might be mistaken as suction pads to conquer tricky rock faces.

'I've been calling your office but your staff keep me on hold and then I get diverted to a voicemail.'

I think I recognise her but – nope it's gone.

'Terrible shame,' Pat whispers as we walk away.

'What is?'

'Only twenty-two and she's ruined her face. The awful thing is she's not alone. There are so many more like her – the freakishly young crowd showing up for auditions with huge puffy lips and frozen foreheads.'

'Women in Hollywood nowadays either look like drag queens or strippers,' I blurt out, then clap my hands over my mouth and dart a nervous look at Pat.

She shrieks with laughter.

'That is very true. I'm not averse to a little bit of work, but not at that age; everything in moderation and for heaven's sake, make it look natural.'

I'm still trying to gauge Pat's age; if she has had work then it's subtle.

'I quite agree,' I say timidly. We sit down at the most lavish poolside furniture I've ever set eyes on. A private Bedouin silk tent furnished with plush pop art cushions, every angle of this palatial setting is the work of sheer interior art; *House & Gardens* is positively drab in comparison.

I couldn't be more impressed than I am now.

'Now tell me about you; I hear you want the role of Roxie Hart.'

This is it. This is my chance. I must not cock it up. I need to sell myself.

'Yes. I'm made for that part. I adore *Chicago*. I could listen to John Kander music all day long.' OK, don't overdo it.

'Have you done many musicals?'

'A few. I was Sally Bowles in *Cabaret*.'

'Very good, West End?'

'I … err …' I take a sip of champagne to avoid having to answer.

Fortunately someone brings over a bottle of Cristal Rose 1995 and Pat's attention is diverted.

'I went to the same drama school as Alex Canty,' I quickly interject, moving the conversation swiftly along.

'Very talented actor. You and him are dating, I understand?'

Oh shit! 'Err well …'

I stop myself, aware that Pat is now giving me a curious look. I want to tell her the truth but I can't, Alex would kill me.

'Yes we are.'

'Bit of a rogue though, so be warned.'

'Alex!' I laugh. 'I've been hearing that a lot. Luckily for me I knew him before fame hit his ego!'

He wasn't like that at drama school; in fact I don't remember him dating at drama school at all. He must be making up for lost time.

'If you are as good as you say you are then we'd be happy to audition you. You've definitely got the right look. Your forehead actually moves, which is always a start.'

I goofily grin.

'What's your vocal range?'

'Contralto to mezzo-soprano.'

'Very good.'

'Have you a business card?'

Shit, why didn't I think of that! 'Eh, no, not on me.'

'Oh you should always take business cards wherever you go. You never know whom you might bump into. Don't worry I'll get your number from Bob.'

'That's great. Thank you.'

'I'll get my office to call you about the audition.'

'Thank you,' I say again. OK, don't overdo it. It's just one professional talking to another professional. But I am

125

feeling a lot of love for this woman. I am of course tipsy. Without realising it the best part of a bottle of Cristal Rose 1995 is now cruising nicely around my veins.

'There you are. I've been looking everywhere for you.' A short, rotund man pokes his head through the Bedouin silk.

'Blake is a notorious PR agent,' she whispers out the side of her mouth. 'He controls most of the A-listers' misdemeanours.'

I'm dying to ask her about those misdemeanours but he literally whisks her off in a grand persuasive PR whoosh. Considering how small he is and how tall she is it's no mean feat. Pat towers over him like a looming praying mantis. She's impressive to watch, her long gangly legs are sporting a pair of impossibly high heels, but unlike me she seems to have been born in them, each stride elegant, poised and effortless. My own wobbly strides on the other hand have as much coordination as a dizzy spider with a blindfold on. Is there some secret I'm missing out on? How do you walk in high heels for longer than an hour? I do feel quite drunk and a little spaced out.

'Where has Pat gone?' booms a voice in my ear.

'Abducted by Blake.' I pivot my tightly bound bandaged bottom around as quickly as I can without breaking out of the seams and face Bob. 'But she said she's going to arrange an audition for me.'

'Good for you.'

'Bob, I don't know how to thank you.'

'Jane, you don't have to. Just prove my instincts right and sing your bloody British butterfly wings off at that audition!' With that comment he raises his glass for another jovial 'Cheers'.

We chink glasses.

'Where have you been?' Alex's voice emerges from behind me.

'Me! You were the one who marooned their fellow shipmate.'

'Can I give you a piece of advice dear boy?' interrupts Bob, as he lifts himself off the chair. 'Do not leave Jane alone too long, the next man might not be so polite as to give her back.'

Alex guffaws. 'I'll remember that.'

As soon as Bob is gone, Alex jumps into the vacated seat.

'Soooooo?' Alex probes. 'How did it go?'

I look at the eagerness on his face and the penny finally drops.

'You did that on purpose, didn't you? Left me alone. You knew Bob would come over.'

'And it worked?'

'Yes. Bob introduced me to interesting people. One was, err ... Barry, Head of M & M's ...'

'I saw. And you met Howard Mears too, he's super-influential, if not a bit ... err ...'

'Lecherous,' I add.

'Be careful around him.'

'Don't worry, I will. He spoke to my boobs. Rude bugger didn't even try and hide it.'

Alex laughs. 'I saw you talking to Pat Goldstein for a long while, what did she say?'

'Well, she said she'll get me an audition for Roxie Hart.' I start grinning.

'That's brilliant.'

'Let's see if she calls.'

'Give it a couple of days and if she doesn't call you, you call her.'

'You think.'

'Definitely. Don't let this opportunity slip by.'

'You're right and we both know I could do the role standing on my head.'

My confidence is escalating. Right now I feel I can do anything. We both start grinning at each other.

'That's my girl,' Alex says, giving me a hug.

'What are you two so happy about?'

And before Alex or I can make an escape Kimberly sits herself down, crossing her legs and giving anyone who cares to look a view of her nether regions. She is dressed in what I can only describe as loose fish-net wrapping. If I thought my dress showed too much flesh, hers is positively pornographic.

'Fab party, isn't it? Although a little out of your league, Alex,' she purposely provokes.

'I didn't know you were coming,' Alex retorts. I can feel the tension rise up and expand in his body.

'I thought I'd accompany my father for once.'

'Alex!' A man in a cravat swoops down. 'Can I have a word?'

Alex jumps up like a springbok. 'Of course, very important to begin discussions …' The man looks slightly taken aback by Alex's enthusiasm.

'It's only dialogue detail, we can do it another time.'

'No, no … no time like the present, Alfie, my good sci-fi pundit.'

'You know it will only ever be a holiday fling?' Kimberly hisses in my ear.

I slowly turn. This girl doesn't like me at all and the feeling is mutual. She's an acidic solution sizzling away, eating, eroding and destroying but I refuse to be ruffled out of my blissful state.

'Don't hold back, Kimberly, say what you think.'

'Alex doesn't love you, he loves me.'

The woman is seriously deluded. 'I'm sorry your plan didn't work out.'

'You're ruining everything,' she says, all but stamping her feet. 'Everything was fine until you came along. Why are you even here? You'll only hold him back.'

She gives me a conceited look that could strip paint.

I cannot believe this woman!

And why the hell am I bothering to be polite?

'Is that right. Strange how he doesn't reciprocate your feelings. Can you feel any more? I've always wondered about Botox misuse.'

'I'm warning you,' she spits shakily. 'Stay away.'

'That sounds like a threat.' I sympathise with Alex, she doesn't seem to be able to take no for an answer. I suspect she is seriously unhinged.

Alex must have sensed the conversation getting out of control; he grabs me by the hand.

'Excuse me, Kimberly, I need to borrow Jane for a minute.'

'Alex, we need to talk,' she stutters indignantly.

'Sorry, Kimberly, let's talk later. OK?'

'OK,' she says, the venom she hissed at me gone back to its lair. Selective bipolar I think are the words to use for her type.

As I walk off I can clearly hear profanities under her breath directed at my back. I join the boys and Alf hands me a full glass of champagne.

'Thank you.'

'You look like you need it.' He gestures with a finger pointing at Kimberly.

'Deluded monster of a woman,' Alex says.

'I see.' Alf contemplates this while pulling crazy faces.

I discover Alf is the sci-fi scriptwriter and he has a level of energy and enthusiasm that is utterly infectious. We spend some time listening to his anecdotes about changing scripts on film sets and prima donna tantrums; he is a strangely entertaining creature, hair all out of place and a suit that either is ill-fitted or skinny pop fashionable. Probably a nerd that accidentally looks in vogue, I settle upon.

'Oh, I got a funny one for yer both ... listen to this ... Once there was a starlet not a million miles away from this spot, you know the one ...' He waits for our acknowledgement but just gets a puzzled look from us

129

both. 'The one who can only pout in reaction, you know ... the camera lingers a bit too long waiting for an actual emotion ... C'mon, you two!' Alex and I look blankly around and then see who he's referring to.

'Oh ... her,' we say in unison, nodding our heads.

'Yeah, well everyone knows that she can't act for toffee – although we never tried that enticement. We've tried plenty of other stuff, believe me. We even wrote her lines, all round the bridge of the star-ship set, but mostly someone had to feed them to her one at a time. Sometimes I'd write a repeat in so she just had to concur or nod, it was demoralising. The camera set-up took twice as long. So there's this one scene where she has to look terrified the ship might be destroyed at any minute, deflector shields are at minimum strength, et cetera. The scene is a long continuous panning shot so to gauge the look of horror on all the cast faces at the prospect of their imminent death, you know a silent suspense shot, it ends with her face as she's the acting captain.' Alf's fervour is mounting; as he tells the tale he even winds himself up.

'So everyone is really emotive, tears running down their faces, sweating ... grimacing beyond what's truly acceptable ... real over-the-top stuff because it's the concluding scene, then the camera gets to her and she looks straight at it and says, "Why is everyone worrying? We have deflector thingies on, we don't die, I read the script." And with that the director throws over the monitor and has a nervous breakdown right there on set. Ironic, isn't it, the only day she actually did read the script. Reading obviously confused the issue for her. The director still hasn't made a film with people since, went into animation after that.'

Alex and I are gob-smacked.

'You hear about these stories but I always thought the media exaggerated them tenfold.'

'Oh no, Jane, if anything they keep the best ones out of the media … welcome to Hollywood!' Alf raises his glass in an impromptu toast.

I leave Alex and Alf arguing over who's got the better vengeance motive, the Hulk, Iron Man or Batman, and go in search of some refreshment – aren't I just picking up Americanisms! I desperately need to eat something before I drink any more alcohol. I'm just negotiating the pillared veranda when I hear a low-pitched question being directed at me.

'Is it Alex or Bob who holds your interest?' Michael's voice is one of his greatest assets, deep, rich and sexy … the kind of voice that could make you do anything. Slowly, I turn. The sight of him makes my heart catch in my throat. Michael is seriously handsome; his DJ fits him immaculately; his stance oozes sophistication.

'Which would you prefer?' I reply coolly, trying to work out if he's a little loaded.

'I would prefer it if it was neither,' he says brusquely.

And why would that be? I want to ask.

'Great party, isn't it?' I force gaiety instead.

'If you like this sort of thing.'

'Why did you bother coming then if it isn't your sort of thing?'

'I've been asking myself the same thing,' he deliberates.

'I see you have all your desirable charms on display tonight.' I'm not about to let him unnerve me. 'Why, don't you like it?' I ask coyly.

His mouth thins and he takes a step towards me.

'I think you've had far too much to drink.'

I pull my glass to my lips and drain the remainder of fizz, lick the rim and grab another champagne flute from one of the ever-circling weary waiters.

'Oh, I've not nearly had enough.' I punch my glass into the night air and raise derisive eyebrows at him.

'Well, I think you should walk it off.'

'Have you seen the shoes I'm wearing? Besides, there's no way I am walking anywhere—' But I don't get to finish my sentence because Michael takes hold of my arm and pulls me to the side of a huge column. Not wishing to create a scene, I let him tug me towards some steps and onto a Japanese garden away from the other remaining guests.

As soon as the last step is cleared I pull away.

'Men have this awful failing,' I lecture. 'They think that they can get you to do what they want by man-handling you.'

'I didn't man-handle you, I simply led you.'

'You dragged me!' I protest. 'I am a grown woman, Michael, so I wear and drink what I like.'

'I can see you're a grown woman, a very beautiful woman, but you're dangerous in this state. I just don't want to see you make a fool of yourself.'

Did he just call me beautiful? I am so stunned by his assessment that I don't register the fool bit, not straight away, and he's definitely been on the hard stuff.

'I'm not in any state, it's you … you … don't like to see people enjoying themselves.' I can't believe I managed a whole coherent sentence in my drunken rage; I'm getting better at holding my liquor.

'Do you enjoy being gawped at?'

'No one is gawping at me … I doubt anyone's even noticed me.'

He treats me to an incredulous look. 'They noticed you, all right.'

'Oh well, GOOD! I didn't wear this dress to blend in with the wallpaper.'

Michael expels a low drawn-out curse and takes a step closer.

'You can't use people, Jane.'

'By people you mean Alex?'

'You don't love Alex.'

132

'Actually I do.' Like a brother but he doesn't need to know that.

'Does he approve of you cavorting with Bob Edwards, or was it Barry?'

'Oh I don't know, there are so many men to cavort with – let me see …' I goad him as my fury rises. 'Contrary to what you might think of me, I am not some man-eater and even if I were it has nothing to do with you.'

He takes another step closer. 'Perhaps I was wrong to not do what I've been wanting to do since I first saw you.'

In a heartbeat the world shifts on its axis and my head begins to whirl. Did he say 'since he first saw me'? Michael leans towards me and my heart starts hammering against my breastbone.

'What are you doing?' My voice cracks in a breathless squeak as his head slowly descends and I think he's going to kiss me.

He is … he's going to … he's going to …

'Ooh, this looks very cosy.' A shrill, nasal voice encroaches upon the space. Michael and I jump apart.

'Kimberly.' Michael gives her a pearly smile. 'I was just telling Jane about the chaparral by the Santa Monica Mountains.'

Impressive, he hasn't even broken out into a sweat.

'Dry and boring,' Kimberly comments.

'Well, Michael, thank you for the insight, I'll bear that in mind. Now if you'll excuse me … must circulate.' I am on the hoof before either of them can comment further.

I no longer have the stomach for food and return to the house in search of Alex, but become distracted by the Miro painting on the wall. I know it's a Miro after two agonising years sitting history of art, where the only highlight was a trip to Barcelona to his museum before I headed off to Guildford to study my true passion, acting. I step backwards for a better view, bumping into a waiter with his arms juggling canapés.

133

'So sorry, madam.'

'No, no it was my fault, I wasn't—' I stop. It's as if someone has chucked a bottle of ice-cold water down my back. Looks like I wasn't hallucinating after all.

'Philip!'

'Sorry, do I know you?'

'You should do, we lived together for two years,' I reply frostily.

Does he really think I could forget what he did, the abusive texts twenty thousand times a day? At one point I even consulted a solicitor, until I saw the hourly rate. In the end I just changed my phone number, my work route, my hangouts and my address.

His eyes widen like saucers.

'Jane!' If I thought he could have changed, showed some kind of remorse ... his mouth curls into a mocking smile.

'You look different.' He gives a little laugh. 'You're not fat. Maybe that's why I didn't recognise you.'

A tiny part of myself starts to shrink inside, turning me back into the girl who let herself be bullied. But the bigger part of me overtakes, the part that has waited a long time to confront him and now it's here I'm not about to let myself down; although I never thought the moment would come.

I pull myself up and eye Philip coldly. 'Is it not enough you try and spoil people's dreams in one country you have to find another continent? Who are you disillusioning this time, you piece of shit?'

Rather than cower, he seems to revel in my anger.

'Really, Jane, it was not like that, I was only trying to prepare you ... I was older; I knew the disappointment of being rejected. I wanted to save ...'

I'm tuning him out ... same shit, different venue. My brain pops with a vivid revelation. JEALOUSY! I had talent, I had fun, I was popular and I am ambitious! Ah ha, by Jove! I think I've got it ... I am ambitious – notice the present tense! I am ... I am. He wanted my life all along, a

134

closet performer. If he couldn't make it then no one would. His constant critiquing of the delivery of my lines when I rehearsed, his frustration over my forgetfulness, his sweaty pawmarks on my music scores, his ludicrous protective male conduct always upstaging me after every performance I did get (nominal fee). He became delirious when the phone went for me, if anyone showed me any attention, professional or not. Jealousy is an inexplicable state and that sums up my relationship with him, INEXPLICABLE! I resist the temptation to throw my drink into his face.

I'm not going to make a scene here with all these people, and with so much at stake.

I swallow several times, getting my words into order.

'You were a bully, Philip. When you finally managed to wear down any aspirations I had left with your constant whining and negativity, you started tormenting me day in day out. You're an abusive excuse for a life form.'

'I don't know what you're talking about.'

'Yeah right, next you'll be telling me it was all imagined.'

'Jane, I know you're still hurting and it was a painful break-up for both of us,' he is patronising and sneering, 'but it's been over three years. You've got to move on.'

Why, the condescending slime pustule. I want to stuff the words back down his throat and let him choke on them. I want to yell furiously, 'Sociopathic fuckwit!'

He's behaving like he's won some sort of victory here. He's twisted, poisonous. I take a slow deep breath then very calmly lean in.

'Took your own encouraging advice, did you?'

His snakelike form contorts, struggling to keep the fake smile on his horrible face. 'Actually, I'm ....'

I don't let him finish, digging my heel into his foot and giving it a twist; I knew these Manolos were worth every penny. I revel as his agonised expression changes to a deeper red. The pain must be immense by now. I feel a wicked satisfaction. He tries to stay poised and just as he utters a sssshh sound I decide I've heard enough and cut him down to size.

'Well, Philip the waiter, go and wait somewhere else.'

'You always did have an inflated opinion of yourself, stuck up cow.' His voice is harsh and bitter, gone is the façade of conceited cockiness, but I am no longer scared of him and he can hurt me no more. I quickly grab flowers out of the closest vase and throw the stale water at his crotch, my head held high as I strut away.

An immense sense of relief sweeps over me and adrenalin drains from my body. Finally I have stood up to the monster that stole two years of my life, stole my spirit. With my heart pounding as I lock the door of the bathroom, I look at my sweating brow in the mirror. Turn the taps and douse my face in cold water. I notice my hands are shaking. I take several deep breaths and when I have finally stopped shaking, return to the party.

I feel a bit timid, nervously circling the party for fear of running into either Kimberly, Philip, or even Michael; I think I've had enough venom spewed at me for one evening. Just then Alex flies past on a pair of roller-skates. Seeing me, he tries to latch onto my arm but misses and ricochets back as he spins an overzealous three-sixty and falls flat on his arse; giving me the biggest laugh of the night, exactly what I needed. All the same I think it's time I went home. Wiping the tears from my face I help Alex to his feet.

'I've been looking for you everywhere.'

'And now you've found me. Look, would you mind if we go home?'

'Sure thing, Janey, I'll just fetch the golf buggy.'

'The what?'

'Won it off Bob, we had a bit of wager when you left, we can go home in it.'

CHAPTER FIFTEEN

It's Sunday lunchtime and a tiny percussion orchestra is furiously practising inside my head. Alex is draped over the kitchen table with his head in his hands and a glass of Alka Seltzer sizzling loudly on the table. He lifts his head just a fraction as I enter the kitchen, peering at me through his fingers. A newly acquired golf buggy is parked rather precariously on the terrace, staring at us through the French doors. The nervous feeling in my belly subsides when I see he is alone.

'You look awful,' I say.

'Likewise,' Alex sniffs.

'That's the last time I'm going to drink.' But we both know that's not true.

'Where do you keep the Alka Seltzer?' I ask with a fragile voice.

Alex pulls a small jar from his pocket and throws it to me. I miss and it crashes to the floor, the noise deafening to our delicate ears. We both wince. Very carefully I bend to pick it up and stagger over to the sink. Even the tap sounds noisy, the drops resonating in my eardrums more strident than thrash-metal.

'Great night though,' Alex chuckles, but the laughter moves his head and he recoils.

'Nice wheels,' I giggle, but this hurts too.

It was a great night but certain parts of the evening I could have done without: Kimberly, Philip, Whiskey boob man, what was his name again ... Bert ... Hugg ... Mears?

'Morning!' bellows a voice from the doorway.

I jump out of my skin and the fizzy remedy splashes over me. I turn around and Michael saunters into the room followed by a dutiful Digger. When the dog sees me he runs over and jumps up, splashing the remainder of the liquid everywhere.

'Digger, down.'

'It's OK.' I reach down and pat Digger's head. 'I'm just feeling a little fragile this morning,' I tell Digger. Michael, on the other hand, looks annoyingly fresh-faced. I sit myself down next to Alex.

'How come you got off so lightly?' Alex grumbles.

'The art is to know one's pace,' Michael chirps smugly.

'Oh very funny, laugh at a dying man,' Alex grumbles, putting his head in his hands again.

Michael chuckles and pours himself a coffee.

'I guess congratulations is in order.' Though his tone is anything but congratulatory.

Alex looks up.

'What are you talking about?'

'The engagement?' Michael prompts.

'Whose?'

'Yours.'

'What?' we both say in unison.

Michael pulls today's newspaper off the counter and we both wince as he drops it on the table, followed by another wince when I see the picture of Alex and me hugging and the caption above:

Canty to Wed English Scanty. Surprise romance shocks Hollywood

I remember that it was taken when we were playing movie charades. I start to read over Alex's shoulder. Alex reads out loud.

'"It's official. Most desirable bachelor Alex Canty has finally been reeled into matrimony."'

'What the hell is she playing at?' Alex hisses, brushing his hangover aside.

'"After playing the field, the domineering stage actress Jane Allen gives our golden boy an ultimatum. One source says it's because of pregnancy after a one-night stand and she is threatening to reveal all to the newspapers, and it's apparent when you see her in the flesh that she is far along. Our source even disclosed her exact words: 'Alex is the father and I'm going to get some money and fame out of this one.' The source, a close friend of Alex's, says this is just despicable behaviour from a self-serving b***h out to further her own career."'

'What ... how could this happen? She's out of control, Alex,' I fume, my head pounding as I digest the possible repercussions of this little stunt.

'Don't worry,' Alex tries to soothe me. 'I'll sort this out.'

'How, exactly?'

He pulls out his mobile.

Michael looks on in bewilderment.

'Who are you calling?' I ask.

'Kimberley, that's who.'

'Don't you think you've done enough damage?' Michael butts in. 'You've already broken her heart.'

'Shit, it's dead. Broken her heart?' Alex says. 'She hasn't got one. She's malicious, obsessive, anything she can't have she destroys.' He is livid. I've never seen him this angry before. Even Michael looks taken aback.

'No one pays any attention to this columnist anyway. I know she can be a bit of a pain but she loves you. She must do ... to do such a thing.' Michael tries to placate Alex.

'A bit of a pain … more like mental. She's fanatical, evil! Look, Michael, you know nothing about it.'

'She's a cheeky mare. Pregnant. It's called eating, you stupid tart!' I'm really talking to myself but Alex half chuckles; probably relieved that I'm not blaming him.

'She told me what happened,' Michael says.

'Her version, you mean,' Alex retorts. 'Michael, I slept with her once, ONCE, and that was when I couldn't even walk, I could barely bloody see! ONCE! And that's only according to her so I think it's a crock anyway. The woman's deranged.' Michael shoots me a sideways glance. 'Don't worry, Jane knows about it. Did she also tell you she hasn't stopped pestering me ever since that ill-fated night?'

'What?'

'Look, I've tried telling Kimberly politely that there is no us but she won't take no for an answer so I figured having Jane as my girlfriend might stop her pestering, her delusions … but it hasn't. Jane and I are not engaged. It was all fabricated … just a cover.'

Michael seems to have trouble digesting this piece of information. 'Fabricated?'

'I asked Jane to pretend to be my lover. I never meant it to get so out of hand. Jane, I'm so sorry.'

But I'm watching Michael. He seems to be still reeling with the shock of what Alex is saying.

'I can't believe you lied to me,' he says, staring at his cousin.

'I'm sorry, Michael. I didn't mean—'

'Dammit, Alex, haven't you grown up at all?'

'Hey now, come on, Michael,' Alex cuts in irritably. 'There's no need to get on your high horse, I can explain everything.'

But he doesn't get a chance as the telephone begins to ring. Alex groans and Michael reaches for the receiver.

'It's Malcolm, your wonder boy,' he barks, thrusting the phone at Alex.

Alex gives Michael a brutal glare.

He turns his back to us, his anger now channelled down the phone. I can feel Michael's eyes on me and reluctantly look up. I'm desperate to know what he's thinking but daren't explore all the possibilities.

'I can't believe you let Alex talk you into this charade,' he finally says.

I massage my weary, hung-over head. 'I didn't exactly approve but he's a friend, what could I do?'

'You could have said no. The publicity machine shouldn't be played with here, it's dangerous.'

'Dangerous seems to be your word du jour, doesn't it?' He looks at me with what I think is perplexed anger.

'Look, Michael! How was I supposed to know Alex's entanglements were loony tunes galore? I came to see him, not work on some elaborate publicity stunt.'

I don't know why I'm defending myself, we haven't really broken any law and I certainly don't need to explain myself to him.

'Sorry.'

The man has apologised – big deal.

'Sorry for a lot of things.'

I purposely remain quiet, letting him stew in his own guilt. He shouldn't have been so quick to judge and it still doesn't explain his behaviour towards me and the disloyalty towards his cousin.

'Jane, I won't be around this afternoon.' Alex is off the phone and kneels beside me. 'I'm meeting up with Malcolm. He's going to sort out this mess.'

'Right.'

'Do you need me to come along?' I cringe at the thought.

'Unfortunately the paparazzi will be hounding me as soon as I hit downtown, then I'm going to speak to Kimberly.'

'OK.'

'The thing is …'

I know that look.

'I have a launch this evening for Harry Winston. I'm their new poster boy, and Malcolm wants me to bring you along.'

'Michael, can you drive Jane there, and why don't you come along?'

NO! NO! NO! For heaven's sake, Alex, you can be so dense sometimes. Maybe the boy can't read people, maybe Kimberly had her reasons after all?

'I'm sorry to have dragged you into this.'

'Don't worry, Alex, it's fine. What are friends for?'

CHAPTER SIXTEEN

The last person I thought would be driving me anywhere again was Michael but here we are on our way to the jeweller's, driving in total silence. Fine with me as I'm still nursing a sore head.

I jolt awake when he hits the brakes.

'I should market myself to GlaxoSmithKline.'

'What?' I say, somewhat groggy and irritated.

'Well if I have such a strong effect on people just sitting in close proximity, they'd make a fortune out of me. Sleeping pills will never be the same.'

I manage a small smile as I let myself out of the car, leaving Michael to speak to the valet.

The store is lit up with hundreds of revolving diamonds. Black feathers adorn the façade, giving the illusion of a nineteen twenties boudoir. We start to walk up the red carpet and Alex bounces out from the six security guards at the entrance. He immediately takes my arm and we're pulverised by camera flashes. Michael hangs back, avoiding any attention – he could be my bodyguard. It's not a comfortable situation but my eyes soon block out any discomfort I might have had when they focus on the biggest diamonds I've ever seen in my life, so big that I can see them shimmering at me from a distance. I'm going to start drooling if I don't snap out of it soon. WOW! Marilyn was right! I never knew what all the fuss was about, but until you see the big stuff ... just save your judgements ... WOW!

We are escorted into the store by a huge, positively rippling-bodied security guard, and they have even bigger stones on display inside. I have quite honestly left my body, and my companions, to look at an art deco diamond necklace encased in glass – no doubt bullet proof. It's ... it's ... I have no words for this objet d'art ... beauty beyond measure. The style is from a time where women were purely elegant, feminine and expert seductresses. It makes my imagination flip out. I stand for what I think is a minute, but Alex is pulling at my arm.

'Jane, JANE ...earth to Jane, come in, Jane!'

'Oh sorry, Alex but look at this.'

'Yeah, yeah, very pretty, c'mon have a drink.'

'I don't think—' He plonks a glass of champagne in my hand. Oh well, hair of the dog!

'Look, Malcolm is going to ease a story out next week about us only being old friends from drama school. He's going to make it a feel-good story, you know: "Alex doesn't forget his roots, the fame hasn't gone to his head" that type of editorial thing.' I look at him, pleasantly surprised.

'So the truth at last – good.'

'Where's Michael?' Alex says. We both scan the heavenly sparkling room.

'Dunno.' Don't care, I silently add. 'Alex, I'm going to look over there, while you're doing your schmoozing and cruising.'

I tiptoe over to a darkened corner where a solitary case is being up-lit with no audience to see it perform. There is a velvet choker sitting on a plush velvet cushion, encrusted with little star-shaped diamonds. It's understated but so pretty, just a twinkle when the light catches the stones. I lose myself in reverie once again, an image of me arriving at my own premiere with the choker on. Oh, there's a cuff to go with it, it has a big blue diamond in the middle – I only know it's a diamond because I'm reading the description, this is better than an art gallery – that must represent the moon, and cascading out from the sides are micro pavéd white diamonds posing as shooting stars – once again nicked it from the description. I love them, I love them. Maybe HW are looking for staff; if my audition goes horribly wrong, I can stay close to the stars in here.

I'm so wrapped up in studying the pieces I don't notice another face peering through the glass cabinet. I promptly stand up.

'Aren't they exquisite?' says the stranger.

'Hmm,' I reply inadequately.

'My name's Eli, by the way.' He holds out his hand and I shake it, firm grip.

'Jane, pleased to meet you, Eli.'

'I work here, if you were wondering, not some oddball who peers at woman through cabinets. I was just checking the halogen light positions.'

'Oh,' I say, for want of a better response.

'Diamonds must be lit in a certain way for optimum sparkle.'

'Really, I just thought they sparkled anywhere.'

'No there has to be light to bounce in through the top down to the bottom point and refract off the facets. That's why diamonds are cut this way. Even the highest grade of diamond needs light. A bit like a flower needs sunshine.'

Jane 'sore feet' Allen talking to a diamond expert now. The closest I ever got to the jewellery world was walking down Hatton Garden to sell an old gold bracelet because I needed tap shoes, now look at me.

'Could I possible try it on? Don't go to any trouble – I'm not rich so I can't buy it.'

'No trouble at all. I thought you looked too enthusiastic for this group!'

145

'I don't understand.' I really don't.

'Well let's say when you've been in the business for a while you get to know body language and you don't look like you've got a stick stuck up your ... oh, pardon me, madam.' I start to smirk. Eli is relieved.

'You must excuse me, I've just flown in from Hong Kong and the last thing I needed was another group of snotty celebs looking at the wonder of mother nature as if it wasn't good enough. You know how they do! A bit too blasé. You should never lose that sense of awe.' I like this man – he says what he thinks; he might be as goofy as me.

'Some people never appreciate anything,' I say, concurring.

'Our representative, though, Alex the TV star, he's nice and grounded. That's why we chose him.'

Eli must have a deluded sense of influence; I know all these houses whether it's jewellery or fashion, speak as though they are one, or as Alex might say, they are 'borg' or 'ood'; they act in one collected consciousness – must be their luxury sales training.

'I know, I'm his friend,' I quietly add.

'English, yes?'

'Yes.'

'You must go and look in Graff's window in London when you're back home. They have wonderful coloured diamonds too and some mesmerising rocks.' I vaguely recollect a small group always standing outside their window in Bond Street. I've never taken a look though.

'I'm not in that league. Really!'

'Nonsense, it's not about who or what or how much, it is about being fascinated, passionate. Marvelling at what carbon has to offer. Trees and tennis rackets are nice but diamonds are far easier to wear!' His humour is gentle and his face sincere.

I'm relaxing – finally, a normal down-to-earth non-psycho person to talk to.

'Have you always loved stones and gems?' My interest is growing in this elite secret glittery world.

'Ever since my father took me to see my uncle who was a diamond dealer on 47th Street in New York, the diamond district. It was like walking into a different world, alive and noisy, and that's saying something in New York! I begged for a job after school and learnt my trade from there. It's the best education you can ever have.' Eli lights up when he is speaking of his youth. He seems far too gentle a soul to come from the bartering world of 47th Street. That much about New York I did know.

'That must have been amazing to see all those stones. So what do you do here in the shop?'

'I help run it.' He seems a little shy now.

'Well you're doing a fantastic job.' I really like him and I want him to be noticed. Maybe he'll get a better commission from his manager if he's seen to mingle well and entertain the guests.

'Shall I sneak you a drink, or aren't you allowed?' I ask cheekily. I don't want to move from this spot, no journalists are here and I have normal company that doesn't scowl at my every word.

'That's OK, I'll get them,' Eli answers. I didn't mean for him to fetch and carry for me, now he'll think I'm a toffee-nosed cow, an aloof pretender like the rest of them.

He puts his hand inside the lapel of his jacket and mumbles. OK, I knew it was going too well and normal … he's mad. Suddenly a waiter appears with an ice bucket. I'm confused. Eli guides me to sit down at a nearby black lacquered table. He pulls a leather tray out and the waiter places silver goblets beside us.

'The silver will keep the champagne cool,' Eli explains, registering my puzzled face. 'You did want to try on the jewellery, didn't you?'

He's such a nice salesman, not pushy but genuinely interested in making you happy. All the staff must have those little microphones on, I suppose, so everything runs smoothly at such a PR event as this. It feels like we are children playing shop. He knows I won't be buying and takes his time to satisfy what is at best a fantasy to me.

He lifts up my hair to clasp the choker and reaches for a mirror. I just gawp at my reflection; the choker makes me feel just ... just princess precious; which it undoubtedly is. (I've gone totally into girly overdrive.)

'Wow.' I keep hold of the luxurious velvet ribbon of stars in case it slips off, my hands slightly shaky at the thought of it dropping to the floor.

'Jane, it's not heavy, diamonds are very light, you can let it go. I think we made the clasp well enough!' he laughs. 'Is this your first time trying on jewellery?'

'How did you know?' I cower with coyness.

'I'll give you a tip: anytime you're about to try on anything around the neck, lift your hair in anticipation, act quite prepared, then the jeweller knows you're used to it!' He puts my goblet in my hand and we chink, well, de-dong de-dong, a cheers. 'Thanks, Eli, I don't think I'll ever forget this.'

His pleasure comes from sharing his gift, his knowledge and I'm mighty glad I agreed to this one last stunt of Alex's. Eli calls over for the jewellery to be polished and put back in the cabinet. Obviously his colleagues rally round when he's trying to impress a girl or make a sale. They are a bit over the top though, saying, yes, Mr Eli, thank you, Mr Eli, you would think they were grateful for the extra duties on such a busy night.

'I have clean hands, Eli, no need to clean it – I did shower!' I jest.

'Oh no, Jane, it's not that, you smell wonderful, but every time a diamond is touched by hand the natural grease of the skin is deposited on the surface dulling the shine. We do it with everything.'

'I bet you have a very polished, glistening clean house.'

'They are.' I'm a bit puzzled by the answer – maybe he didn't get the humour.

Two of his colleagues are trying to get his attention – I can see them out of the corner of my eye. Eli just chats away casually and I don't want him to get into trouble by devoting his attentiveness solely on me, the poorest person here!

'Eli, I think your colleagues want you.'

'Right, OK. Jane, I'll come and find you later. I do have some duties to attend to.' He's so sweet about it. I follow him with my eyes as he walks away – nice bum!

Alex is in the middle of a large group of plastic-pumped pariahs, charming the pants off them, I suspect. He's in his element. I casually walk past the group, hanging back from the perimeter, just making sure he spots me, and signal to him that I'm fine and he doesn't need to stop the schmoozing any time soon. This gig is his first major sponsorship and he needs to concentrate.

I glide over to the next magical cabinet to take a peek at some more carbon bits and pieces. This time it's a pair of chandelier earrings with two huge drops at the end. They make Oprah's look like H. Samuel's Christmas crackers.

I'm enjoying the evening so much that I am unaware Michael is standing at my side.

'Nice, aren't they?' His question abruptly lifts me out of my girls' world daydream.

'Good grief, there you go again creeping up on people.' I'm not impressed with his feeble efforts at an olive branch … uncharacteristic small talk. He might as well stick his olive branch back into its hard-crusty case where it's obviously happier.

'Your ears would have to work out to wear those!' He tries to engage me again and despite myself I laugh, as I visualise little ears pumping iron and taking aerobics classes.

'As if it weren't expensive enough at the gym,' I add. 'Imagine yoga for ears: now listen in and listen out slowly and rest with plugs for five minutes.'

He lets out a bit of gnarf laugh. I start giggling like a mad woman.

'Look at Alex, he should have been a ring master, keeping those hyenas at bay!' His humour takes me by surprise – the fact that he has one. I'm so surprised that I snort champagne up my nose. I look across at Michael and he is doubled over in laughter and you know what it's like when you see someone laughing so much that it makes you laugh even harder, and the fact that we are where we are makes the laughing almost sacrilegious, and that's it, I'm gone, we both are for several minutes.

Tears streaming down my face I reach in my bag for a tissue.

'You've ruined my mascara.'

'Oh, I don't know, I'm quite partial to pandas.' He's beside himself with hilarity. I hit him on the arm, still giggling. 'I'm going to the toil— restroom.'

Michael and I actually having a laugh; can't believe we have the same humour.

I move towards the restrooms but get distracted by a sparkling siren. I would marry diamonds; they are now my favourite things – much more enticing than soggy raindrops on roses and far more inviting than whiskers on clawing kittens. I follow the prism of rainbow light; it's a striking brooch from the twenties, and I can just picture the original owner with her bobbed hair and cigarette holder. The fantasy and romance draws me into this glamour world more and more.

I can see Eli in conversation with the press. He must be acting as a buffer before the bigwig takes questions. I concentrate on a diamond chart; if I'm ever going to get a rock I better educate myself so maybe I'll know what to buy. Yeah, I'm an independent woman but seriously lacking any Beyoncé foxiness. There, there, so much for you thinking I was imagining silly white horses and equestrian princes again, I reckon they are all a bit camp: white iPod horse, ruffles and frills, far too groomed for a straight guy anyway. Has any woman ever picked up on this?

'Jane, can I interest you in a book?'

'Excuse me?' I answer, unaware of who's asking. I turn and see Eli.

'Oh, hi again. Is it a good evening for you?'

'It's had some highlights.' His eyes sparkle at me, although this could be a side-effect from all the diamonds.

'Listen, Jane, I'm a bit tied up this evening. Could I interest you in a coffee sometime?'

'Me?'

He leans in and gives me the book.

'It's a book about the history of gems, thought you might enjoy a browse through. You can give it back to me when you agree to meet me. See, I've laid a trap: now you're obliged to have coffee with me otherwise you'll be absconding with the property of H. Winston and those beefy guys will detain you.'

I can't refuse him even if I wanted to. He is modest with his confidence; he half expected a no, it's such a gentle dupe.

'Sure, why not.' He gives me a business card and I put it my purse.

He is then ushered away by a rich-looking sheik. He must be their top salesman or something. I take the card back out and have a sneaky read.

Eli Strasberg — Global Director of Retail

Oh my God ... he is the big noise ... His manner was so mild and unassuming. I thought he was ... oh fiddly-dee. Oh! But OH!!!.

CHAPTER SEVENTEEN

A couple of days pass and Alex's media frenzy is finally calming down. I've spent my time loosening up with dance exercises, jogging and swimming, generally preparing for the audition I'm told is going to happen any day now. I'm just having a smoothie in the kitchen when there is a ring on the thunderous doorbell. Alex jumps up and I stay where I am, slurping through my straw nosily.

'Jane, come and look,' he yells excitedly from the hall; he really is a puppy in human form. I reluctantly step into the hall and see the biggest bunch of multi-coloured roses ever; there must be over fifty. They cover Alex's broad chest. Michael comes out of his study to see what the fuss is all about.

'Wow, Jane, someone must really like you.' Alex nods with approval.

'Are they really for me?' I'm shocked – I thought they were for Alex; it's the type of thing that happens to movie stars.

'Yeah, and there's a card.' I rip it out of Alex's hand before he has a chance to read it. It's handwritten in eloquent calligraphy:

You didn't call and now my bookcase is unsymmetrical and it's bothering my neat polished mind! If you are holding it to ransom I shall be forced to meet with you and discuss terms. Meet me at the Standard on Flower Street at 7 pm.

I smile to myself. Here is a man who doesn't take himself so seriously ... how refreshing!

'C'mon, Janey, who's the mystery admirer?' Alex is flapping around like a big girl. I give him a quizzical none-of-your-business glare.

'Alex, you don't need to know everything. You don't tell me everything!'

He grabs the card out of my hand.

'Well, I think they're from Eli. He wouldn't stop asking questions about you at the launch.' He shuts up and reads on.

Michael retreats back into his study without saying a word. Alex, on the other hand, has turned into an excitable gay version of himself.

'What are you going to do, are you going to go, what will you wear?'

'Alex, I'm not sure, now stop it, you're freaking me out. This stuff with Kimberly hasn't made you switch teams, has it?'

Alex pulls his flappy hands down and butches up by pushing out his pecs.

'Very funny, missy! I'll leave it to you. I've got a meeting with my agent tonight so I hope the entertainment isn't too shabby in my absence.' He struts off all Neanderthal and he-man. I chuckle, watching him quiver into macho mode ascending the stairs, then I stand just admiring the flowers. They are truly beautiful, I don't think anyone has ever made such a grand gesture like this before.

I start thinking about what to wear and an hour slips by. It can when you're in that floaty pondering mood – not that I've experienced it too often. I go downstairs and help myself to a drink. I try following the recipe for a cosmopolitan but end up with sharp-tasting red gunk. I sit down outside and phone Eli's number. Michael walks into the kitchen and starts fixing a drink without looking over.

'Hi, Eli, thanks so much for the flowers, you shouldn't have.' I can sense Michael's half listening.

'Jane, I'm glad you called. Don't thank me, I should thank you for introducing me to you! But unfortunately I've been called away on urgent business. I can't really refuse either.' His voice is calm but hang on, what did he say?

'Oh.' My stomach sinks.

'I've tried bucking the job to my associate but the guy is one of our most preferred VIP customers.'

'Well it can't be helped, I suppose. Who is he: Lawrence of Arabia?' I joke.

'Something like that. I think he likes to be addressed as Premier Putin!' he adds with that modest and shy manner that doesn't really fit into his world. 'I did tell him it was inconvenient but he is a very hard man to say *nyet* to.'

I giggle at his Russian accent. 'I understand completely, Eli. I hope you have a good trip. Where are you going?'

'Oh, I never know, I just get picked up with the goods and taken to a jet.'

'Wow.' I am impressed.

'Can I give you a call when I get back? These things can take a few days.'

'Yes. But you do know the ransom might be extortionate by then!'

'I thought it might, the English are such villains. I guess I'll have to think of something extraordinary.'

'You could ask your friend Putin for strategic pointers.'

I hear Eli laugh. It's so easy to banter with him, no strain, just natural.

'Well, Jane, I'm not sure even he can help, despite his reputation. I shall devise a cunning rescue mission. Much as it pains me to say I've got to run now, speak to you soon.'

'Bye, Eli. Look forward to it otherwise I'll start ripping the front cover slowly and painfully.' I hear him chortle and what I think is a kiss noise but I'm not quite sure.

I sit back in satisfaction and take a sip of the bloody awful drink I made. Michael is still making what looks like a mojito; he's going to town on some green foliage in a pestle and mortar. He's quite handy in the kitchen. I sigh and gaze at the pool.

'Mind if I join you?' I jolt up from my stupor.

'Err ... no,' I answer, a bit taken aback at his politeness.

'No plans for tonight then?' He almost sounds happy about it.

'What? Oh no, Eli was called away on urgent business,' I reply without a trace of disappointment.

'That's a pity ...'

'Yes, well, that's life.'

'So, errmm, would you, errmm ...' Michael stops and seems almost surprised that he's struggling to get the words out. 'Would you like to have dinner with me tonight?' He speaks so quickly that I'm not sure I heard correctly. 'I mean, as we're both at a loose end and we both need to eat something later, I thought ...' Michael's suggestion is the last thing I expected. He is even quite humble in his offering.

'You don't have to entertain me! I'm not your guest.' I catapult his very own words back at him.

Michael seems regretful. 'I would like to take you to dinner. I do know a nice quiet, paparazzi-shy place.' He shrugs. 'Up to you.'

Now it looks like I'm the one being unreasonable. I suppose burying the hatchet for Alex's sake wouldn't be a bad thing.

'OK,' I hear myself say. 'Let's do dinner – should be such a laugh.'

I am being so rude. Even a little mean. Nothing he doesn't deserve but he is trying.

'That's great. I'll book a table for eight.'

'OK,' I respond, and with the evening's activities arranged he slinks off back into his study.

He's an odd one.

CHAPTER EIGHTEEN

Calm down, it's only dinner, I tell myself as I raid my wardrobe looking for something pretty to wear, trying on and discarding several outfits before settling on a sleeveless pale blue summer dress by Chloé.

Modern fairy godmothers come in the form of rectangular flexible plastic with a security number written on the back these days.

'It is only dinner, just dinner, consuming food …' I repeat over and over like a mystical mantra while I put my make-up on. 'Just dinner, only food,' I chant as I fasten a diamante bracelet onto my wrist.

I take a slug of G&T, for Dutch courage. I have terrible butterflies in my stomach. *Glee*'s 'Don't Stop Believin'' comes blaring through the radio and, needing to shake off the nervous energy, I turn up the volume and start moving to the beat. I love dancing. It always makes me feel better. I sway my hips and arms, then, feeling like a tramp with a fiver, I really let go, jump onto the bed and start giving it what my Welsh grandmother would say 'some welly'. Grabbing my brush and using it as a microphone I give it some seriously lewd foxiness. I feel fifteen all over again.

'Lovely. Can anyone join in?'

My imaginary pop world comes to a screeching halt. Michael is leaning lazily against the doorjamb trying very hard not to laugh.

Well this is embarrassing!

I bring my hand, which is still clutching the brush, to my chest, as if I could somehow hide the fact that I'd just been caught in full impresario.

'Don't you Cantys ever knock?' I clamber off the bed in an ungainly manner.

'I did,' he answers. 'You didn't hear me.'

'Well you should have knocked harder.'

'And miss all the fun?' He shakes his head.

'Laugh it up, Mr Canty, but if zombies chase us, I'm tripping you up. What do you want anyway?'

'Just came to see if you're ready.' I jump to attention after noticing the clock above his head.

'Oh, right. Yep, just need my shoes and then I'm all yours. I mean, erm ... ready.'

I slip on my Manolos, grab my white cardigan from the bed and dash under Michael's arms.

Descending, or ascending for that matter, the stairs in high heels is a tricky little beast but I've been watching John Partridge do it on YouTube, and with a lot of practice I can now walk it out like a pro.

Michael joins me at the bottom and I'm tempted to ask if he is impressed with my seamless glide down the staircase.

'Just for the record, you look stunning.'

'Err ... thank you ... likewise.' Oh, brother! What a thing to say.

But he doesn't look bad himself. He has on a pair dark grey trousers and a pale blue short-sleeved shirt, which is open at the neck. His dark hair gleams from a recent shower, and he smells fresh and manly.

This time I manage to stay awake during the drive and we arrive at a tiny shack of a building, tucked away up a dark remote hillside. Now I think he's gone completely mad and driven me to nowhere for some power kick. I'm just about to embark into battle cry when I see the flickering of candlelight dancing in the thick terracotta window arches.

Michael opens the passenger door and I climb out and silently follow him towards the obscure little shack. My heart soars as we enter the Italian restaurant. I'm consumed by the heavy romantic atmosphere; lamp-lit tables placed in funny nooks and dim crannies. The rustic wooden tables spaced widely enough apart, giving each the privacy desired. Stop it, Jane, this is not a date and you are not his friend. But the setting seems so intimate. What a strange place to take me.

The proprietor's wife comes forward and greets us warmly. We both tower over this small old woman.

'Michael, Michael,' she chants in a thick Italian accent.

'*Buonasera*, Isabella,' Michael says in an impeccable accent, leaning down to kiss her rosy cheeks. 'How is my favourite lady this evening?'

'*Fermarlo*! *Fermarlo*! My dark *bambino bello*,' she chastises playfully in her muddled language. '*Non dire, non dire* ... You shouldn't be saying things like that to a *vecchia signora* ... I mean an old woman like me when you 'ave *molto bella bella signora* tonight. *Si*, eh!'

She grabs his cheeks in the manner only an Italian mama can; she seems rather fond of the moody writer. Her eyes glisten at him and he appears modest for once.

'OK, you're my second favourite.'

Isabella tuts. '*Prego, prego* ... come along I 'ave the *perfetto* table for you.'

She shows us to a secluded table in the far corner. As soon as we are seated a bottle of ice-cold Rancho Sisquoc Chardonnay arrives.

'Do you come here often?' I instantly go bright red as it sounds like a cheesy chat-up line. 'I mean … They seem to know you very well here.'

'I like to come here whenever I can.'

Which doesn't exactly answer my question. It's not the sort of place you dine alone.

'It's my mother's favourite restaurant. Whenever she's in town I like to bring her here.' I glance down at the menu as my heart does a little song and dance – fool. I thought I'd got over that little skirmish. There's no denying we have some kind of chemistry thing going on but he really has been appalling to me … and I would do well to remember that. Concentrate, Jane, you are not easy fodder.

'I'm starving,' I blurt out. The tantalising aroma of fresh herbs has been seducing my nostrils from the moment we stepped into the restaurant. 'I'm surprised that you haven't heard my stomach rumbling.'

'Is that what it was. I thought my car needed servicing.'

I look at him in surprise. He's just told a joke, not a good one, but this is a side to his character I'm still trying to get used to. He's been a different person since Alex revealed our love affair sham, but I've seen the darker side to his nature and I've still to be convinced.

'Have you made up your mind?'

Startled, I look up from the menu. 'To eat?' Michael prompts gently, slightly confused by my gormless expression.

I blink. 'Eh, yes, I'll have …' I quickly select the truffle and wild mushroom risotto with a green herb salad and Michael orders the macaroni of lobster.

'I need to tell you how sorry I am.'

'What for?'

'I haven't given you an easy time.'

Understatement of the century! I shrug my shoulders in a nonchalant manner.

'Doesn't matter.'

'Yes, it does.'

I look at him carefully, conscious to keep my curiosity on tepid.

'Why did you then?' The anger that I've been trying to suppress all afternoon simmers just beneath the surface.

'Let's just say it has been a misunderstanding on my part, a huge misunderstanding. But I plan to make it up to you.'

'How exactly do you plan to do that?'

'Wine and dine you, of course.' His mouth pulls back into a confident grin.

'Really, is that what you think this is, an acceptance?' I solidify my fortress; if he thinks he can just make it up to me by buying me dinner, he has a big surprise coming.

'I didn't mean … I was only kidding. Of course I know …'

My God, Mr Moody is lost for words.

I watch his Adam's apple bobbing with tension and I quell my rambunctious tendency to make him suffer fully.

'Shall we make a toast?' he placates. I decide to play along out of courtesy to the other guests – and Alex doesn't need any more aggro surrounding him.

'How about toasting to the success of your book,' I offer up.

'OK – to success,' he says.

'Success,' I echo. We touch glasses.

I sip my wine, enjoying the cool crisp taste, and relinquish the anger that has consumed me in favour of some pleasantries. I know I shouldn't let him off the hook but it's too exhausting being angry all the time so I feign polite interest in my dinner companion.

'How long did it take you to get your first book published?'

'When I first started writing I was doing odd jobs here and there and then writing in the evenings. It took me four years to write my first novel – now it takes me about a year.'

161

'Four years!'

'Yeah, nothing happens overnight. I lived on nothing but tinned ravioli and cigarettes. Oh and let's not forget the stereotypical Mr J. Daniels and coffee by the gallon.'

I'm caught off guard by M. Canty admitting flaws and anxieties.

'Did you ever lose focus?' Now this is interesting only because it draws a parallel to my own life.

'I had bad days. In fact, I had bad years ... no one is unflappable, Jane.'

I must admit I don't know how to react so I grab my glass of wine and take a sip.

'I read *The Beast* while you were away.'

He seems surprised. 'You did? I'm flattered. I thought horrors weren't your cup of tea.'

'They're not,' I say. 'But then I thought since I was living in your house it would be the polite thing to do.'

His lips hover over the wine glass and there's a smile about his mouth. 'How very gracious of you.'

'It was very good, by the way,' I impart.

'Despite the incredibly gruesome bits?' he teases.

'Yes, well, there were some very incredibly gruesome bits but I didn't expect them to be within the mind. I can't imagine how you think up such dreadful things.'

'I think in all of us lurks a dark side.'

'Yes, I suppose,' I say. 'It is sickening that people can be so cruel. You only have to turn on the news to see children killing children, pensioners being mugged, horrific wars in aid of cornering a dollar.'

'I agree,' Michael says. 'Unfortunately humanity has a failing, and that is the desire to dominate so as to make themselves feel powerful and untouchable; the mortal crave invincibility. Self-preservation rules above all.'

'Doesn't what you write ever frighten you?'

'It takes a lot to frighten me nowadays. Sometimes I get a certain chill but because I have control over what I write I hardly ever get spooked by it.'

'I wouldn't mind reading another.'

His eyebrows flicker. 'Have I converted you?'

Damn, I didn't mean to pay him a compliment.

'Maybe,' I say casually.

'Now it's my turn.'

'For what?'

'To ask the questions.'

I bite my lip nervously and look beyond him. 'Sure, fire away.'

'Can you remember what drew you to acting?'

I smile. That's an easy one. '*The Sound of Music* ... I saw it when I was a little girl and my mum couldn't shut me up, I was forever singing "These are a few of my favourite things". I told my mum I wanted to be a nun because I thought being a nun meant you got to sing all day. That's when Mum took me to my first dancing and singing lesson ... Silly, huh?' I give a small self-conscious laugh, aware of his intense scrutiny. 'Well, needless to say I fell in love with singing and acting.'

I'm relieved we are on an even keel now, past events safely tucked behind us. If only it could have been like this from the beginning.

'When I used to act it was always a chance to explore the human psyche. Humans are fascinating and I'm riveted by human behaviour, whether it's in a crisis, some odd situation or love—'

I didn't intend to break off at the word 'love' but it made me falter. Michael is watching me closely. I try and make the mood matter-of-fact again.

'When I act I would always lose my own identity. Sometimes I actually think and feel like the character I'm playing, and that's when you know you're in tune with the emotive self.'

'It sounds like you really have a method passion for acting.'

'Not intentionally but yes, I really do,' I enthuse.

A timely Isabella arrives with our dinner. It's steaming and looks mouth-watering – by this point I am ravenous. We both look incredibly appreciative of the arrival, much to her delight. I try to eat like a lady rather than wolf it down; careful to lick away traces of a delicate porcini sauce that escapes down my fork.

'This is tasty,' I mumble through forkfuls of rich risotto. 'How's yours?'

'Delicious. Want to try?'

'No … No. I'm OK—'

'But I've already selected you a bit,' Michael insists, his dark eyes challenging me. I have no choice but to lean over and open my mouth, enabling him to feed me. 'Mmm, you're right,' I agree, chomping down, trying not to be mindful of the intimacy, 'delicious.'

We eat the rest of our food in silence and amazingly it feels natural.

'I still can't believe you and Alex did what you did.' He leans back in his chair patting his full but noticeably taut belly.

'Yes, well, believe me I wasn't happy about it.' I chirp away, relaxed in his company for the first time. Must be the bottle of Prosecco he craftily ordered after the wine.

'But you know Alex, he always has a cunning way of getting you to agree to all sorts of things.'

Michael laughs. 'So, there's no special man in your life?'

Didn't expect that question.

'No,' I say.

'What about … Eli?'

'We haven't even been on a date. What about you?'

'I do have someone in mind.'

'Oh.' I swallow hard. Well, good for him. Am I relieved? On some level I must be.

'I'm really glad you agreed to have dinner with me,' he says after a pause.

'That's OK, it's good to be finally on the same page! No pun intended.'

He stares at me with confusion.

'So we are on the same page, as you put it?' he remarks, tentatively. His face is awash with an expression I haven't witnessed before.

'I'm having a good time, are you?' Is that uncertainty I hear in his voice?

'Would you care if I wasn't?'

'Yes.'

This conversation is getting too weird.

'You have beautiful eyes,' he suddenly announces.

And weirder still, I laugh. 'Err, thank you. Green,' I offer up unnecessarily.

'*Bien dans sa peau*,' he suddenly announces.

'Sorry?'

'The French have a saying: "*Bien dans sa peau*." It means literally, "happy in your own skin",' he swiftly translates. 'Are you happy in your own skin?'

How do I even begin to answer this!

'Let's just say I'm beginning to, but I have my days. What about you – are you happy in your own skin?'

'Yes.'

Of course he would be. 'Now why don't I find that hard to believe,' I laugh.

'There's nothing wrong in having a healthy opinion of yourself.' He takes a big swig of prosecco. 'Who was it that gave you a low opinion of men – a past boyfriend?'

His questioning is certainly keeping me on my toes.

'You hardly have a glowing opinion of women.'

'Touché. I had a fiancée once,' he confesses. I'm a bit shocked at his revelation but manage to hide the fact whilst pretending to sip my prosecco. I wait for him to say more but I've lost him.

'It's hard, isn't it?' I empathise. 'You give so much to a relationship and when it doesn't work out you feel such a … failure.'

He looks at me, surprised. 'I never thought myself a failure, I just doubt very much that I could ever fully trust a woman again.'

That's one hell of a personal statement!

'But you have to trust your partner,' I say aghast. 'If you don't have trust, the very core of respect, then the relationship is doomed from the start. Jealousy causes so much grief.'

'Was your old boyfriend a jealous type?'

I don't want to divulge too much but why pretend otherwise?

'Yes,' I reply, leaning back as the dessert is set down on the table, glad to have a distraction. Keeping my eyes lowered I spoon up the tiramisu.

'Delicious,' I comment after my first bite.

'Mmmm,' he agrees readily.

And neither of us speaks until we've devoured our desserts. I place my napkin neatly on the table and heave myself out of the chair.

'Will you just excuse me?'

On reaching the Ladies, I place my hands on the sink and breathe in deeply. I'm definitely getting mixed signals from the man. Perhaps he's trying so hard that I'm reading too much into it. Or maybe Eli has rocked him enough to up his game. But that's silly – Michael didn't seem that bothered Eli was going to take me out.

Just get on with it, Jane, and take it for what it is … stop analysing every little detail. I'm getting far too LA for my own good. But I really like him and I can't ignore the calm feeling I have now he's humanoid. I trash the thought that he's still attracted to me. I wash my hands and scoot out to finish the biscotti before Michael chomps them all away.

There is a cognac and coffee waiting for me on my return. Michael looks self-assured and loose in his body.

'Now there's a contented man.' I bumble out, tripping over the terracotta tiles. 'Whoops, nearly lost my shoe. I would make some Cinderella!'

'You could make a serial Cinderella with your footwear troubles.' We both crack up at my innate clumsiness. I sit down and we look over at each other, my stomach nerves are bubbling away again. He is handsome – especially like this. I decide to break the moment before I lose myself.

'So its cognac for you and bacon for Digger – I've got you two sussed.'

'How perceptive you are, we are but humble simple creatures.'

When we leave the restaurant Michael grabs hold of my arm in a gentlemanly way and swoosh, the air becomes charged and I can't ignore what is happening.

It's a short walk to the car but when we get to it neither of us make a move to get inside or even step apart. He turns me around to face him and stares into my eyes, as if he's testing the terrain.

'Thank you for a lovely evening.' And then slowly he bends forward, his lips hover sensually above mine, and he kisses me gently on the mouth. I close my eyes and sigh deeply, feeling his breath mingle with mine and kiss him back, savouring the taste of him, the feel of him. My knees buckle with desire as he pulls me closer, my breasts crushing against his chest, my nipples pushing through my dress, demanding to be free. I arch against him urgently, wanting to be rid of it. He cups my bottom and brings me closer.

'We can't do this here,' he pants, breaking away.

I take deep, shaky breaths and lean back against the door, my fingers trembling as I smooth down my dress and hair, afraid to look in his eyes in case I see rejection.

'Yes, you're right,' I say quickly, fumbling with the latch on the passenger door.

He puts his hand over mine. 'Jane, I want you. But not like this. Not here in the car park. You deserve better than some awkward fumbling of a hormone-raged teenager.'

'You mean your car is too precious.'

'I mean it's too constrictive for what I have in mind for you.'

Enough said. We scramble to get into the car, passion ignited on full blast, and drive back in total silence, the air between us thick with unsatisfied desire. I have never felt so charged in all my life. I'm not going to think about tomorrow, I'm going to throw caution to the wind and go with the moment, grab the sort of sexual pleasure that I have never experienced, and not likely to again. After all, I've been telling myself this holiday is all about new experiences.

It feels like an eternity before we reach the house, neither daring to touch one another until we are safe behind closed doors.

'Where have you two been?'

Like children caught with their hands in the cookie jar before lunch we abruptly swing round; I can feel my cheeks heating with embarrassment. I look over to the sofa and Alex is lying there with a beer in his hand and Digger stretched across his legs.

'How was dinner and what happened to Eli?' Alex says.

'Eh?' I really wish I could think faster and answer with some morsel of eloquence.

'Dinner?'

'Oh, that ... fine ... yes ... lovely ... thanks,' I fluster. (My above point disastrously proven.)

'Am I missing something here?' Alex's grin is wide, as he looks between us.

I look everywhere else but at Alex. Thank God Michael pipes up.

'Alex, don't you have to be up early tomorrow?'

'No.'

'I really do think you do——' he says again.

'Actually, you know what, I feel quite tired.' I stretch out, pantomiming a yawn. 'I'll think I'll be off to bed.'

'I might join you,' Michael says. 'I mean … not with you … not in your bed … my bed … alone.'

Alex chuckles. 'Michael, you're a lousy actor,'

Digger gets up but Alex grabs his collar. 'No, Digger, you're staying with me tonight. Don't do anything I wouldn't,' he says, and his saucy cackling follows us all the way up the stairs. But at this point I'm beyond caring.

CHAPTER NINETEEN

This is it. Blimey. I gulp. We're going to do it – suddenly I'm incredibly nervous. I think I'm going to faint. What if all the suspense was the passion and that's it? What if I've forgotten to, you know, how to ... well it's been a while and I don't want to disappoint. What if— STOP with the 'what ifs'!

I look at Michael and our eyes lock and before I can think another thought he pulls me into his arms and kisses me, and any dumb reason to be self-conscious is instantly forgotten.

I feel the zip on my dress go down and he discards the fabric as if it were nothing but tissue, his eyes focusing fiercely on mine. He then drops fervent kisses on my stomach, his arms reaching around my back as he pulls himself up. He swings me up in his arms then lays me down on the bed, stepping back to admire the somewhat naughty view. Thank God for the scanty Agent Provocateur ensemble.

My body writhes helplessly. I don't care. I've never felt so animalistic. It wills him to join me and I pounce on top of him, ripping off his clothes. I've become a wild tigress.

I actually do rip his shirt, which seems to ignite him even more. I stifle the giggle that's on my lips, not wanting to spoil the moment. He looks magnificent, sweat glistening on his chest and the fire playing freely about his hips, pulsating and eager. I had no notion of how hungry I was for him. He engulfs me with his body and I feel so aroused I tear my underwear off in desperation.

We can't hold each other tightly enough; it becomes a sweaty struggle, rough, obsessive and all the while we are touching and holding and tasting and sucking until we draw away from one another, panting hard and fast.

'You are beautiful,' he rasps.

How does he have the energy to talk?

And then it's back down to business; our hot wet kisses growing more ardent. Michael scoops me up from the bed and I wrap my legs around his waist, I move against him, twisting and arching, feeling as if I might explode. Still just about on the bed, although I am halfway off now, we are touching, biting, kissing and caressing. I want him inside me. I want him inside me – now! He draws away.

I groan in protest.

'Patience,' he whispers. I hear the rustle of a condom wrapper and then he's back with me. He changes momentum to savour the moment and places whispering licks all around my hips. I draw him up for a kiss and before our mouths touch I gasp loudly as he enters me. I pull my legs around him, squeezing them tight as he pushes deep inside me, deeper and deeper as we race towards the same goal. Moving harder and faster, the tension in my body increases, the frantic rhythm goes wild, closer and closer towards an orgasm, until finally, our worlds explode, spilling deep within.

We stay interlocked, there is no rush to part, I can still feel him … this is a wriggly wet heaven I've never been to before, didn't even know it was on the same menu. WOW!

'Beautiful.' Michael pushes a strand of hair gently off my face. I smile back.

We did it. I remembered. Only it's not how I remember it any time before.

This time was different. I never imagined it could be like this, this perfect.

In slumber we are as comfortable as dreamy spirits gliding along a cloud of wonder. There is no awkwardness, no rush to entertain, contentment circles and fills the room. The closeness that we have is ... is ... well, no words describe it; we are at one and both serene drowsy cats in the sun although we are in moonlight. The light reflected from the ocean shimmers through the window, our body outlines are still, peaceful but entwined, occasionally stirring to secure each other's limbs. Nothing could have prepared me for this moment, no wining or dining, no stupid dating for months on end, no books or history ... Nothing.

CHAPTER TWENTY

I wake early, my leg hugging Michael's thigh, my arm resting over his chest.

I carefully disentangle myself from him and sit up, rubbing the sleep from my eyes. I look down at Michael's sleeping form. I don't think I have ever seen him look more handsome or more relaxed.

I look around me: a writing pad and a pot of spilled pens (they must have been knocked over last night), a tower of medical books on the bedside table, and on closer inspection I see a whole pile of psychology papers trickling out from under the bed. There are some strange yet attractive mobiles undulating over an architect's desk in the corner. The whole space dwarfed by an enormous industrial lamp. Other than that his bedroom is much the same as mine; the same expansive window facing the Pacific Ocean, the same long cream drapes, and lush carpet, except his is littered with our discarded clothes. I look back at Michael's muscular body barely encased by the silky sheets. He's so peaceful. I can't help thinking, I did that. I put that look of contentment on his face.

Finally I know what all the fuss is about. Sex can be fantastic. Just got to do it with the right person. A familiarity with women's physiology is always a big plus, adds to the dynamism, if you know what I mean, ladies, wink-wink! I want to rejoice, I want to sing, I want to shout out the window I had the best climax of my life, dear Lord. Good grief, I sound like an evangelist. Maybe that's it … this is where God is and that was heaven. I reach down and kiss Michael lightly on the lips. I can't help myself. His eyes flutter open.

'Good morning.' My voice sounds husky.

'Good morning.' His own voice is thick and heavy with sleep. 'Sleep well?'

I give him a feline smile. 'Yes, eventually.'

He smiles and it hits me: I love him. Someone I barely know, and yet I have fallen, madly, deeply, crazily head-over-heels in love with him. Of course I have the good sense not to say it out loud. I know, I know, most women release that crazy love chemical post-bonk but I'm impartial. I flicked through all my crazy earlier, and now a powerful connection remains.

I lean over and quench my desire to kiss him. It's about half an hour later when we come up for air just in time to hear the knock at the door.

'Are you two decent?'

Alex! Fuck! I quickly gather the sheet, tucking it under my arms, my cheeks bright red. Michael pulls himself up, not the least bit embarrassed by his nakedness.

'Don't you think you should …' I cough, 'cover up?'

He gives me a wicked smile, then seeing the desperation on my face pulls the sheet over him.

'You can come in, Alex,' Michael says.

I slouch against the headboard as if I could somehow merge in with the leather upholstery.

'Well, good morning, my noisy lovebirds. Is the pecking feast over?' Alex gloats. 'What do you want, Alex?' commands Michael, targeting Alex as an unruly infant.

'A phone call for Jane.' Alex grins at me. 'Thought you'd want to take it.' He walks over to me. 'It's Pat's office.'

Pat's office! I sit bolt upright and snatch the phone away from Alex's grubby hands, pressing the phone to my ear.

'Hello, this is Jane Allen.' I try to sound as confident as possible.

I listen intently to the voice on the end of the line, aware that Michael and Alex are watching me. 'Pen. Paper,' I mouth silently, flapping my hands at them. The sheet slips out of my grasp and I tug it back into place.

Michael hands me a notebook and pen from the bedside table. 'Sorry, could you repeat that?' I flip through the pages of scrawl until I find an empty one and start scribbling away. At the end of the call I hand the phone back to Alex who looks back at me expectantly. I look down at what I've written and manage not to whoop for joy. I mean, it's not like I have the gig or anything but just fantasising about it for a brief moment is thrilling.

'Jane?' Alex says, running out of patience.

'They want me to audition for the role of Roxie Hart,' I blurt on a giant breath. My mind flicks through the abundant daydreams I had looking out my bedroom window – all my most loved reveries from girlhood are coming true, maybe just for this minute and this minute alone but I feel alive, expectant and frightfully excited.

'They want me to send over my résumé and headshot.'

'That's brilliant. You're bound to get it.' Alex is as excited as I am.

'It's just an audition,' I say, trying to contain my hopeful excitement.

'Yeah, but you were made for the part,' Alex enthuses and I'm grateful for his faith in me.

'The audition is in …' I look at the date on the pad, 'two days' time …' And then it dawns on me. Two days' time, I am not ready.

'Oh God. I need to rehearse. I need a résumé. I don't have a résumé. I don't have headshot—'

'Don't worry,' Alex interrupts. 'Let me make a few phone calls.'

He pulls Digger by the collar and leaves Michael and me alone once more.

I sit cross-legged on the bed and stare at the magnificent scribble; my eyes can't look anywhere else. I voice my thoughts calmly but with trepidation.

'If I get it, which let's face it is a big IF, I'll have to move to New York. Imagine that.' And I do. I can't help picturing that I already have the part and a swanky pad in New York and Michael by my side.

I realise Michael hasn't said anything. I look at him and he is frowning which is a little disconcerting.

'How did you get the audition?' The question is casual enough but if I'm not mistaken a little suspicious in its connotation.

'I had lunch with Bob Edwards and he thought I'd be great for the role so he made a few phone calls, orchestrated a meeting with Pat the casting director at the party – and hey presto.' Which just goes to show it's not what you know but who you know in this business!

'I didn't know you had lunch with Bob Edwards.' And there it is again, a flash of suspicion. I find myself feeling guilty, even though I've done nothing wrong.

'It was while you were away in New York. He took me to Chateau Marmont and we talked over my future ... I mean my aspirations ...' I ramble on and on; I'm not even going to mention bumping into my ex.

There's silence. Michael seems awfully interested in the small details. 'This could be my big break, aren't you happy for me?'

'Of course, it's great, well done.'

'Well I haven't got it yet.'

Michael seems to go off into a trance and I want to ask him what he's thinking but whatever it is it doesn't look particularly pleasant.

176

'Right, I suppose I should get up.' I try to hide my disappointment and start to move but Michael puts his hand on my arm to stop me. His fingers begin tracing the curve of my arm, moving across my shoulder blades and down my front, tugging the sheet loose.

'Don't go.' I'm not about to go anywhere now that his other hand is wandering up my thigh, creating havoc with my insides. If he's not happy for me he's certainly happy with me!

CHAPTER TWENTY-ONE

'Come on, time for a break,' Michael says, barging into the lounge. I've been going over my Roxie Hart monologue all morning and I thought I had it memorised but now I keep forgetting my lines. Not that I'm freaking out. OK, I am freaking out but that is perfectly normal. This audition is important to me. I have to get it right – this might be my only chance.

'I can't,' I protest as Michael hauls me off the couch onto my feet. 'I have to get this right.'

'You need a break.' He prises the lines from my hands. 'A walk on the beach then you can carry on rehearsing.'

He's right, of course. I'm just getting myself into a state. A bit of fresh air will do me good.

'OK.' I let him pull me into a kiss and for a while get lost in how it feels to be in his arms. Sometimes I think I could stay like this for ever but with the audition set for tomorrow I untangle my arms from his neck.

The past couple of days have been the happiest and busiest of my life. If I'm not with Michael then I'm singing; when I'm not singing I'm with Michael. I'm not so much walking on air as dancing in the thrills of life. I am seriously loved up. My audience of three – Michael, Alex and Digger have been extremely enthusiastic about my talent, which is working wonders for my self-esteem. I also spoke to Sian last night and she gave me a good tip: imagine everyone is fighting to sign you and they are naked and ugly. I think she's been reading another self-help book entitled *Confidence for the Crazy*.

As for Alex, he's been good as his word, made his phone calls and managed to arrange a professional photographer to take my photos who just happens to shoot for *Vogue*, *Harper's Bazaar* and all the other top magazines. Another phone call was to a top make-up artist – how lucky am I?

The photos have turned out pretty good; actually, they're amazing – who knew I had cheekbones? My résumé has been a complete nightmare though. It took me several agonising hours, and then Alex had to cast his expert eye over it and proceeded to tart it up. Well I say tart it up, I mean fabricate the truth; a little stretching he said was a total necessity. Résumé and photos were then swiftly couriered to the casting agent. I'm so nervous – what if they find out my West End experience are actually East End fiascos?

Michael hands me his shades and I slip them on, shielding my eyes from the powerful sun. He squeezes my hand and guides me along the beach, Digger running ahead. I know we've only been together two days but I think he's *the one*. I know, I know, don't fall into that false trap but you can't help your feelings. Neither of us has broached the subject about my impending return to the UK but if I get the gig in New York and if he wants to continue this whatever this is … then it's going to be a lot easier than having a massive transatlantic ocean between us.

'Penny for them,' Michael says.

'Oh nothing.'

'It's natural to be nervous but you'll be great.'

I smile. 'Thanks.'

Michael suggests a game of Frisbee, a ploy to take my mind off the audition. And it works for about half an hour but I really need to get more practice in.

'One last throw then I really must go back in,' I shout over to Michael.

'OK,' he hollers back.

He aims the Frisbee and it flies over my head and lands in the ocean.

'Whoops!'

I plant my hands on my hips. 'You did that on purpose.'

'I did not!' he chuckles unreservedly. 'Aren't you going to run in and get it?'

'No. I don't want to get wet.'

'But the wet look suits you.' He grins unashamedly.

'Always the gentleman,' I yell, as I head into the water.

But I have a plan. I sneakily sink the Frisbee so it fills up with water. Michael has bent over to scratch Digger so he doesn't see what I have in my hand.

'Not playing anymore.' I say, as Michael lifts himself up. Before he has a chance to realise what I'm about to do I flick the water straight at him. It drips comically down his face.

'Serves you right.' I snort with laughter.

I make a run for it while I still have the chance, giggling as I speed up and sounding very much like a merry congested pig. But my cleverness is short-lived as I realise Michael is fast on my trail.

'I didn't mean it,' I squeal, as he grabs me firmly around my waist, swinging me to a stop.

'Yes you did,' he says. I am laughing and he is grinning although he's trying to act menacing.

I don't know how I thought Michael scowled a lot. He doesn't scowl all that often and when he does it's usually because he's in deep thought about something. He has a great sense of humour, playful and exciting – he's so much fun to be around.

'You think that's funny, do you?'

'No,' I say, shaking my head, but unable to control the incessant grinning.

'I think you need to be taught a lesson.'

'What, to respect my elders?'

He growls and I blurt out another mirth-infected noise, somewhat nasal in origin.

'I promise I won't do it again,' sensing the danger I'm in. I batter my eyelashes in an exaggerated flirty manner.

'Now why don't I believe you?' And quick as a flash Michael tips me over and I fall onto my bum with a thud.

'Sand shower for you, impertinent young lady!' It's no use, he's pinned me down.

'No!' I screech. 'I said I was … SORRY!' I scream but Michael just laughs as he sits astride me, his powerful long legs gripping my waist. Then I see the bottle.

'What are you going to do with that?'

He slowly unscrews the lid.

'That's not fair,' I shriek, 'I only threw a little drop of water at you!'

'Your inept choice of a vessel is hardly my concern, Miss Allen! One must learn strategy from the master!'

'Right like you're the grr—' He tips the bottle upside down; water pours all over me. I splutter as it splashes into my mouth and up my nose. 'I caaaa-n't believe you did th-th-that.'

He chuckles, enjoying his one-upmanship. I try to wiggle from his grasp but he has a really strong grip, and I'm not a weakling – FYI, arm-wrestling champ down my local pub. Most men say my strength is freaky. It's not often I'm helpless. Michael tilts the bottle again, threatening more spillage.

'All right, you're the master, now stop, you buffoon!'

A single drop falls onto my nose.

'No. Don't. Please! I'm begging you.'

'Begging?' Michael flashes his teeth at me. 'I like the sound of that.'

'Sadist.'

The teasing and laughter have now gone and in their place is pure lust. Michael brushes his thumb against my cheek, removing the wet sand from my face and slowly across my parted lips. My pulse starts quickening.

'Michael, I really need to practice.' But I only half mean it because I've always wanted to re-enact the beach scene in *From Here to Eternity*.

Michael bends his head and traces kisses over my wet face.

'We can't. Not here,' I gasp. 'What if someone comes?'

'No one will.'

He continues his delicious onslaught and I'm a goner … Eurgh! What's that! Michael and I reluctantly pull away.

'Digger!' Michael growls.

I giggle. Digger lunges forward and slobbers me with another kiss.

'Eurgh!'

Michael grabs my hand and pulls me to my feet. *From Here to Eternity* will just have to wait.

CHAPTER TWENTY-TWO

Excited chatter fills the air of the theatre café. People order skinny cappuccinos with soya milk, Frappuccino's, lattes with half fat, decaf and cinnamon, double-shot espressos … the most elaborate coffee requests I've ever heard, all the time staring over in our direction whilst pretending not to look. Their attentions are focused on Alex, but he shows no awareness of this; he seems preoccupied. In fact he hasn't said a great deal since we sat down.

'I'm not about to shoot the rapids then follow on with an unequipped base jump, you know!' I attempt to lift the daunting silence of our little table, to no avail.

I get rewarded with a grunt from Alex and a half-hearted chuckle from Michael. 'Come on, guys, lighten up – it's me who's auditioning.'

I suppose I should be touched that they are nervous for me but they needn't be – I am as ready as I'll ever be. I've come to the conclusion this is really a long shot and it's possibly only out of duty to Bob Edwards that they're seeing me at all. But I'm going to give them one hell of an audition, the performance of my life. No way am I going to let Bob Edwards or myself down. It's not me being negative. I am incredibly excited and positive about it all but I must be realistic – I have to be prepared. And if nothing else, at least it will be good practice for when I get back home. I have already faxed over my resignation to work, deciding I owe it to myself to make a proper go of it, regardless of what happens here today. Although I am still seriously considering Alex's offer to up sticks and move to Hollywood, but I haven't discussed this with Sian or Michael yet; we still haven't spoken about me going back home to England.

'How about another coffee?' Michael jumps to his feet.

'No, I'm fine. Any more and I'll be whizzing away with the caffeine fairies.'

Michael sits back down and Alex starts jiggling his leg, the table wobbles. If anything is going to get me nervous it's sitting here with these two.

'If you two carry on like this I am going to sit elsewhere.'

'What?' Alex is indignant. 'I'm not doing anything. Are you sure you've learnt that monologue? Shall we go over it one last time, I sensed a delay in the middle, didn't you, Michael?' He starts biting his wooden stirring stick apprehensively.

'Right, that's it.' I push my chair back and get to my feet.

'Where are you going?' Michael looks up in alarm.

'To the toilet … bathroom, I mean restroom,' I translate. 'Away from you two bags of nervous twitching.'

'Confidence is key,' I tell my reflection. Remember you are smart, talented, and gorgeous. As it happens, I do feel more confident. I am dressed for the part, head to toe in comfortable yet stylish jersey black cat-suit in case they want me to razzle-dazzle them with some funky jazz moves. I've sleeked my hair into a blunt bob and spent ages on my make-up, opting for a vampy red-carpet vibe.

My preparation, presentation and poise have never been more polished. I feel more mature about my approach to this audition. I breathe deeply and a gasp of air gets stuck in my windpipe. I start coughing then my eyes begin watering profusely and I fear for my make-up. I stumble to the sink and drink some water quickly. I shake myself and resume professional deportment.

It's no good though. I'm now riddled with nerves. I need a pee. This is all Alex and Michael's fault, with their incessant fiddling and twitching. What fine overanxious company to be around when you're trying to remain calm and composed for the biggest event in your career to date.

I wash my hands then pace the length of the toilet, all ten feet of it, taking deep gulps of breath. The butterflies are now playing volleyball inside my stomach. Time for desperate measures. I lie down on the floor with my legs raised above my head. I take another gulp of breath and let it out slowly. I repeat the exercise and close my eyes as if I was taking a yoga class. When I open them again a lady with huge boggling eyes is peering down at me.

'Are you OK, honey?'

I jolt up in embarrassment. 'Oh yes, fine, thanks.' She scrutinises my arms and nose, checking that I'm not some crackpot OD-ing on the floor. Only in Hollywood would they have this checklist down to a non-intrusive sophisticated art.

'Well, as long as you're OK, you carry on.' She steps over me and takes her make-up bag out as if this is nothing out of an ordinary day for her.

There is a knock at the door and Michael enters.

He looks at me lying on the floor. 'What are you doing?'

'Breathing.' As if that wasn't obvious.

'And you can't do this standing up because?'

'I need to concentrate.'

The boggled-eyed lady turns around. 'Oh yes, it's much better to lie down and concentrate, then you don't have your feet to deal with.' And she returns to her mission of make-up application without the slightest sense of interruption.

I love Hollywood!

'Right.' He surveys both of us silently for a few seconds and I get the impression he's trying not to laugh. 'We were getting worried because you've been in here for ages.'

'Well whose fault is that?' I say in irritation. 'You two have been fretting all morning and now I'm nervous. Satisfied?'

The boggled-eyed lady walks over me then stares at Michael.

'Don't make people nervous, honey, it's not nice for them.' With that final sweet yet cheeky little statement she leaves us alone.

Michael holds out his hands and pulls me to my feet. 'It's perfectly normal to be nervous. I would be concerned if you weren't.'

I look in the mirror, smoothing down my hair.

'Besides, I know you're going to be brilliant,' he says, standing behind me and running a hand down my back until it rests on my bottom.

'Drama. Dazzle. Dirty. Delicious ...' he murmurs, nuzzling my neck, his breath hot against my skin. Our eyes hold in the mirror and there's a block in my throat. I love this man. There it is again, the inescapable truth. I lean back against him, feeling the strength of his body, so solid so reassuring, so right.

I step away. 'OK. I'm ready.' I head for the door.

'Just a minute.'

He stuffs his hand in his pocket, shifting uneasily from one foot to the other. He pulls out a black antique-looking box.

'Not quite the environment I envisaged but I want to give you this.' I take the box. 'It's no big deal,' he quickly adds. 'Think of it as a good luck charm.' He's nervous.

My own nerves are jumping all over the place and my mouth has run dry.

I prise the lid open. Inside is the choker from Alex's launch night – the one with diamond stars on. WOW, real diamonds and lots of them, this must have cost him ... a small fortune. I can't speak and tears prick the back of my eyes. This isn't the sort of gift you give to someone you have no intention of seeing when they fly back home. My heart contracts as I fixate on the box's contents: this is no ordinary good luck charm!

'Michael ... you really shouldn't ... I mean, it's um ... this is the nicest ... IT'S BEAUTIFUL,' I blurt out. I can't help myself.   'IT'S BLOODY MAGNIFICENT!'

I am having the ultimate *Pretty Woman* moment. I wasn't expecting this at all. Movies are one thing but this is ...WOW.

'And so are you,' he says, touching my cheek. 'Beautiful and magnificent.'

I flush with pleasure as he gently takes the choker from my grasp and fastens it around my neck. He turns me towards the mirror and slides his hands slowly from my shoulder down to rest on my waist.   I've never had a boyfriend buy me anything except when it's been my birthday. Even when it's been my birthday the presents have always been pretty lame. Philip bought me a blender, and another boyfriend gave me gift vouchers, no thought behind it whatsoever. What a lot of time-wasting jerks I've been out with. Now my boyfriend – can I call him that now? – buys me Harry Winston jewellery ... it sort of makes up for it. BIG TIME!

'How did you know?'

'I saw you looking at it for half the evening, so I thought you might like it.'

I turn around and slip my arms around his neck. 'Thank you,' I whisper, overcome with emotion. 'I love it. I love it.' I love you, I silently add, reaching up onto tiptoes and planting a kiss on his lips. The kiss lingers, only breaking when another woman enters my temporary yoga sanctuary.

'Don't mind me,' she winks.

'Michael, can you keep it while I audition? It's too precious to be worn now.'

He unclasps the choker and places it back in the box. Momentarily I stroke its faded suede top as if it were a prized exotic cat. My hand reaches up to his face, capturing it for another frenzied kiss.

'By the way, you're wearing my lipstick.' I wipe the red smudge from his lips and we head back to our table, giggling like teenagers, only Alex is not alone.

'Oh, err … hi, Kimberly,' Michael says. 'This is an unexpected surprise.'

'I was in the neighbourhood.' She shrugs her jagged bony shoulders. I look at Alex for explanation but from the thunderous look on his face he's not at all happy by her sudden appearance. It's not exactly your typical celebrity hangout. Seems a little stalker-like to me.

'And I came to wish Jane good luck.' To my utter astonishment she air-kisses me enthusiastically on both cheeks.

'You look great,' she tells me. 'Love the cat-suit.'

'Err … what? Erm … thanks.' I sit down. Kimberly smiles at me as if we are the best of friends.

'I love the auditioning process. I always find it exhilarating, I just fall into the part very quickly. I don't rehearse much before, either, it comes so naturally to me …'

It is strange to think that Kimberly could even consider talking to me on a friendly basis given how she's behaved when she thought I was Alex's girlfriend, the hypocritical boneshaker. I suppose now that I'm not Alex's girlfriend I'm no longer a threat. I suspect that she assumes the whole charade was just a vehicle to get her jealous and that Alex is playing hard to get. Poor Alex.

'My friend is auditioning for the role of Roxie Hart too. She's amazing. She's won like a ton of awards and is a true singer, you know, naturally gifted.' Oh great. This woman really is devoid of tact. 'But I'm sure you'll be good too.'

'Jane, I think you should head over,' Michael says. 'It's nearly time.'

'Is it?' I glance at my watch then leap to my feet. 'Ohmigod, so it is.'

I lost track of time. I start gathering my things in a flurry.

'And you'll both wait for me here?'

Alex pulls me to one side and gives me a hug. 'Don't let that bag of bones faze you. The friend is Daddy's goddaughter and they let her audition so it keeps her on the wagon. They've been doing it for years,' he whispers.

'Want me to walk with you?' Michael says.

'No. You'll only make me more nervous.'

He wraps his arms around me and pops a kiss on my lips.

'Just be yourself and you'll be great. I mean, your natural acting self, err … you know, be like you were … in … ummm.'

'I know what you mean, thanks.' I pop him a kiss in return.

'I'll come with you,' Kimberly offers, grabbing her bag and following me to the door. 'I was going to say hi to Cherry anyway.'

The last words I hear are from Alex. 'Break a leg.'

.

CHAPTER TWENTY-THREE

Which I very nearly do, if it wasn't for Kimberley pulling me back from the reversing Hummer I would have been a very flat two-dimensional Roxie.

Oh God, now I owe Kimberly my life.

'So what songs are you singing?' she enquires politely, whilst threading an arm through mine as if we were bosom buddies and guiding me across the road.

'"I Can't Do It Alone" and "Me and my Baby".'

'Good choices.' Maybe I was wrong about Kimberly, maybe she was just seeing the ugly green monster but now she knows Alex and I are not an item she can put her claws away.

I push through the double doors and into a huge foyer. In the corner is a stand with a sign: *Chicago auditions.* A stern, efficient-looking woman sits behind a table.

'Hi.' I approach briskly. 'My name is Jane Allen.'

She reaches for her list and ticks me off.

'Kimberly Roberts, here for moral support,' she announces in a buttery tone. The woman beams at her.

'I love your show.'

Kimberly smiles at the woman kindly.

'Thank you. That's very kind of you.'

The woman continues to beam at her in awe then turns to me.

'If you take a seat, they'll call your name when they are ready for you.'

As we walk towards the row of plastic seats Kimberly sniggers.

'Did you see her hair, and those awful clothes, she should get a stylist.'

There are half a dozen women already sitting down, including Cherry, Kimberly's friend. She is stunning and has that little-rich-girl look. Kimberly struts over and starts whispering. I get the sense they're talking about me; I could just be paranoid, but they do keep glancing over.

'Jane, isn't it?' I look up to see a tall, wiry man and I recognise him instantly.

'Howard Mears.' He presents himself again.

Yes, yes, Bob Edward's friend who spent a good part of our introduction staring at my boobs. He holds out his hand and I plaster a polite smile on my face.

'Hi,' I say, shaking his limp hand.

'You're auditioning?'

'That's right.'

'Well, good for you.'

Kimberly comes over and kisses Howard on the cheeks.

'Hi, Howie.'

'Hello, Kimbo, you're looking radiant. New facial doctor?'

'Oh yes, you simply have to try Dr Zarousou down on Fifth. Wrinkles will be yesterday's worries and the worries of today won't have a chance.'

I listen intently – could Kimberly have some hidden depths? She's so lucid in her delivery, actually rather humorous. I've never heard her carefree and comical before.

'Here, have this card, darling, it's his motto. Such fun, isn't it, and he only charges peanuts … nine hundred an hour, it's a steal.'

I knew those words came from another being!

'Ms Allen, they will see you now.'

Gulp!

I enter the auditorium; my stomach is riddled with nerves. I think I'm going to be sick.

BURRRRRPP.

No, I'm not. That did the trick. Too many lattes with carbonated water chasers.

Three judges sit in front of me and I feel like an experiment for the *X Factor*. I head straight over to the accompanist at the piano and hand him my sheet of music.

'A major?'

'Naturally,' I reply with a smile, my confidence gradually returning.

I walk to the centre of the stage. The room is in total silence and I'm almost afraid to look up but I do and I force my lips to stretch into a smile. I feel so happy that even the tepid reception doesn't scare me. You can do this, I tell myself, this is your chance.

'My name is Jane Allen and the two songs I will perform are … "I Can't Do It Alone" and "Me and my Baby".'

They look down at my résumé.

'You're English?'

'Yes. But I can do an American accent.'

They want to hear me sing first. The accompanist gives me a starting pitch and off I go.

I give it some welly from the belly and look up to the heavens in short prayer to my Granny Myfanwy – a fiery Welsh one.

I grow not only in stature but also in my self-belief – it finds a route through my entire body and I get wholly consumed in the Roxie spirit. I can feel that twenty-year-old

192

fighting out of me, my ambitions rumbling back to real life, the way I felt when I got my place at drama school. This transformation is welcomed. My body is still tingling when I come to the end of my song but I am greeted by deadly silence and have no idea how I am doing.

Next comes the monologue and my throat dries. I swallow hard and count to five then start talking.

Then it's over and I have done all I can. They give nothing away but I think I catch a hint of approval on Pat Goldstein's face – it could be just politeness, or worse still, wishful thinking. I thank the accompanist and step off stage. Scarcely before my feet leave the wings I am accosted by Howard Mears.

'That was amazing, Jane,' he enthuses.

'Oh, eh, thank you.' I blush, trying to contain the release of excess adrenalin whirling round my head.

He steps closer and I resist the urge to step away. I don't like the way he encroaches on my space and the last thing I want to do is be rude but there is something snakelike about his demeanour, he unnerves me … yuk.

'I want you,' he breathes. At least that's what I think he says. I give him a sharp look.

'On my books,' he adds with a wolf-like smirk.

'Oh right … um, thank you.' I take another step back. No doubt he has charmed a number of women in his heyday and probably still does with his influence and money, but I'm definitely not one of them.

I hear a nasal voice approaching fast. Kimberly butts in, and this time it's appreciated.

'Are you interested in taking Jane on?' Kimberly asks Howard directly.

He looks me up and down and I shudder. This man is giving me the creeps.

'I've yet to decide,' he replies.

Kimberly titters. 'Oh, but I think Jane's got hidden talent.'

'And some not so hidden,' Howard responds, looking at my boobs.

Kimberly titters again but I don't laugh.

'How did the audition go?' Her tone is sweet.

'Good, I think.'

'They never give anything away, although my friend said they cheered after she finished. 'Did they cheer for you?'

'Um, no.'

'Oh. Well, I'm sure you were great too.' She flashes her false veneers at me momentarily.

'You should stop by at my office,' Howard suggests, offering me his card.

Kimberly snatches the business card from him. 'I'll make sure she does.' And she weaves her waif-like arm through mine, steering me out of the building.

'Howard Mears wants to take you on.' She sounds stunned. 'That's a really big deal.'

'It is?' I respond doubtfully.

'Oh yes,' Kimberly reassures me, thrusting the business card into my hand. 'You really should consider meeting him, he's super-influential.'

'I'm not sure ...' For once she has a valid point but my body shudders at the thought – maybe I ought to just grow up. I'll have to think about it. You can't like everyone you work with and I know he's connected.

'But you have to have an agent in this town if you want to succeed. An agent promotes you, an agent will find you work, will fight for the right rate. You know it's very rare to just be spotted without having done anything of significance before.'

As I push through the heavy door into the café Alex springs to his feet then slumps back down again when he sees who's with me. I shrug a what-could-I-do face.

'What happened to your friend?' I ask Kimberly.

'Oh, she had to go and meet her councillor. Want a drink?'

I can understand how difficult it's been for Alex to get her to take no for an answer – she's the human equivalent of Velcro.

'I wouldn't mind a water,' I say, just to be rid of her.

She trots off to the counter and I run over to Michael and Alex. Michael smiles at me but I can see he's nervous.

'What's SHE still doing here?' Alex hisses through his teeth.

'She just tagged along.' I shrug. 'What was I supposed to do?'

He slinks back into his chair, grunting. 'She's up to something.'

I sink into the chair next to Michael.

'Well?' he asks.

'OK. I think.'

'I'm sure you were sensational.' He kisses the top of my head.

'Did you remember to make eye contact all around, even the empty seats?' Alex barks.

'Yes,' I yap back. 'Look, can we talk about something else? I don't want to analyse the audition into sub-atomic particles. What have you two been up to?'

I catch a shifty look between them, then Alex starts to smile broadly before catching himself and biting his lip.

'Nothing much, just sitting here listening to the stomach rumblings of your inferior wannabes! Luckily you never suffered stage fright to that extent, otherwise Michael would have been in for a right treat in the bathroom! Shocking the smells ladies can produce. Pooh!' And he mimes an ungodly stench coming from the next table.

'Aren't you so high and mighty. I seem to recall a vomit pool just before *Henry the Third*!'

'That might be so, but wasn't that just after the infamous monologue, a purely medicinal side-effect ... I think you'll find the term is.'

'ALCOHOLIC POISONING is the term you are looking for, dear Alex!'

I don't get a chance to interrogate them further because Kimberly arrives.

'Jane might have herself an agent,' she trills.

'Wow, Jane, that's fast.' Alex beams at me proudly.

'Oh I'm not—'

'Oh yes,' Kimberly butts in. 'He was really impressed with you. It must be fate, you two meeting again.'

'Who is he?' Alex probes.

'Howard Mears.' Kimberly offers up the information.

'Howard Mears is a slime-ball,' Michael snarls.

I'm surprised by Michael's outburst but am in total agreement.

'He is a bit creepy,' I admit.

Kimberly titters. 'No, he isn't. Anyway, he was rather taken with our Jane.'

Kimberly's use of the possessive unnerves me; from arch enemy to endeared family member is a hell of a stretch in one and a half hours, even by Mother Teresa's standards.

'All over her like a rash and you seemed to really hit it off.' The woman is unstoppable; how desperate can one be to hog centre stage with propaganda – well, misinformed storytelling.

'What makes you say that?' I'm aghast.

'You should watch out, Michael,' she giggles. 'Howard has a way with women.'

'We hardly talked at all,' I exclaim, getting slightly annoyed with the exaggerations.

'Of course,' she embellishes. 'You were just talking,' she says with a wink.

I roll my eyes at Michael to show that Kimberly is exaggerating but I catch the frown on his face. I look back at him, quizzically. If Michael is jealous he needn't be. I couldn't possibly. Eurgh, yuk ... the very thought. I squeeze Michael's hand.

'Are you OK?' I whisper.

'Fine.' Only I can tell from his tone he is not.

Kimberly starts rattling on about some girl's breast enlargement going terribly wrong when thankfully she spots a fellow stick insect ... I mean an actress that she's in competition with, and swarms over to invade her space.

'Shall we get out of here?' Alex chips in, breaking the frozen atmosphere between Michael and me.

'Good idea.' And before I have a chance to get hold of what is happening Michael steams out of the café, quickly followed by Alex. I pick up my stuff and rush after them. I can see them in a vigorous animated discussion as I slowly catch them up the street.

'What the hell?' I grab Michael's arm and Alex discreetly occupies himself with a non-existent text message on his phone.

'Hey, I'm talking to you. Could you have the decency to explain your sudden mood swing?' I surprise myself by going straight for the confrontation.

'What?' He looks at me as if I'm the one who's insane.

'You just stormed out,' I cry, indignantly.

'What? Oh, I just, eh ... just remembered somewhere I have to be. My publisher. I have an appointment with my publisher.'

I don't believe him for a second.

'I have to go,' and just like that he leaves ... no explanation, nothing.

A leopard doesn't change his spots; his rudeness, arrogance and moodiness revisit quicker than Angelina Jolie at an orphanage. I feel another rush of indignation. How dare he. HOW DARE HE!

'Jane.' Alex grabs my arm. 'Let's get a proper drink.'

I'm too annoyed to resist Alex's substitute offer and walk off, confounded at the beast's uprising.

'Listen, about Michael—'

'Alex, don't. Don't even dare to rationalise his behaviour. I don't care, he's schizo. I'm done ... finished. I'm not wasting another moment on the self-indulgent loopy fruit and that's that – do I make myself clear?'

Alex is flabbergasted. 'Jane, it's not what—'

'Alex, just buy me a drink. Subject closed.'.

CHAPTER TWENTY-FOUR

I enter the kitchen and Michael is already there, nose in a newspaper. I feel a prickle of annoyance. The fact that my heart still soars at the sight of him only fuels my annoyance. He is still wearing the same khaki shorts and crumbled navy T-shirt but his hair is damp from either a shower or a swim. While I check him over his head remains lowered. I stomp over to the kettle. Fine. If he's not speaking to me then I'm not speaking to him. I'll play his childish games if that's what he wants. I drum my nails loudly on the kitchen surface, waiting for the kettle to boil.

'How was your afternoon with Alex?' I didn't even notice Michael approach.

I spin round, half jumping with surprise.

'Oh, so you are talking to me now?' I scowl.

Michael gives an awkward cough. 'Yes, why wouldn't I?'

'Oh, I don't know, suddenly rushing off like that all moody and wretched.'

His head tilts as if I'm insane. 'I told you I had to see my agent. I spent half the day with you, Jane, and delayed it twice waiting for you to come out of the audition.'

But I'm not about to let him off the hook. I cross my arms and glower.

'That's not how it was and don't pretend otherwise. You never mentioned a meeting. Your mood swings are unpredictable.' I turn away, pouring myself a cup of tea, hot water spilling everywhere. Now I feel like I'm going to cry.

'I'll make it up to you,' he says.

'I don't want to be made up to. I want you to talk to me.'

'OK,' he says simply. 'Maybe I'm not used to communicating my dull scheduled meetings to everyone!' And as if that explains the whole incident he lowers his head and kisses me on the mouth and like putty in his hands I kiss him back.

Am I falling into another doormat trap?

'Oh good, you've kissed and made up.'

Michael draws away, smiling down at me. I smile back, breathless.

'If you happen to have the time, Miss Allen, I have Jim, Pat's casting director, on the phone for you. You know I might start charging you for the use of my secretarial services, now that I don't have a regular income!' Alex says casually as I try and reach for his hand.

'The casting director?' So soon? I didn't anticipate this, it can only mean one thing – NO.

I snatch the phone from Alex, swallowing the bile scratching the back of my throat.

'Hello, this is Jane Allen speaking.' I listen to the voice at the other end intently, nodding mechanically. I'm sure the rhythmic movement is all that is required for what is bound to be a sullen exchange.

'Yes, that's fine, no problem. Really … right … Ahuh … mmm … yes … OK … Bye.'

I politely hand Alex back his phone and draw in a breath. I think I need to sit down. Michael and Alex follow. Michael hands me a cup of tea as I try to absorb the telephone call. Both standing over me like expectant parents.

200

'They want me to see me again. Tomorrow,' I eventually disclose.

'That's brilliant.' Alex pulls me out of the chair and into his arms.

I laugh. 'It doesn't mean I've got the part.'

'As good as,' Alex rejoices.

Michael tugs at my waist. I turn around and wrap my arms around his neck. He hugs me tight. 'Well done.'

'I knew they'd see you were perfect for the part,' Alex asserts.

'I haven't got it yet, it's just a call-back,' I say, somberly, but I can't stop the bubbling of excitement flooding my veins.

I am more nervous second time around but Michael is a welcome distraction and sits patiently with me, not saying anything, just being a steady confident presence. The audition is over-running by about forty minutes and Michael is content to read his e-mails, do a crossword and basically just hold my hand. He knows better than to ask me inane questions this time round. We sit together in our own worlds harmoniously until I hear someone bellow my name.

I hear the chords on the piano; I hear the intro finish ten bars in but nothing comes out of my mouth. Oh no, I've frozen. The pianist stops and gauges my panic.

'My fault, everyone, wrong key. From the top.' He winks and urges me to continue on the count of five. This time I bellow out what is possibly the loudest audition. When your voice gets trapped inside you its final release overcompensates. Luckily for me it's a big song and you have to belt it out otherwise I would seriously be out of favour … phew!

After my finale I squeeze back out through the auditorium doors, quiet as a slipper-wearing mouse; the next call-back is already in song. My feet freeze to the floor midway as I see Michael engaged in a heated conversation with a beautiful statuesque dark-haired woman. I hang back for a minute; the woman leaves abruptly after Michael points a furious finger at her. I casually walk up to him and he gets up hastily.

He smiles at me. 'How did it go?'

'OK, I think.'

'Shall we go?' He's already setting the pace as he leads me out of the building and I hurry to keep up with the swift tempo. I'm dying to ask him who he was talking to but I don't.

As we drive in silence I have a brain wave. The woman was Raquel Delaney. Only the most bankable actress in TV since Calista Flockhart. The journey home is very quiet, only broken by intermittent auto-questions about my audition.

'So you think it went well?'

'I guess so.' I can tell he's not really there with me.

'It went well then?'

'Sure, it went great,' I answer, but it falls upon deaf ears.

I figure if he wants to tell me he will, so I leave it well alone..

CHAPTER TWENTY-FIVE

Things are on the up! Life is fantastic. I got the part.

I can hardly believe it. I feel like high-fiving everyone I know ... or strangers, I'm really not fussy. I feel like dancing the fine fandango. I am going to play Roxie Hart on Broadway, isn't that just insane? Of course I've told everyone, it's on my Facebook status and everything, I'm even thinking of setting up a blog. My parents are delighted for me and Sian squealed for a full ten minutes and then cried for a further ten when she realised she would have to advertise for a new flatmate.

It isn't a dream either. I know because I pinch myself several times a day. And the best bit of all is Michael; we are rarely out of each other's company. We've had endless lazy walks along the beach, made very saucy love many times, and talked about anything and everything and yesterday, completely out of the blue, when we were walking Digger by the beach, he said that he will join me in New York because he has a book launch in SoHo and we might as well make use of his apartment overlooking Central Park, no less. He then gave me a long intense look and asked me what I thought about living with him? I didn't want to just jump in and say yes I'd love to live with you so I said I'd think about it and I did for all of five seconds then leapt into his arms and said YES I could keep him company so he doesn't get lonely.

I wish I were with Michael now instead of this party in the hills.

I was hoping for a nice, romantic meal together but he had some last-minute thing he needed to take care of and told me to go with Alex and he'll join us later. To be honest he was acting a little weird and I can definitely tell when there is something on his mind but I didn't want to intrude. I mean, how irritating is it when someone constantly asks you what's up when you just need to think? I don't want to put him off us living together. This time I'll do it right: maintain a little space and separation so as to ease into the change. I asked Alex but he said I was being ridiculous, and I had to get used to being with a moody writer type! Now I come to think about it, even Alex was acting a bit shifty. I still have no idea what the heated exchange was with Raquel Delaney but it really doesn't matter, I trust Michael explicitly; jealously is a terrible thing. And one doesn't need to know every little detail of the past, people should concentrate on the future, it would save a lot of relationship aggro. I figure Michael is a here-and-now kind a guy, and that suits me. If I had to rake through my past it'll probably send him running.

So here I am, feeling like a fish out of water and about to be crushed to death. Some bloke the size of a quarterback is standing in front of me and not budging. 'Can you please move?' I dig a sharp elbow into his back but he doesn't hear me. The party is heaving like a pregnant walrus, I am giddy and claustrophobic and the people here are on the edge – not just out for a good time, they want to push the limits. It was nice enough when we first got here but the atmosphere changed when a wild rehab group turned up. This wasn't what I had in mind when I put my diamond choker on tonight, its premiere to the world should have been calm, serene and adoring. I try to move to the side but I'm blocked again, this time by a hyperactive weirdo. I am being pushed, bumped and terrorised from all angles. I feel like a Chinese Olympic ping-pong ball, and to top it all I have lost Alex. Just when I think I'm going to faint or be sick or both, someone behind pushes up against me. I stumble forward, nose pressed against the quarterback's back, my hands frantically checking the whereabouts of my choker. I then start to panic, there's no air and it's so hot in here, I can feel the room collapsing in on me and I struggle for breath. Oh God, this is it, just as I'm about to make my Broadway dream come true I'm going to suffocate to death.

I feel my knees begin to buckle when a hand from nowhere grabs me and pulls me through the crowd. I cling on desperately, squeezing through the blurring room towards a door, literally tasting the oxygen. We push on, digging a fist into any bodies that won't move. Eventually we make it outside. I look around me – I'm out in the garden. I gulp the air greedily.

'Thank you,' I gasp, astounded when I see that it is Howard Mears.

'You looked like you could do with some help there.' He flashes a row of dazzling white teeth at me.

'I was, I mean, I did,' I gasp. I lean over the railings; my head is still spinning and it takes a second or two for the desire to vomit to pass.

'I've lost Alex. You didn't see where he went, did you?

'I think he went into the VIP room upstairs.'

'I should go and find him.' The last thing I want is to re-enter the hell pit but it seems more attractive than spending any further time with Howard.

'Not so fast.' He lecherously sidles up next to me so that his arm is touching mine. I involuntarily take a step sideways. 'You didn't call.'

'Oh right ... I've been busy.'

'Yes. Congratulations on your role.'

'You know about that?'

'I know everything,' he says rather pompously, while checking out my boobs.

'Of course.'

'We should arrange a meeting.'

I know an agent is a good idea and I know he's a major player but I really don't like him. I don't trust him, and if I needed any further evidence of why, the abhorrent ogling is really getting on my tits – literally.

'I had an enlightening conversation with Kimberly,' he suddenly announces.

'Kimberly?' I take a step back and hit the railings.

He steps towards me, putting his hand on my arm. He smiles, teeth gleaming in the darkness. Then he puts the hand on my boob.

I slap his hand away. 'What do you thinking you're doing?'

He laughs. 'Such coyness, Miss Allen, you know you want to. Think of it as a private audition.' The audacity of this disgusting man!

'I'd appreciate it if you keep your hands to yourself, you old lech.' My voice is devoid of any politeness. Friend of Bob Edwards or not I'm not going to put up with this. I go to leave but his hand shoots out and grips the top of my arm.

'Oh, come on, don't be like that. I'm just being friendly.'

'I think you have made a mistake, old man.'

'Kimberly said—' He stops.

'Yes? Kimberly said what?'

He ignores my question and tries to kiss me.

'For God's sake, leave me alone.' I jerk away.

'Playing hard to get, is that it?'

'Not playing at all,' I say coldly.

'Oh I get it.' He produces a low-pitched nasty snigger. 'You like it a bit rough.'

I don't like the way this conversation is going and there is an aggressive glint in his eye. I try to side step past him but he clasps his hands on my waist and twists me round, aiming for a kiss.

'I said NO!' I twist violently from side to side. 'Have you lost your mind?'

'Stop squirming, my little temptress.'

His hands grip me harder and I find myself really struggling now. I try to yell but his mouth finally clamps down on mine as he pushes his tongue in, rubbing himself against me. Survival instincts kick in and I go limp in his arms, ready to yank away when he loosens his grip.

'What the bloody hell is going on?'

Michael. Thank God.

Michael grabs Howard's shoulder and rips him off me. His face is furious. In fact, he looks as if he wants to murder Howard — and me come to think of it.

'What the …' Howard piffles out, choking on his breath.

'Oh, Michael, aren't I glad to see you——'

'Save it, Jane!' I am so shocked by the venom in his voice that I flinch.

'Michael?' I question, totally bewildered.

'Decided he wasn't as nauseating as you first thought?' Michael's eyes fix on me with a cold, hostile stare.

'Nauseating eh?' Howard wheezes and splutters.

'I was being polite.' I am shaking with anger. I turn to Michael. 'It's not how it looks.'

'It never is.'

'But it's true the wretch forced himself——' I reach out to Michael but he pushes me away.

'It's exactly how it looks,' Howard says, straightening his tie with his fat, hairy hands. 'She wanted it every bit as much as I did.'

'No I didn't, you repulse me!' I roar, rounding on Howard, spitting for his blood. 'You forced yourself on me.'

I turn back to Michael. 'Michael … you have to believe me.'

'I don't think so,' he says, curling his lips contemptuously. 'Kimberly was right about you.'

'Kimberly has been busy,' I retort.

'I think you should leave.'

I'm not sure if he is talking to me, or Howard.

'Gladly.' Howard's self-assured sarcasm returns. 'Another time, baby, just for fun, eh!'

But I'm not about to let him get away with sexual harassment. I swallow back the tears that are stinging the back of my throat and straighten my shoulders.

'When a girl says NO she means NO,' I snarl. 'If you're not careful you could find yourself up against rape charges.'

'I wouldn't go saying things like that if you want to work in this town, baby.' His voice turns nasty and he walks right up to my face and sneers. 'You simply misconstrued a romantic liaison and that is slander.' Leaving me feeling like it was somehow my fault.

'Michael?' I say, gently touching his arm.

Michael recoils from my touch, his eyes are murderous.

'It's not how it looks, you've got to believe me.'

'Decided he'd be a good career move after all?'

'Why are you being like this? That's not what happened.'

'At best you're a calculating tart, at worse a predatory bitch flaunting your body for roles.'

His harsh words are like a cold sharp slap across my face and I have a sudden case of déjà vu. Isn't this something that my ex would do; accuse me of throwing myself at some guy? How, oh how, can he believe that of me?

'Is that what you really think?' My voice is flat and cold. I search for any sign of compassion and for a moment there's a flicker of hesitation but then his jaw tightens and an ugly scowl appears across his face, shooting an icy dart straight to my heart.

'Right ... well, I guess that's that then ... I'm not staying here to listen to this, I'm leaving.'

'I think that would be a very good idea.'

But I'm unable to move. My legs stay motionless, my stomach is as cold as steel, my arms like lead. Basically I'm a compound of heavy inert metals. My iron head is going to explode. Is this it then, the end of everything? Our love affair?

'You know what, you need to learn to control that anger of yours.' And with one last fleeting look I run for the exit. I can't run fast enough; spotting a yellow cab waiting outside I make a beeline for it.

'Claudia Von Helsing?' the taxi driver enquires as I pull open the door.

'Yep, that's me.'.

CHAPTER TWENTY-SIX

I'm not prone to hasty decisions but the need to get away, far, far away is so great that I know what I must do. I ask the taxi driver to wait for me while I go inside to fetch my belongings, surviving on raw energy as I rush around my room and Michael's room throwing all my clothes into my suitcase. The very last thing I do is unclasp the diamond choker, placing it safely in its box and leaving it on Michael's bed – it would be wrong to keep it.

On my way to the airport I leave a message on Bob Edward's phone and enlighten him about the type of friends he keeps. I'm surprised when I get a call straight back. Does this man not sleep? I recap what happened and not once does he doubt that I'm not telling the truth. Apparently Howard has done this sort of thing before but one of these days he is going to get his just desserts.

The flight back to London Heathrow is a different experience. This time I don't take advantage of the perks that first-class has to offer – I am too numb with grief. I keep replaying the incident over and over in my head, wondering if there was anything I could have done to prevent Howard's advances, if there was anything I could have said to make Michael see sense. I think until my heart and head throbs. You can't have a relationship without trust and if Michael chooses to believe a low-life like Howard then this is proof enough that the relationship is doomed. Always pay attention to the early indicators; I should have known from our first encounter that he had anger issues. However much I might love or think I might love Michael I can't allow myself to fall for him, a man that allows incensed jealousy to control his reasoning. That said, it doesn't make the pain any easier to deal with. I don't realise I am crying until the stewardess asks if I want a tissue. Gratefully I take it from her and blow my nose noisily.

I drift into a doze, exhausted from shock, only to wake up five minutes later as my ears pop on the turbulent descent.

I have a zillion voicemail messages waiting for me when I let myself through the little nondescript London door and they're all from Alex, wanting to know where I am; none from Michael. I text Alex back and tell him that I'm OK, that I'm back home, in England, that I'll explain later, and then switch my mobile off and fall into my bed. I pull the duvet over my head and shut the world out. The flat is small but familiar and I need familiar right now.

CHAPTER TWENTY-SEVEN

'It's for you.' There's a crash as Sian swings the door open, knocking over my wine glass, which I put on the floor while I pulled my tap shoes out of a box.

'Who is it?'

'Alex.'

'Can't you tell him I'm out?'

Sian covers the mouthpiece. 'No. Not this time. You need to speak to him.' What I need to do is finish packing.

Over the past few days I have been able to keep myself busy, getting ready for my move to New York, sorting out visas, work permits and all other legalities. It has enabled me not to think about anything that happened at that dreadful party. Night-times are a difficult kettle of fish; I feel wretched without Michael but I will get over it. People get over broken hearts all the time.

'You need to tell Alex what happened.'

Of course I told Sian everything and she has been my rock, my shoulder to cry on. I glance at her desperately but seeing that she isn't about to budge on this I reluctantly take the telephone from her.

'Alex!' I exclaim, with fake enthusiasm.

Alex is livid. 'Why the hell aren't you taking my calls?'

My voice jumps in panic. 'I … err … I've just been really busy.'

'Bullshit.' I stare down at the phone. 'I've been worried sick,' he says. 'You promised to call and explain. What the hell happened?'

I know the question is coming but I still don't know how to answer it.

'Why don't you ask Michael?'

'I have tried but he's been in a foul mood since you've left – weird and remote.'

'OK. You want to know what happened. Here it is. You left me at that party alone and Howard Mears sexually harassed me.' I shudder with revulsion as I recount Howard's fat, grubby hands all over me. 'Michael walked in and automatically assumed the worst, jumped to the wrong disgusting conclusion, and hates me. I couldn't bear to stay a second longer so I ran. There you have it in a nutshell.'

When I finish I hear Alex expel a deep cursing oath.

'The fucking bastard,' he yells. 'He needs a fucking leash.'

'It's OK. I'm OK.'

'It isn't OK. That man is a sex fiend. I shouldn't have left you alone.'

'No, you shouldn't have.'

'But why did you jump on a plane and head for England? Why didn't you just go back to Michael's place?'

'"At best you're a calculating tart, at worse a predatory bitch flaunting your body for roles",' I say, recounting Michael word for word.

'Michael said that?'

'Yes.'

'The stupid idiot, he's such a ****, a ******'

The profanities Alex rants down the line make a Tourette's sufferer sound like Ghandi. I never heard him like this except when he had that episode with Kimberly.

'Oh yes, I forgot to mention Kimberly's generous helping hand in all this.'

'She did what?'

'She more or less told Howard Mears I was up for anything.'

'Fucking scheming piece of rubbish. But we'll come back to that bitch later. I need to talk to you … about … umm … Michael. He was just angry.'

'And that gives him the excuse to—'

'No,' Alex jumps in. 'Jane, do you love Michael?'

I wasn't expecting this question. I'm stunned into silence.

'Jane, you still there?'

'Yes,' I whisper.

'Michael loves you.'

'He has a funny way of showing it.'

'He's a prick. But I know he loves you because he was on his way to pick up …' He stops, as if realising he's already said too much.

'Alex, you weren't there. You didn't see the look on his face.'

'Do you love him?'

'I did love him, I mean …' No sooner than the words involuntarily spill out of my mouth, I start welling up. I try and disguise a sniffle but there is no point in hiding my true feelings, the little good that ever does. I wipe the tears that are now free-falling down my face.

'I could never be with a man who treated me with such contempt again.'

'Again?'

I pause, as I try to decide how much I should tell Alex about my past. In the end the need to get it all off my chest is overwhelming.

When I am finished he sounds as distraught as I am. He lets out a strangled cry.

'Jane, why didn't you tell me? Michael is nothing like that. He would never hurt you. He loves you. He said those things ...' he pauses, 'in the heat of the moment ... I know, it's not an excuse and when I speak to Michael I'll tell him, but Jane, I am going to tell you something very important and I think you will understand why Michael reacted the way he did. It doesn't make it right but you'll understand his odd behaviour a bit more. As for Kimberly, I am going to give her a few home truths via the gossip columns and believe me she's not going to like it, nor is her daddy when she becomes the next YouTube hit,' he informs me, relishing in the thought. 'Did Michael ever tell you about his ex-fiancée, Raquel Delaney?'

'Raquel Delaney, THE Raquel Delaney?'

'Raquel De-lay-me, more like.' His disdain is apparent.

'Michael found out that Raquel had been cheating on him, but not with just one man. She slept with anyone who could accelerate her career: producers, directors, casting agents, anyone to secure a part in their TV show or movie, and one of those men was Howard Mears. She used Michael and everyone knew except him. She took him for a ride. When I arrived in Hollywood Michael had just finished with her and it had hit him hard. He said he would never trust women as long as he lived; he was no one's cuckold or career ladder.'

I digest everything Alex tells me and while it explains his reaction it only makes me sorry for what could have been.

'So you can see why he reacted the way he did, can't you?'

'Yes. Sort of.'

'So you see you need to talk to him.'

'No. Too many things have happened.'

'But you've got to. You two are the real deal. The Burton and Taylor, the coffee to his crème, the neutron to the electron ... the star in his galaxy ...the ...'

I cheer up at Alex's pitiable attempts at romantic links. 'Enough sci-fi, Captain, it won't change my mind. Why don't you have this conversation with Michael?'

'I can if you want me to.'

'No! Look, Alex, I really appreciate what you are trying to do but I think it's best we leave it alone. When you've had this many obstacles at the start, or should I say non-start, the finish is going to be bloody awful. I'm not putting myself through its greedy jaws again.'

CHAPTER TWENTY-EIGHT

I've been rehearsing for sixteen hours a day, six days a week for two weeks and it is the most fulfilling experience of my life. As a late replacement it's much harder work than I expected, breaking into an already established theatre family. Knowing I only have two weeks instead of six certainly puts the pressure on, greater than Venus's atmosphere. (I learnt that from Alex when he was going over his lines with me the other night.) But I am keeping up with the pace.

Despite eating, breathing and sleeping the role of Roxie Hart, it still hasn't stopped me thinking about Michael. It doesn't help that Alex and Sian call me nearly every night talking about the beast. I swear they've agreed on some sort of Rota between themselves. They are driving me mad. What they need to understand is that Michael hasn't tried to contact me, he hasn't had the decency to explain his behaviour, he's not called to say sorry, nothing, nada. And it hurts. It hurts to love someone and have emptiness fill that tender place solely created by him. But we all know it takes time to totally eradicate a complicated love mess.

My long working hours have also meant that I haven't had the opportunity to explore much of New York.

I'm just in the midst of changing into normal non-sparkly clothes when there is a knock at the dressing room door. Julia, my understudy, comes through with the most amazing bouquet of flowers. My heart quickens. Has Michael finally submitted and sent an apology? She dances over to a dressing table and plonks her sequined bottom down right on a chorus girl's headdress.

'Julia, watch the feathers!' She has about as much finesse as ... as I do really.

'Open the card, Jane, we're all dying to know.' With that eager request three of the ensemble fall through the door, stumbling over their tap shoes, their faces expectant and excited. I've met some nice people here; it wasn't what I anticipated from fellow performers – that's why you shouldn't believe tabloid junk stories.

I look at them all with motherly censure and hurriedly pick up the card to appease my audience. I start reading aloud.

'"To my Dearest Jane ...

"I realise the futility of this poor gesture, in the sheer ridiculousness of keeping a single shred of hope ..."'

I break off, looking at the wide-eyed dancers.

'It's the writer ... it's the writer! Oh listen to him go,' they all coo.

'He might be finally apologising, girls!' I pipe up as I clasp the card to my chest, fully realising how dramatic and luvvie I'm becoming.

'Read on, Jane ... quickly. We have another scene in ... err ... well now!'

'OK ... OK ... keep your sequins intact.' I continue, trying to heighten the suspense (theirs and mine), '"that my book is still remotely intact."'

'WHAT?' they all shout in perfect toned unison.

218

Oh … the penny drops noisily and loudly in my vacuous mind.

'Is he writing a book about you?' Julia asks.

'It's another guy,' I explain to the false eyelashes that furiously blink at me. They remind me of a bunch of Bambis wading through a stinging mist.

'What other guy? You never mentioned another guy. Tell us later … shit, we got to go … c'mon, Lara, Sara and Clara.' (Only in America!) As quick as they came they were all gone and there was me left in a picture that Flemish Baroque painters would burn their brushes on. I finish reading Eli's message.

To my Dearest Jane,

I realise the futility of this poor gesture, in the sheer ridiculousness of keeping a single shred of hope that my book is still remotely intact. (I understand you people do not take kindly to rearrangements.)

If there is the slightest chance of negotiation — even if it has no index left! — I would be willing to arrange a rendezvous. Will be in touch.

E..S.

A P.S from ES as soon as I've found a suitable briefcase with the required clicking noises so often heard on these dramatic exchanges.

I gather the bouquet up and inhale the wonderful fragrant lilies: this has certainly stamped a smile on my face. I walk out to the theatre foyer. Normally I would leave by the stage door but I have to pick up some tickets for my mum and dad, they're coming over in three weeks. Enamoured by my flowers I don't realise I'm dripping water all over the floor.

'Jane, are you that nervous you've developed a little incontinence problem?'

'What? Oh.' I look up at Marvin the ticket vendor sitting in his booth and trot over to talk to him. He hands me an envelope.

'Hey, Miss Allen, we had one person today buy a ticket for every show next month. Some folks are whack, far out, man.' I show a cordial look of understanding and smell the air to see if anything herbal is lingering in the little plastic room. He could use it as a massive bong – it's not so far-fetched if you saw him in the flesh. I quickly wave goodbye and make for the doors.

'Is it that the stakes are so high now?' Who said that? I look around me and see a figure, obscured by a pillar, holding a *Herald Tribune*, and sporting a Humphrey Bogart fedora and a rain mac.

'You lost your nerve, kid?' I strain to see the face as I approach, half chuckling to myself. I reach the column and back onto it, ready to play the role of Lauren Bacall. I try and recall some of Slim's lines in *To Have and Have Not* but I don't want to do the obvious whistling one. Many times I have watched her on film – I even tried to mimic her for a year.

'You know, ES ... you're not very hard to figure, only at times. Sometimes I know exactly what you're going to say. Most of the time, the other times ... the other times, you're just a book hoarder.'

'Jane, I thought you'd be too young to guess!'

'Eli, there is such a thing as TCM and I am an actress. We do study film history, you know.'

Eli takes his hat off and gives me a firm hug; it's good to see a friendly face.

'Eli, how did you ...?'

'I did keep my end of the bargain and called you after my trip; Alex told me all about your success and as I was in the vicinity I thought you might want that cocktail I promised you all those moons ago.'

He is so sweet – the world feels better when he's around.

'In the vicinity, really, Eli!'

His eyebrows rise. 'Well yes, Jane, I have some work to do at our Fifth Avenue store.'

'Yeah, of course,' I mumble. I feel like a right pilchard. Just shows you ought not to get ahead of yourself and keep your ego tied up tighter than Houdini in a water tank.

'I'm not dressed for cocktails.' I panic, feeling self-conscious after my inflated ego pops.

'You look just fine, Jane, shall we go?'

I actually feel really pleased. I haven't given my love life a forward thought since Michael and now hope makes my stomach somersault.

I take his open arm and we walk down the steps of the theatre. Eli has a driver waiting but opens the door to the limo himself. This is another world, I feel glamorous and pampered. We drive up Broadway and take a right through Central Park onto 5th Avenue. Eli asks me all about the auditions and how I am settling into New York life. We chat and chat until the chauffeur stops the car.

'I'll be one minute, Jane, I just have to pick up a little thing.' We are outside H. Winston. I goggle at the imposing marble façade, the huge doors tall as giants, following their form upwards to discover four more floors of jewels. That is some shop!

Eli springs back into the limo with a dark-suited burly man and two square velvet boxes.

'Jane, this is Ivan, our guardian angel.' I shake the towering man's hand. My bones feel crushed and I look at Eli. 'Ivan, go easy when you shake hands.' He gives the beefy wall a frown.

'Sorry, Mr Eli, I lost feeling in my right hand after Bājíquán tournament, opponent paid high for his mistake.' He has a thick eastern European accent and he is very scary. Eli grins at me, his eyes full of mischief.

'Don't worry, Jane, he's only the runner-up in the deadliest of martial arts. The world master beat him, he's nursing a bruised ego today.'

Ivan gives us a steely glare. 'Tragic, my opponent my master. I think more training next time. He no good if I'm not better than him I get money back.'

Am I in a *Stars Wars* movie? Have the Russian Jedi invaded New York City? Ivan is smiling at his stilted joke. Eli pats him on the back.

'Better luck next time, Vlad the Impaler!'

'Mr Eli, I'm Russian not Romanian. Dracula bite flesh, I merely maim.'

The two men laugh at some in-joke. I shift backwards; this fairy-tale world has its ogres also.

CHAPTER TWENTY-NINE

We pull up outside the Museum of Modern Art. We've barely driven two blocks. I give Eli a puzzled look.

'We should have just walked!'

'I don't think the insurers would approve, Jane.' And with that he pops open one of the boxes. Woooah … an emerald and diamond tiara sparkles back at me in all her glory.

'We're giving it an evening out.' He lets Ivan get out of the car first then invites me to join him.

The people here are very different to the LA bunch. Mature ladies dripping in jewels glide around the foyer discussing various fundraisers and their varying degrees of success. This is New York's elite, the old money; the powerhouses; the trustees of the city's art and culture. Eli is in conversation with the curator and someone who looks suspiciously like Donald Trump.

Ivan looms over two podiums displaying the tiaras; you would be an idiot to mess with him, I'm sure he's armed. I mosey around in the modern spacious foyer, lost in my own thoughts. The architecture reminds me of Michael's house, clean sharp edges and expansive windows. I walk towards a huge sculpture in the middle of the room – it sucks me in for a closer look. I can't see the back – it is an optical illusion. Eli interrupts with a martini glass.

'Thanks.' I turn to make an impromptu toast but I'm too late.

'Here's your cocktail, Jane, a few weeks late!' I smile; he is so thoughtful. I look at him for a moment and I'm just about to ask him about the evening when he is captured by an intimidating character, a man, must be in his seventies. People have been circling him all evening – maybe I would know who he was if I perused the financial papers. Eli seems pleased with the uninvited interruption but I'm getting a bit peeved being left on my own. Oh grow up, Jane. He's a very connected businessman with a very busy schedule; he's made a tremendous effort just to see you.

'Jane, I'm just going to speak to Mr Oppenheimer, be back in five, I promise.'

I force a 'no problem' face on and pretend to be really interested in a glossy four-metre-high brain sculpture that's oozing oil from its frontal lobe. Sometimes I just don't get modern art but it was the easier thing to waffle about in the history of art exam.

After another fifteen minutes I wander over to where Ivan is. Eli breaks off another encounter and heads my way, at last.

'Sorry, Jane, a big part of my job is networking. So I get pulled in different directions constantly.'

'That's OK,' I lie. 'Are you making big deals?'

'No, it's not quite like that, unfortunately, you have to network regardless of potential sales. You're the company's face, similar to you being the leading lady. Without you there is no show, people listen to the narrator not the typist.'

'Must be fascinating to meet such influential people.'

'It can be.' Eli is very untouched and in control. A waiter comes over with some more martinis, Eli hands me a glass. We make a toast to 'encounters of the book kind'. I spin around to admire the view and a thinning mop of curly hair passes beneath my chin.

'Excuse me, miss; I was trying to step undetected between all the money puddles vaporising out from the stiffs. There's so many Abe Lincolns on the floor, are we in another civil war, did I miss something on the news, did something happen between Wall Street and Waldorf?'

I don't understand the joke (history was never my strong point) but I'm not concerned. I am completely star-struck, paralysed ... it's Woody Allen.

He greets Eli as an old friend would and they start chatting.

'Really, Eli, these are magnificent stones, but good grief my uncle's stomach hernia is smaller than that – you mean people still wear this? Didn't that die out with the Tsars?' I hear Ivan mutter under his breath. Woody is really ribbing Eli.

'Style advice from a man who has a wooden microwave and deems corduroy a lavish treat fit for kings, you've worn the same glasses since the Apocalypse.'

They laugh and give each other a hearty hug. Another amazing experience; these tend to happen when Eli is around. He introduces us and I'm tongue-tied. I listen to the two men bicker and enjoy the little sideshow. A middle-aged couple greet Eli from a distance, then scoot over and start wittering on about the commodity markets – will gold prices go lower, will the dollar rise, is it a good time to buy diamonds now, that type of thing. Woody Allen is entertained, watching the intensity of the couple. He chips into the serious debate with a morsel of advice.

'If you buy the baguette diamonds at least you get a free lunch included in the price.' He is very funny – it's an education standing next to him.

I pluck up the courage to talk to him.

'Mr Allen, we have something in common.'

'We do? Well it's not our neurosis, dress size or our taste in men!'

I laugh, he's exactly like you expect him to be.

'Only our surname, I'm afraid.'

'You're far too tall for my family tree, apart from when they wore platforms in the sixties, that's the only time they had the height to get on rollercoasters. My mother still wears them on Sundays, confused birds circle her, thinking their emigration route's been shortened. They spy a perch on what they think is a Canadian redwood, (her wig colours have more choices than deluxe) all in less than twenty minutes from Newark. Really you should see it! Alfred Hitchcock should have just hired my mother.' I giggle as he puts me at ease. We chat about Broadway and New York: this is the quintessential New York experience. All I need now is Liza Minnelli, SJP and David Letterman.

A few admirers have spotted Woody and are edging our way. He tries to dip his head out of sight but too late, we are surrounded. I look across to find Eli but he's occupied with what I can only describe as Money on Heels. I wander off and look at a laser installation. I spend the next hour by myself.

I'm dazzled by the event but spend most of it on my own. As the evening draws to a close I try to get Eli's attention. I really must leave now as I have an early rehearsal tomorrow and my feet need warm water. Eventually he manages to unravel himself from some heiress's grasp.

'Sorry, Jane, I've said that too many times tonight. I hope you've been enjoying the evening, despite my flawed qualities as a host.'

'That's OK, Eli. You're a man in demand.'

'Jane, I'm here for another week, I'm going try and shift some appointments around so maybe you can join me for a picnic in Central Park and we can make the swap?'

'I have rather a busy schedule myself, Eli. We go into technical rehearsals this week.' I am flattered by the invitation but somehow not excited at the prospect. He's wonderful to be around (when he's around): funny, smart, sophisticated and handsome, but ... C'mon, Jane, make an effort. Am I taking the fantastic out of the fabulous ... Am I taking opportunities for granted?

'I know, I know, you felt ignored and I am dreadfully sorry. Please let me make it up to you.' His face is serious.

'OK, Eli, give me your card and I'll phone you when I know my schedule.'

'Perfect, let the driver take you home – I have to finish some business here.'

He leans in for a kiss and I turn my face so it hits my cheek. It feels nice and secure but no electricity. Perhaps this is the way of mature sophisticated relationships, this is the proper way it happens. I've finished playing with the clumsy Duplo blocks and gone straight to Lego. Is this how it's supposed to be, a bud that grows in fertile soil, not a bloom that lasts a few days?

I wave as I skip down the steps and he blows a chivalrous kiss.

I sit back in the limo but can't help feeling a little disappointed. I really need to grow up. At least his temperament is constant. I shouldn't expect the whole world to be one constant firework after the next. And anyway, I met Woody Allen ... wait until I tell Sian. My life is one big firecracker!

CHAPTER THIRTY

Brilliant, the tech rehearsal goes well and we don't have to do a re-run this afternoon so I ring Eli and we arrange to meet at two by the pond in Central Park. I have an hour to spare so treat myself to a facial. My skin is under duress after all the plastering of stage make-up. Feeling relaxed and enjoying the walk through the park, I check the Google map on my new iPhone to make sure I'm in the right corner. My sense of direction is pretty hopeless at the best of times so New York is one of the easier cities to navigate for the geographically challenged; an avenue and street grid-system, thank heavens.

I sit on a bench next to a leafy tree and soak up the sunshine, which is temporarily obscured by a man on a unicycle with a huge hat on. New York is a place where anything can happen. The other day I came out of rehearsals and a small parade of golden midgets were stopping the traffic to hand out Height Awareness leaflets.

Fifteen minutes later and I have to presume Eli is detained by some major diamond emergency. I take my shoes off, lay my wrap on the ground and sit down on the grass, admiring my pedicure and the sights around me. Another ten minutes pass so I lie back and sunbathe. I have dozed for a few minutes when my iPhone starts jumping about in my pocket.

'Jane, Jane, are you there?' Good, I was getting a little agitated. Glad he's on his way.

'Hello, Eli, you're late.'

'Well, yes … but I'm afraid I've been summoned by a client.'

'So when will you get here?'

'Well, that's the point. They've requested a private viewing now as they only have two hours in New York.'

'Can't you ever say no?'

'Afraid not … not in my position, I'm—' I hang up. This is the second time he's bailed on me, and the other night I was more or less by myself. I'm pissed off; maybe if I arranged a viewing with my American Express card I might have actually got to spend time with him. I know he's the all-important, indispensable jewellery man and a great guy but I'm not interested in playing second fiddle to an all-consuming job 1000 per cent of the time. OK, that's an exaggeration: by my calculations he's failed 83.33 per cent of the time so far. The fullest conversation we've had was at Alex's launch and he was working then. I'm busy but this guy is a workaholic. I hear my phone ring and I ignore it for as long as I can, before finally conceding and picking it up.

'Yes.' My tone is impatient.

'Jane, can you forgive me, I have a very demanding job.' He sounds genuinely sorry.

'Eli, I do have things to do as well. It's not often I have an afternoon off.' I keep my voice controlled and level.

'Can I call you later? My driver is here. Please say yes, Jane.'

'Sure.' I hang up, but I won't be taking his call and I don't feel any regretful twinge at what might have been. I pick myself off the grass and start walking with purposely long fast strides and don't immediately hear my name being called. The choreographer of the show is yelling at me exasperatedly.

'Jane, stop, hang on. Miss Allen, really … would you stop already.' He picks up his fully costumed Chihuahua, places it in his Louis Vuitton dog carrier and sprints over to me. It's quite a vision.

'Hi, Nicholas, what you doing here?'

'Oh darling, darling … you … shouldn't make me run in these jeans. They nearly split at the crotch,' he playfully jokes as he catches his breath. 'I haven't had a chance all week to cruise the park with Tula!' The tiny Tula yaps and growls at me. 'Oh Tula! Naughty girl. Stop it, you feisty little fluff-ball.'

You need not ask: yes, Nicholas is as gay as Michael Douglas is straight.

'My date didn't show.'

'What, the bling-bunny?' He campily flips his hands around.

'Yeah … too busy.'

'Why don't we go to the Russian Tea Room for high tea? Come along, let's you and me go and drink tea. My treat,' he trills.

He grabs my arm and I have little choice, 'no' is not in his vocabulary. He made me do a kick this morning that nearly gave me an internal injury. The afternoon turns out to be fun in the end. Nicholas can be incredibly lewd about cucumber and he swaps the tea for champagne. It's like having a one-man-and-his-dog show all to myself. Tula sneezes on her curried chicken and dribbles the yoga water for dogs all over her bag.

CHAPTER THIRTY-ONE

I'm in my dressing room when Julia bursts through the door – she's making a habit of that.

'Look, Jane, more flowers. He must really like you.'

I look at the beautiful floral creation and hand it back to her. 'You take them home.'

'Really, Jane?'

'Absolutely, if you promise to stop barging in like someone's put dynamite in your corset! You'll give me a coronary.'

'If you're sure. You sound very New York now, Jane, it's nearly authentic.'

'Thanks, honey, kiss my hiney.' We both start to giggle in an infantile manner. I take the card out of the bouquet and stuff it in my bag, at the bottom with the loose tissues and chewing gum.

Up on stage I fail to hit a big high note and my voice feels raw. The vocal coach is drowning me with honey, boiled water and salt, olive oil, brake fluid, whatever she can lay her hands on. I am sitting out the next scene while Julia takes my place, nestling down in one of the auditorium's seats, when I feel a tap on my shoulder. I twist round to see my illusive co-star Penelope, who plays Velma Kelly. She's been very nice and easy to work with but she keeps herself to herself off stage. I don't feel I know her at all and all the other girls pile into my dressing room, which makes me think either she is alone or she has all the boys!

'Hi, Jane, how's the voice holding up?'

'Not good,' I whisper.

'Better to let it rest today, otherwise you'll lose it tomorrow and the producers will get jumpy because of the show's closure mid-run. Look, I have this flask – it's just boiled water and pomegranate rinds, my grandmother swore by it. Drink it, it helps, and here's some eucalyptus capsules – I always carry them.'

'Thanks, Pen—'

'Jane, really! Not a whisper. The chords have to rest.' She's a very serious young lady but genuine in her concern. I rummage in my bag for a pen and write *thank you* on a napkin.

'You're welcome. I need you back on stage – Julia treads on my toes!' She leaves for her next scene.

Some of the girls think she's odd, and I have to agree with them but she seems really sweet and she's an amazing performer. Funny that she avoids being sociable off stage, shunning big groups; peculiar as she's the centre of attention on stage. But that can be the case with some actresses; they are more comfortable in a role and with a group of strangers. It's the perfect cover.

I sit out for the rest of the day and look over the new stage directions. The voice failure has actually allowed me to catch up quite a bit and I feel more prepared.

It's the end of the day and we're all heading to the East Village. Nicholas is having a cheese and whine evening. Yes, that's right, whine. All the girls are going over to moan about men. Nicholas has recently broken up with his lover of two years; he said he was such a bitch about it. His brownstone house is amazing; Nicholas is a bit of brand name in the dancing world: he has a private dance school and runs workshops downtown for underprivileged kids. The list of credits to his name is outstanding, Madonna recruited all her dancers from his underprivileged domain. Anyone who means business (in the dancing world) has a Nicholas Delarue Dancer – it's the most coveted Michelin star of the dancing profession.

All of the girls are lounging around on his sun deck, drinking health drinks and smoothies. I spy a vodka bottle coming out of Lara's bag. Nicholas sashays his way across the sprawled bodies and claps his hands to summon silence.

'Now, girls, I know the last two weeks have been hard work and a lot of you have been whining about the changes and everybody's love life has taken a nosedive, but just think: this is your career, not theirs, and if you have a partner that is inconsiderate now, what will he or she be like when we're in full production again? So this is a party to shovel out the shit if you haven't already done so.'

Everyone shouts cheers. I raise my glass – my voice is coming back but I'm not taking any chances. Nicholas is the peacock among his brown clucking hens; the girls love and admire him. He is their demi-dance-god. I sit back and enjoy observing them. They are such a lively bunch of souls, some of them are only eighteen so Nicholas's paternal guidance is in play here – granted with a very big gay lollipop – but he sincerely cares about his troupe. I kick off my heels and put my feet up on the sunbed.

'Hi, Jane, is the voice any better?' Good grief, it's Penelope, she never comes to any social events.

'Much better, thanks to that magic potion you gave me,' I whisper. She looks tense and fidgety. 'You OK, Penelope?'

'Fine, just fine, quite a gathering.' She is terribly awkward at making small talk – I wish my voice was stronger.

'Oh, you missed Nicholas's "damn all the world apart from your life" speech!' I whisper towards her ear.

'Well he's not far wrong,' she says sombrely. I'm puzzled at her response.

'I suppose you're used to the life though?'

'Yeah, all successes have a price.' She takes a seat by my feet, then without warning tears start filling her big brown eyes and her cheeks go blotchy.

'What's the matter?' I try and speak softly but it comes out as a bit wolfish.

'Oh, Jane, I can't do a duet with a tenor!' She manages a little joke and quickly regains her composure as if her emotions momentarily got free without prior permission.

I resort back to whispering, 'Better out than in, girl, believe me. I've just had my heart broken, with a disappointment chaser on top. The turmoil is unbearable, but the last week has given me strength to stop speculating over silly men.'

'Really, Jane, who would break your heart? You're lovely! If you can't keep one, how will I?' Penelope's deadly serious.

'Pen ... do you mind if I called you Pen?' She seems delighted.

I swing my legs down and move in closer, she's such a private being.

'It's not us, it's them!' I joke. I point over to Nicholas who is sitting in the sideways splits and tapping a glass – ever the showman.

'Now, girls ... hush. If a man or woman doesn't appreciate this type of agility what are we going to say?'

They all shout back, 'Screw you! You just got in the way of my arabesque.'

There's a roar of laughter and they mimic falling into each other backwards into rude positions. Penelope has a quiet giggle.

I attempt another approach. 'Did someone do the dirty on you?'

She's taken aback by the frankness of my question.

'Well … err … not exactly. I don't have anyone to talk to about it.'

'You can talk to me, I can keep a confidence.'

'My partner thinks I'm frivolous.' I gulp my drink in disbelief; this is a girl who's dedicated, serious, professional, very talented and above all never frivolous.

'But, Pen, you're the most sensible one here!'

She smiles shyly. 'I know I'm not much of a party girl, and I know the other girls think I'm strange but when I leave the theatre I go directly home.'

'So what, if that's what you want to do that's what you want to do. Were you partying too much then?'

'Never, Jane, I never party.'

'Oh.' Her answer surprises me. What is it that she's unhappy about? 'So you're not frivolous under any circumstances and your partner says you are?'

'Yeah, he thinks everything that I do is frivolous; my career isn't a real one and that I waste my time on make-believe, rubbish, nothing consequential to the world.' The words start to chill my bones and I feel a slow anger burn from the pit of my belly. I already despise this man.

'Now listen here, Pen, I lived with a monster like that. He did everything he could to jeopardise my chances and I fell into oblivion for two years; it was the biggest waste of time and effort of my life. Don't let someone else dictate the rules to you about your life, your needs, or aspirations. Can't he see you're a star in one of the most famous musicals of all time?'

'He just thinks I need to get it out of my system then settle into an academic life like him. You see we met at college then I dropped out to concentrate on my dancing. He was disappointed in me and said I didn't have the gumption to finish the course.' The tears are rolling down her petite face.

'Surely you've proved your gumption by now.'

'That's just it. He says this must be my last show. He wants someone around that he can discuss ideas with, not costume fittings.'

'Pen, why do you put up with it? He sounds like a prison warden.'

'He's a theoretical physicist – he writes for the universities.' I gulp harder, another irrational writer. I wasn't about to get into that episode with Pen, I had to fill her with hope.

'I have packed my bags.'

'You have?'

She nods, tears still free-flowing.

'Sounds to me like you've done the right thing, good for you.'

'I'm scared.'

'Why?'

'I've lived with him for five years. I don't have any friends because each day I must return home without fail immediately after every performance, otherwise my head will get filled with junk and nonsense if I associate with anybody from this heinous pretend world. This is the first time I've been out for years.'

I want to give this guy a piece of my mind and a piece of my heel – preferably embedded in his odious, spewing mouth.

'Stay there, Pen. I'll be back in a minute.'

Pen sits there as lonely and lost as a girl can be. I keep my eye on her, making sure she doesn't bolt. A few minutes later I return with Nicholas. Penelope is horrified. Nicholas assesses the situation well.

'Look, Penelope,' he kneels down, 'Jane hasn't told me why or what or when or who but how would you fancy shacking up with a full-on gay boy? My place needs some grace and there are so many bedrooms not getting the use they deserve. To be truthful you'd be doing me the favour. I can't rattle around with my pink lycra cat-suit on with nobody to appreciate its glory.' Nicholas stands up and puts his hand over her mouth before she has a chance to say no. He goes over, collects her bags and we both follow him up two spiral staircases. We reach a beautiful sunny attic room with a balcony and a bathtub right in the middle.

Nicholas throws his clothes out of a closet and hangs her things up with the speed of a Japanese bullet train.

'These can go to the dressing-up box at school.'

He grandly gestures with his hands. 'C'mon, we have a celebration of human rights to attend.' He grabs our hands and floats down the stairs.

CHAPTER THIRTY-TWO

Pen and Nicholas are the most unlikely roomies but it seems to be working well for both of them. Pen is still reserved but much lighter in her step; she even visited my dressing room with some fairy cakes. She said Nicholas insisted they were fairy cakes not cupcakes. Because of the progress in rehearsals we got off at five. I'm going to have a sensible early night. I have a little studio apartment just off Broadway with a narrow view of Central Park, which you can spot if you stick out your ostrich head from the makeshift balcony. It's a bit of a hovel but I like to see it as artistic, bohemian and very, very New York. I grab a bagel from my local deli and head on up the six flights of stairs. I settle down for the evening, just dozing off when the phone rings.

I groan down the phone.

'Fine way to greet your most treasured flatmate.'

I just grunt because I know what's coming.

'Alex called,' she announces all mysteriously. Honestly, that girl is a soap opera in her own head.

'So what's new?' The two have become the best of phone pals.

'Well …' she begins. She has the most dramatically charged phone manner I've ever encountered.

'That is … we both feel—'

'So it's "we" now, is it?'

'Yes "we",' Sian's patronising teacher's voice announces down the line. 'We—'

'Stop right there.' I'm exasperated with this conversation – I know where it's going.

'Shut up and listen. Michael is in New York and the address is—'

'I'm not listening, la la la … not listening …' but before I have a chance to hang up she blurts it out quicker than an EasyJet boarding call.

'Apartment 237, Central Park, Seventy-second Street, Upper West Side, GOODBYE, love you, sweety.'

She'd make good money in sales if she decides to quit her teaching job, the woman can't take no for an answer. Flat 237 … the address keeps circling my mind. Trust him to have such a spooky number; that scene in *The Shining* freaked me out when I was young. Now my head is full of unpleasantries, I won't sleep easy tonight.

The next day we finish at four thirty. I'm not quite sure what to do with myself so I take a leisurely walk round Central Park but midway it starts pelting down with monsoon rains. I'm at the other end of the park so I hail a cab, relieved when one pulls up nearly on my feet. I jump back.

'Central Park, Seventy-second Street, Upper West Side,' I shout out as I jump into the back. I instantly realise I've mistakenly given Michael's address, the address which has been swimming around in my sub-consciousness all day. I'm just about to change it when the cab driver swerves across the road and my body is thrown onto the floor. I get up, panicking, then see that the driver is talking on the radio whilst driving one-handed. I grip my seat tightly.

The yellow cab zips through the traffic and I bounce about in the back trying to keep the contents of my lunch down. Do all cab drivers have to drive about in this manic way, and why isn't there a gridlock when you need one? I clutch my stomach as the cab takes a sharp left. If he'd just slow down then maybe I could think this through properly because I've decided I will go and see Michael, if I get there in one piece. I, Jane Allen, am no longer a coward, my head is held high and no man or his demons are going to shit on me, and I can get the closure I need. I'm resolute about this and I must practise what I preach, I walk in BIG shoes. I look down at my trainers and realise I have my Manolos in my bag. How appropriate. I pull them on. Now I am ready to face Michael.

'Here we are, lady, Central Park, Seventy-second Street, Upper West Side.' The West Indian cab driver smiles at me through his rear-view mirror. I drag my eyes over to the tall exquisite building and the knot in my stomach twists tighter.

It's now or never.

I pay the driver and stride purposefully to the building, so preoccupied I nearly bump into a lady and her dog.

'Hey, watch it, you crazy broad, you got eyes, ain't you?' Another so quintessentially New York moment that you can't take offence.

The cab speeds away and I face the imposing building, certain that this is a very bad idea. In fact, if I stop to think about this properly, it is complete and utter madness. Firstly there is no telling whether Michael will see me and secondly, despite Alex's insistence that Michael loves me I have no actual proof. He hasn't made any attempts to contact me but I know I need to do this. I need to exorcise this demon and kill it off once and for all.

Right now I have more pressing matters: how the hell am I supposed to get inside?

'Good afternoon, ma'am,' the smartly suited security guard addresses me.

'Good afternoon,' I say. 'I'm here to see Michael Canty.'

'Dr Swansborough?'

Dr Swansborough? Is Michael ill? No he can't be, Alex would have said something.

'Yes, Dr Swansborough, that's me.' I cough up in the most doctorly voice I can muster. Fortunately at that moment the security guard turns to assist a lady struggling with a buggy and two small children into an awaiting car. I take this opportunity to slip into the lobby and run into the opening lift, I mean elevator. Quite proud when I manage to remain upright especially on marble flooring, (no mean feat, no pun intended!).

At last I'm actually a dab hand at running in high heels. Long gone is the wobbly woman at Arrivals, I might even enter a stiletto race, I believe they're popping up all over the place. Such a pro now, each step professionally accomplished without the slightest waver. Wish the confidence would percolate down the rest of my body. My palms feel clammy and perspiration runs down my back. I nervously wipe my hands against my jeans.

Even the elevator has a marble floor, art deco in its decoration – this is some building! I'm trying to find things to occupy my mind so I don't turn around and flee.

The upward journey stops at the twentieth floor and the door pings open.

A little old man and his wife get in; she has a walking cane so he guides her gently in. She gives him a tender kiss and they both smile at me. I mean to step out but my legs don't move.

'Which floor, miss?' The old man gallantly stretches his hand out towards the buttons, his wife as proud of him as the day they married.

'Umm … ground floor, please, thank you,' I mumble.

I can't go through with it, I can't handle more rejection, more irrational behaviour. Why would I want to expose myself all over again, rehashing turmoil, hate and disgust … No thank you, ma'am.

As we descend I watch the elderly couple closely. They are so in love with each other it's adorable – they must be eighty plus. I can detect a tear rising up. Why oh why am I such a sentimentalist? We reach the lobby and they totter out arm in arm. The lady turns around and looks right through me.

'So, you going up after all?'

I was unaware I hadn't moved.

'You go up and find out.' Her parting words to me. How on earth can she tell? I suppose the cliché is right – wisdom comes with age. I'm flabbergasted.

Standing now in the corridor on the twentieth floor just outside Michael's apartment I am finding the idea of putting one foot in front of the other and ringing the bell increasingly difficult. I take a deep breath and with a few jerky steps forward I punch the doorbell before I have a chance to change my mind. The door flies opens and the look on Michael's face says it all. I am the last person on earth he is expecting. My hearts slams so hard against my ribcage that I think it's trying to make a run for it. That's not such a bad idea.

For what seems like an eternity neither of us speak.

Oh crikey, I shouldn't have come. It is absolutely futile. I've made a mistake.

'I was … you know … in the neighbourhood, but I can see it was a stupid idea …' I back away but he steps towards me.

'Don't go! Come in!'

There is anguish in his voice and I wonder if he really might be ill. There are purple bruises under his eyes and his face is drawn as if he's suffered angst or bereavement.

'I thought you were someone else,' he says, as I follow him inside.

'Dr Swansborough?'

'Yes. She is helping me with some research for my next book.'

'Oh right ... so you're fine ... good health?'

'I wouldn't say that, exactly.' He gives me a wry smile. 'What about you ... are you ... fine ... good health?'

'I didn't come here to exchange pleasantries.' Surprising myself with my brusqueness.

'Of course ...' He stuffs his hands in his pockets in a rare moment of awkwardness.

I get straight to the point. 'I have never nor would I ever sleep around to get a part. I certainly didn't encourage Howard Mears' harassment. *He* grabbed *me* and forced himself onto me. The fact you chose to think differently is wrong, sickening and downright insulting.' I rush the words out in case he tries to cut in but he doesn't. He doesn't say anything so I continue. 'You hurt me. Beyond hurt. I thought we ... I thought you ...' Now the words fail me. 'You're the only man I have ever ...' Gosh, this is harder than I imagined.

'When I saw you with that greasy Mears I saw only what my mind wanted me to see ...' he suddenly says. 'I thought history was repeating itself. I couldn't bear the thought that you were capable of behaving exactly like Raquel.'

'But I wouldn't – I—'

'I know, and as soon as I cooled off I realised that but you were gone and I knew I had blown it.'

This is the apology I came for, the closure I need to move forward, but why does it feel far from over?

'Shall we shake hands and forget all about it?' I force out, although it's the last thing I feel like doing. 'Maybe one day we can meet for a coffee ... as friends?' I say, holding out my hand.

'When I picked you up at the airport I was completely thrown by this wobbly-hobbling beautiful woman,' Michael suddenly says, grabbing my hand; the charge of electricity bolts up my arm stronger than ever.

243

'You were all tipsy and gorgeous and you stirred up all these feelings in me that I thought were well and truly buried and I resented it, I'm sorry.' His mouth quirks into a rueful smile. 'It seems I spend far too much time saying sorry to you.' He entwines his fingers into mine and my world feels like gravity has absconded into outer space as the revelation dawns on me.

Michael's gaze probes mine.

'We did have something special, didn't we?'

'You know you are the only man I have ever loved ... I mean ...' Oh well, it's out there now.

Michael's whole demeanour changes; gone is the look of anguish and in its place hope, which dissipates quickly.

'You used the past tense.'

'Well what do you expect after all these dramatics?' My throat constricts. 'I loved you.'

'Loved?'

'Yes,' I say, unshed tears now blurring my vision, 'with all my heart. I know that it's daft because we weren't together very long ... and now too much has happened ...'

'I love you.' I look at Michael in disbelief; did he just say he loves me? 'I love you but it was easier to believe you were like Raquel than to admit how much I love you.'

'Yo-uu looo-ve me?' I have trouble getting the words out.

'Yes,' he says, his face crinkling into a familiar warm and tender smile.

'But you can't love me,' I insist.

'But I do.'

'But ... how ... you haven't even tried to call me.'

'I wanted to but I didn't think you'd want to speak to me. Then Alex gave me fresh hope after a well-deserved ear-bashing. Oh Jane, these past few weeks have been utter hell.' He suddenly breaks away and swoops over to his desk, taking out a large envelope from his drawer.

'I did have a plan though.'

'A plan?'

'To win you back, of course.' He hands me the envelope. 'Go on, open it.'

My hands tremble as I empty the contents onto the table. I look at Michael, quizzically.

'They're tickets for *Chicago*?'

'I bought a ticket for every single night.'

Marvin was right and not confused by herbal distractions.

'That was you?'

'After behaving like a bad-tempered idiot I really didn't think you'd want to see me again so I thought I would try and win you back by showing you complete and utter devotion. I hoped by showing up every night you'd realise how much I love you.'

For several minutes I can't speak. Michael loves me. HE LOVES ME. This is the last thing I expected when I made the subconscious decision to come here.

'Sounds a bit stalker-ish to me,' I eventually say.

'I am a desperate man,' he says. 'Jane, I have been going crazy these past few weeks, trying to figure out how to make it up to you. I didn't dare hope that you felt the same way ... and here you are.' His hands go to the desk drawer again. 'That night I was going to ask you ... I was about to give you ...'

He pulls out a jewellery box, a sumptuous black box with the initials HW engraved in a subtle relief.

'I was going to give you this. Now is probably not the right time ...' But he flips the box open all the same. Inside is the most beautiful ring I have ever seen and my heart starts thumping really fast.

'It's a trilogy ring,' he says.

I nod; surprised that I can move at all.

'Isn't that ... past, present and future ... for ... err ...' I falter mid-sentence, my nerves cracking and I resort to humour. 'Isn't that kind of a hobbit thing?'

Michael looks aghast until he sees the smile slide across my face.

'It's what you usually give to the woman – not a hobbit, I'd like to stress – when you love them madly and want to ask them to marry you.'

Did he say marry? Now my body starts to shake from head to toe. I look at the beautiful ring and I can feel my nose start to prickle like it does when I'm about to cry with happiness.

'I know this isn't the right time and I need to make it up to you but I do love you and when you are ready …' His face is etched in seriousness and I know I want to marry this man.

'Yes,' I say, and I watch as his body tenses.

'When I am ready I will marry you.' I step into his open embrace, laughing as he gathers me into his arms and I bury my face into his chest. 'We could have a themed wedding.' I'm getting excited at the thought. 'I could get married in a dress like Lady Galadriel and we could have the whole wedding party dressed as elves and hobbits …' I feel the tension in Michael's body mount as he tries to figure out if I'm being serious. I can't hold out any longer and my face cracks into a smile and he laughs with relief.

Although now I come to think about it, a themed wedding would be fun.

ACKNOWLEDGMENTS

Without the pure vision of the outstanding Mr Blahnik this book might not exist at all; a special thank you to those at Manolo Blahnik who generously gave us permission to use his prestigious name.

To the Bare Ninny in us all, you know who you are – your perseverance is unstoppable!

To James for his artful digit, and D for his patience.

To proof-reader extraordinaire, Liz H and Sarah J for being so utterly brilliant. Thank you for sorting out the nitty gritty grammar. You are both amazing.

ABOUT THE AUTHOR

Nina Whyle is writing duo - Nina Bradley and Clare Whyle. They have been finishing each other's sentences since 2010 - but have been friends a lot longer.

You can follow them on Facebook, Twitter and Instagram.

Want to read more books from Nina Whyle?

Moving Up On Manolos
Fighting Love
When Life Goes Pop!
My DisOrganised Life

www.ninawhyle.weebly.com